For my mother and foremothers: Shirley, Virginia, Lois, Countess, Estalyn, Julia, Mildred, Ida.

For my father and forefathers: Bruce, Carlton, William, John, Hiram, Herbert, Percy.

I speak your names.

CHAPTER ONE

THE CLOCK HAD BARELY ticked past 11 p.m. when the door to the break room creaked open and a woman poked her head inside. I glanced up from my paperwork, and when I saw Lucy's expression, my stomach turned.

"Something wrong, Lucy?"

Lucy chewed nervously on her bottom lip. She was young; she'd only been in this business about six months and hadn't yet grown the thick skin she'd need to weather the many deaths that lay ahead of her. I saw misery and exhaustion all over her face, but it wasn't my job to coach her through this. She had to learn on her own.

"It's Mrs. Harrison," she said, her eyes liquid and unfocused. "She's ready. And she's asking for you."

I pushed myself away from the table and got to my feet. "Thanks, Lucy. Do you want to come? It might be good for you to get more final moments practice."

But the younger woman shook her head, cringing. "I don't think I can," she said, her voice breaking. "Mrs. Harrison was so nice."

I nodded and waved her away, watching her disappear from the doorway. I didn't understand why people like that got into hospice work. Would she only be able to stomach death when the patients were mean?

I followed Lucy out into the hall to make my way quietly toward Mrs. Harrison's room. Mrs. Harrison had been at the hospice for the past three months, and in that time, she had become dear to me. I liked to think she was my friend. I had so few.

I knocked but didn't wait for a response. I pressed the handle to Mrs. Harrison's door and let myself in. It took my eyes a few moments to adjust to the room's dimness, but when they did, I saw Mrs. Harrison lying on her back, her eyes closed, her breathing slow and steady. My soft-soled shoes barely made a sound against the linoleum, but Mrs. Harrison sensed my presence, her eyes fluttering open, a slight smile settling on her lips. She turned her head toward me, and my heart beat faster.

I stepped forward, forcing myself to smile. Inside the room, my hands began to buzz, indicating that the death current was active, preparing to decompose, deconstruct, and end my patient's life. I folded my hands in front of me and cocked my head to the side. "How are you feeling, Mrs. Harrison?"

The old woman gave me a long blink in response, and when her eyes opened again, her smile had widened. "My time on this earth finally comin' to an end," she said. There was no fear in her voice. She had no family, or if she did, they had never come to see her. In the time that Mrs. Harrison had been with us, the only people I'd ever seen with her were a couple strangers who had dropped her off on her first day. But whoever they were, they had never returned, and Mrs. Harrison had never spoken of them.

I came to the edge of the bed, close enough for us to speak intimately. "Is there anything I can get for you? Would you like some water? Maybe I can make you some tea," I said.

Mrs. Harrison shook her head and made a shooing motion. "Naw, I don't guess I got time left for alla that. By the time you boiled that water, I might have gone on."

"You wouldn't wait till I got back? I know how much you like that Sleepytime blend," I teased.

"I'm about to sleep for long enough," came her reply. "You got any children, baby?"

I side-stepped that question with one of my own. "Do you?"

"Naw," she said, her eyes bearing no regret. "Never got around to it. Had too much to do, I guess." She slipped her hand in mine and gave my fingers a gentle squeeze. "Well, you got time. You busy?"

At first, I thought she was asking if I was too busy to have children. But then I realized that conversation had passed; she was only asking if I had time for her now. "Nothing in the world to do but be here with you," I said.

Mrs. Harrison closed her eyes. "If you don't mind, Kezia baby, I'd really like it if you sat and talked with me a while."

It was a typical request. A lot of times, when the old people feel death is near, they just want to talk and tell stories: growing up during the depression, giving birth to their first child, watching their friends and family die one by one. But Mrs. Harrison had never been much of a talker. She was always more disposed to hearing my stories, though I was never very inclined to tell them. I don't know if that's a personal proclivity or something I got growing up like I did. In our community, keeping one's business to oneself is sort of a prime directive. "Mind ya business," Big Ginny would say, cutting her eyes at me. "And don't you go tellin' folks mines, neither." Big Ginny had several trust issues. One of her favorite sayings was, "You can't go around trustin' nobody ain't got some kinda kink to they hair." To tell the truth, I had no idea what hair texture had to do with trustworthiness, but anyway, I'd always been hesitant to share the details of my life with anyone. Even other Black folks like Mrs. Harrison.

I made myself comfortable on the edge of the bed and returned the old woman's gentle squeeze. Her skin was soft and weathered, and without thinking, I found my thumb stroking her knuckles, caressing her as though to offer comfort. Most of the time, I tried to avoid touching the patients. That had nothing to do with how I was raised. But it had everything to do with who I was.

"Would you like me to read to you? I've got a novel in my purse—a romance," I said with a grin.

Mrs. Harrison chuckled and gave a slight shake of her head. "Naw. Ain't never had much use for them stories anyhow. I ain't tryna meet St. Peter with beautiful lies ringing in my ears. 'Specially not them horny lies," she added with a grin. "Naw, tell me something, girl. And make it true, baby. Whatever you do, make it true."

I hesitated, not knowing exactly how much I wanted to share with Mrs. Harrison. I could tell by looking at her she was right; she would pass on soon, maybe even within the next few minutes. Certainly she wouldn't last out the hour, let alone the night. Big Ginny taught me it was a sin to deny a dying woman a final bit of peace. And for some reason, I was in a giving mood.

"I wanted to be a marine biologist when I was little," I said, "because I didn't know then that poor Black kids from the inner city didn't get to become marine biologists. When I finally figured that out, I decided a regular biologist would be fine."

"What do marine biologists even do?" Mrs. Harrison asked.

I shrugged. "I have no idea. At the time I thought they all worked at Sea World and Marineland training orcas and dolphins. That was good enough for me."

Mrs. Harrison laughed. "I bet your mama woulda liked that. Daughter runnin' around in a swimsuit all day." She clucked her tongue at the imaginary disgrace.

"Well, it never came to that, and anyway, my mother died giving birth to me. My brother and I were raised by my father's stepmother—we call her Big Ginny. Which is funny because she's about the size of a toothpick." Both Mrs. Harrison and I chuckled at that. "Her Christian name is Ginevra. She's from South Carolina."

Mrs. Harrison grinned and raised an eyebrow. "Yeah? Whereabouts? You know I'm from Charleston."

"I didn't know that," I said with a smile. "But it explains a lot. You remind me of her." I squeezed Mrs. Harrison's hand. "She can sing like a country music star. When I was little, we used to have competitions, and my brother Lamont would be the judge. I always thought I got my talent from her; I was a teenager before I figured out we weren't genetically related."

"Your daddy wasn't in the picture?"

I shook my head. "Nope. I know he's alive, but that's it. Big Ginny won't even speak of him," I said with a sigh. "Can't choose your family I guess. Ain't that right?"

Mrs. Harrison sucked her teeth and made a shooing motion with her hand. "Aw, shit, just cuz he donated some swimmers don't mean he's your family. Family's what stick around to clean up your mess after everybody else done hitched up they skirts and gone on."

I nodded. "Well, I guess you got that right. Anyway, around the time I turned sixteen, I started looking for my mother."

The old woman at my side tilted her head and blinked in confusion. "How's that? Ain't you just said she died giving birth to you?"

"She did," I said, nodding my agreement. "But for someone like me, death is no obstacle. It just turns a local conversation into a long-distance one."

Mrs. Harrison intoned a little cooing sound like she'd put two and two together. "Ahh, I see it now. You're a necromancer."

I nodded. "That's right. I found out when I was in the fourth grade. It was scary at first, and then fun. Some of the kids from school would ask me to relay or receive messages from their loved ones. But after a while, it stopped being a game. It's serious business." I paused, caressed Mrs. Harrison's fingers with my thumb. "You know much about necromancers?"

Mrs. Harrison whistled and rolled her eyes like I'd asked a stupid question. "Lawd, yes. Ain't been in a while, but when I was comin' up, we used to go to Mr. Freddie's parlor and get our gifts every month. My family always went on Sundays after church. And after we got our gifts, we'd have breakfast at IHOP. My brothers and sisters and I would compare gifts to see who got the best one."

"That sounds like fun. Which gift was your favorite?"

"Silver tongue," she answered without hesitation.

I grinned. "Ahh, the ability to talk your way into getting what you want. That's one of my favorites, too."

Mrs. Harrison's grip tightened around my fingers. "Kezia,

baby. You want to grant a dying woman a wish? Lay that gift on me one last time. Just for fun," she said, a twinkle in her eyes.

I sighed, regret pulling the corners of my mouth into a frown. "I wish I could," I said. "But I haven't received my Godsend yet."

Mrs. Harrison's expression melted. "Oh. You still green? Ain't that unusual at your age? I hope you don't mind me sayin'."

I shook my head. "I don't mind. You're right; it's very unusual. To receive the Godsend, you have to make contact with your nearest deceased ancestor. That's my mother. But for some reason, I've never found her on the other side. I've found dead grandparents for coworkers, dead sisters for people at my church, but never my own mother. And until I do ... "

Mrs. Harrison made no move to let go of my hand. "Being a necromancer's got to be a hard life," she said. "I don't know why the Lord would put that kinda burden on a person."

"It is hard," I agreed. "But it's also a privilege." *In theory.* "At least I know what my purpose is."

"That's right. You followin' Miss Ruby's footsteps."

I smiled at that. The first recorded natural-born necromancer was born in 1927 in a Black neighborhood in Mississippi. Her name was Ruby Thompson, and her gift was discovered in 1935 when she began carrying messages from her dead grandmother to her father. The local church deemed it the work of the devil and tried to have Ruby exorcised. But pretty soon, other cases of Black children speaking with the dead were discovered. A pair of twins in Gary, Indiana, a blind boy in the Bronx, a pastor's daughter in Mobile, Alabama. Newspapers across the country were filled with stories of children who could commune with the dead. Among Black folks, Ruby Thompson was a folk hero.

Mrs. Harrison closed her eyes. She was slipping. "Well, if you a necromancer, I guess that's how you ended up here. Because of your devil's breath and all. Can't kill nobody if they already dying."

I tensed but didn't respond. Admonishing a dying woman not to use a derogatory term for a person's disability seemed cold and unnecessary. These final moments were about her, not my easily bruised feelings.

Though I really did hate the term *devil's breath*. It and the other colloquial terms—witch's shadow, black cloud, and grave calling—were just unnecessary salt to our injury. They were meant to describe our affliction, the downside to being a necromancer. And our affliction was bad enough.

I ought to know.

"It's my choice to be here," I said. "I really do love end-of-life work. I'm honored to be here with you now. But you're right. It can be hard. I've had to make sacrifices most people never have to think about. And sometimes that weight is a burden."

I hadn't meant to say any of that, and if my boss heard me speaking this way, she'd write me up for sure. But Mrs. Harrison didn't look like she minded. Instead, she beckoned me closer.

"Maybe I can help you. Come here."

She lifted a hand, and I leaned in low, allowing her to place her palm on my cheek. Her skin was cool. "The Lord bless you and keep you," she prayed. "The Lord make His face to shine on you and be gracious to you. The Lord lift up the light of His countenance upon you, and give you peace. Amen."

The buzzing in my hands became a cold throb. The energy shifted, and I felt mortic energy gathering around Mrs. Harrison. I held my breath. This was natural. Mortic energy would dissolve Mrs. Harrison's vital spark and allow her soul to slip from her body.

I'd been here many times, but the process still felt sacred. I stood upright, watching a succession of biological processes taking turns ushering in Mrs. Harrison's death. Some people think death happens instantaneously, that the moment the person stops breathing or the heart stops beating the person goes from being alive to dead. But in reality, death is a process. It's a cascade that begins with one small trigger, one cell failing to find homeostasis and finally ends when all the processes in the body have stopped. It's not instantaneous, and it's different for everyone.

For Mrs. Harrison, death came in gentle waves. First her breathing slowed. Then her heart. Her brain's electricity guttered to a stop and mortic energy bloomed thick and fragrant—like a dozen extinguished candles—and finally, with a last shuddering breath, Mrs. Harrison's vital spark—her life force—silently dissipated, flowing back into the death current, allowing the rest of her soul to leave her body and cross over to the other side.

Only then was Mrs. Harrison truly dead.

Carefully, I removed my hands from her body and adjusted her gown, her hair, the position of her arms atop the thin sheets. I brushed the backs of my fingers against her cheek, admiring the soft skin and the full lips which had been so used to smiling. She had been a beautiful woman in life, and she was beautiful in death, too. "Rest in power, Mrs. Harrison," I whispered, laying a kiss on her cheek. "Goodbye."

WHEN I ARRIVED HOME, I entered the house quietly, stepping over a thick line of brick dust Big Ginny had spread earlier that day. It was supposed to keep out those who would do us harm. "This here dust is better than some police-calling alarm system," she'd say smugly. "The hell you gone do *after* the murderer done already killed everybody? Best to stop 'em fore they come in the house in the first place."

You couldn't really argue with that logic.

The door clicked closed behind me, and I heard voices coming from the kitchen. It was almost midnight, and at this hour, I knew what voices meant.

Big Ginny had a client.

I trudged into the kitchen to find Big Ginny and another woman sharing what I hoped was decaf coffee at the table. I recognized the woman from church. Her name was Peaches Henley, a friend of my grandmother's.

"Hey, Big Ginny. Hey there, Ms. Peaches," I said, sliding out of my shoes. "What y'all doing up this late?"

"Oh, we just sharing some gossip, you know how we do," Big Ginny answered. I glanced at the table between them, surprised to see there were no magical accouterments set out. No candles, playing cards, or bloodied bones. Big Ginny was a Conjure woman, a practitioner of hoodoo, homegrown African-American magic. Certain works could only be performed at the crossroads—physical and temporal intersections. As a transition from one day to another, midnight was a powerful crossroad.

But no tools meant no works. So this was a friendly visit? At this hour?

"It's good to see you, sugar," Peaches said. "How you been?"

"Oh, just fine," I said. "Working. Tired."

"Hoo, chile, you and me, both." Peaches grinned. "I

planted two trays of azaleas today. I'm 'bout to feel that in the morning."

"I know that's right," I agreed. "Well, I'll leave you two ladies to it. I'll just—"

"Before you go, Kezia," Big Ginny interrupted. "I was hoping you could do a favor for Peaches."

Here we go, I thought. I should have known this wasn't a friendly visit.

"What kind of favor?" I asked.

Peaches began wringing her hands. "Well, I got me a little problem. A dilemma, you might say. A developer offered to buy my house for a good sum. My daughter says I should sell and buy a place closer to her out in Wyoming. It would be nice to be closer to her and her family, but I ain't sure about all that cold. Plus, I like my home here. I'm not sure I want to move."

I nodded. "Sounds like you've got a decision to make. How can I help?"

"I was hoping you'd contact my husband and ask him what he thinks I should do. We always made these decisions together, me and Norris."

I sighed. "Ah, Ms. Peaches. It's late, and I—"

But the old woman touched my arm, her rheumy eyes imploring. "Please?"

I dipped my chin. "Did you bring something personal of his?"

Peaches opened her purse and retrieved a bolo tie, inlaid with turquoise. "Most of his things I put away years ago," she explained. "But I kept this. Will this work?"

I accepted the tie, closing my fingers around it. With my intuition, I reached out to the death current. My fingers grew hot, and I smelled Old Spice, hair wax, laundry detergent, and moth balls. "This should work fine," I said, returning the tie. "I need a moment to prepare," I said. "I'll be back."

"Kezia," Peaches said. "I hate to be vulgar, but how much is it? Your services?"

I smiled and leaned down to kiss Peaches on the cheek. "Ain't gone be no charge for you tonight, Ms. Peaches," I assured her. "This one's on me."

I slipped away from the kitchen and went into my room to get ready. I undressed completely and threw my uniform in the hamper. Next, I wrapped a silk scarf around my hair—this kind of work was likely to wear me out, and I wanted to fall into bed quick as possible. Then, I donned a thin muumuu I saved just for my death work. Dressed, I pulled a bottle of Florida water from my closet and began wiping down my doorway—essential to making the space sacred and safe, warding off any energies I didn't want hanging around. The scent was astringent and floral with cinnamon undertones. I followed the spiritual cleaning with an act of physical cleaning. I squirted lemon Pledge onto a handkerchief and quickly wiped down my doorway and altar. When the room was cleansed, I pulled a bottle of attar of rose from my cosmetics drawer and anointed myself at the crown of my head. And finally, I lit two cones of incense: palo santo and copal.

The mingled scents of incense, rose, and Florida water flipped a switch in my mind. Fragrance had a way of doing that. One minute, I was a night-shift nurse's assistant wearing a mundane nightgown with a scarf wrapped around my hair; in the next, I was a Conjure maiden, ready to do my sacred work.

When I was young, I attended a funeral with a little Mexican girl who lived down the street. This was how her home smelled: sacred woods and cut flowers mingled with lemon furniture wax. This, to me, was the smell of death. Not decay or rot but funerary rites—perfume, flowers, tears, and alchemical transformation.

I sat down at my altar and lit two candles, one for each of my patrons: Papa Jinabbott and Mama Fat, an uncle and aunt respectively. These were not, strictly speaking, my ancestors. Fat was Big Ginny's cousin, and Jinabbott was Fat's lover. Papa Jinabbott was a magic worker in his own right, a witch doctor who had the ability to possess animals. Aunt Fat wasn't magical at all, but I'd loved her fiercely in life, and that kind of love was its own magic.

I closed my eyes and prayed for the protection of my ancestors.

When I worked alone, I didn't need any of this ritual. But working with other people introduced uncertainty; you could never be sure if they brought curses, ill intentions, dark energy or whatever into the ritual. It was better to be prepared. It was better to be safe.

I stood and returned to the kitchen. Big Ginny had turned the lights out, and now candles flickered on the table. I sat down next to Peaches and took the tie in my hands once more. "What's your husband's full name?" I asked.

"Norris Triumphant Henley," she answered.

I closed my eyes and let my head loll back. I opened myself to the death current, the natural energy of decomposition, deceleration, and decay, and let it activate some hidden ability at my core. I reached for the veil, the thin membrane separating the world of the dead from the living.

Crossing over wasn't trivial. It wasn't a matter of wishing it and magically materializing among the dead. It was more like dragging myself through a dark, twisty crawlspace, shuffling along on hands and knees. But the more I did it, the less arduous it became. It was always tricky, though.

In the darkness, the sounds began.

They started low and distant but quickly picked up volume and urgency. My ears, attuned to the vibrations, perked at the sounds. Drums. A descant of ululations. Feet stomping earth. Hands slapping bare thighs. Laughter.

So much laughter.

My pulse quickened; I had to bite back my enthusiasm. New sounds joined the others, lending their fuel to my fire. So many voices: mothers, fathers, aunties, uncles, all coming together to guide me through. To help me find them. I smelled clay and dirt, manure and oily water. Fat burning over a fire. Roasted plantains and sweet potatoes. Tobacco. I sensed more than saw the ancestors as they gathered near the veil, shouting at me to pass through.

My body was still in my kitchen. But my consciousness had passed over to the other side.

I was standing in a garage. It smelled of motor oil and turpentine. A man stood at a workbench wearing grease-stained coveralls with his name embroidered on the chest: Norris. He'd been old when he died, but now he looked to be in his early fifties, close-cropped hair shot with gray, almond skin scattered with freckles. The dead could appear to be any age and I found them in myriad settings. I'd never found rhyme or reason in any of it.

"Are you Mr. Norris Triumphant Henley?" I asked.

The man smiled and beckoned me closer. "That's right. I recognize you. You're Ginevra's grandbaby. That necromancer. Did Peach send you? That why you're here?"

"Yes, sir," I said. "She asked me to come speak to you because she doesn't know if she should sell her house and move to Wyoming to be near your daughter, or if she should stay where she is. She wants you to tell her what to do."

Norris sighed and rubbed a hand over his face. "I think I married Peach too young," he said. "She was eighteen; I was twenty-three. Not a whole lot older, but enough. She always had the disposition of a child, and when we got married, I guess I kinda took over everything. I worked, paid the bills, did the tithing, fixed things round the house ... and now I wonder if that wasn't a mistake."

I frowned. "Why's that?"

"Because she never had to make her own choices, and now I don't think she knows how. My daddy used to say that what separates a man from a boy is a man makes his own choices and accepts responsibility for the consequences. That's the only freedom we really got in this world. I took that away from her. I ain't never given her the tools to make her own choices. Now here she is, sending necromancers to talk to dead people to tell her where to live."

"I see," I said. "Well, what should I tell her?"

Norris shrugged, turning back to his workstation. "Tell her you couldn't find me," he said. "Otherwise she'll just keep asking."

"Mr. Henley—"

"Does she seem happy to you?" he asked.

I shrugged. "I don't know her very well, but I'd say she seems as happy as can be, all things considered."

He was silent a moment. "I tried to make her happy," he said.

"People always say that, but the truth is, you can't make other people happy. They have to do that for themselves."

Norris pondered that before nodding. "You probably right.

But I didn't say I made her happy. I said I tried. And trying made *me* happy."

I waited for him to continue, but when he didn't, I said, "What should I tell her?"

"Tell her you couldn't find me," he repeated. "Go on, now. I ain't gone change my mind. You go on, now. Bye bye."

I was fading. Before I knew it, I was back in my body, blinking myself to wakefulness. Peaches and Big Ginny were staring at me, faces expectant.

I cleared my throat and reached for Peaches's hand. "I'm sorry," I said. "But I couldn't find him. It happens sometimes. I'm sorry."

Peaches swallowed, her eyes growing damp with tears. "But I need to know. I need him to tell me what to do."

"Not this time," I said. "From now on, you have to make these choices for yourself."

"But what if I make the wrong one?" Her voice was hoarse.

I offered a small smile. "You might. We all do, sometimes. But it's your choice alone to make. And at least you'll know *you* made it."

Big Ginny patted her friend on the arm. "Kezia's right. And she should know. She's had to make her own hard choices. When Lola got sick—"

"I think I'll head to bed now," I said, interrupting. I stood so quickly that I shook the table. I caught my grandmother's eyes, giving her a pointed look. She glanced away. "Good luck with your decision, Ms. Peaches. You're gonna be fine. Good night."

I retreated to my bedroom where I blew out my candles and thought of my own choices as I climbed into bed, praying that at least for tonight, my choices would not haunt me.

CHAPTER TWO

B Y THE TIME I WOKE UP the next morning, it was almost lunchtime. I staggered into the kitchen bleary-eyed, yawning hugely as I slid into my seat at the kitchen table. Big Ginny was at the stove, stirring grits and frying up bacon and eggs. My stomach growled in anticipation.

"You feel like making me some coffee?" I asked with a grin. She absolutely loved it when I treated her like a house servant.

Big Ginny turned to me and cocked her eyebrow. "You got two feet," she said with a huff. "And make me a cup while you at it."

Standing, I ambled over to the coffeemaker and set the percolator to brewing. I took two mugs out of the cupboard and set them on the counter. "How'd you sleep?" I asked.

"Oh, fine. You?"

"Like the dead."

Big Ginny chuckled. "You working at the hospital today?"

I shook my head. "Naw. I'm not on the schedule today, thankfully. I lost a patient last night."

Big Ginny clucked her teeth as she flipped the bacon. "Somebody you cared about?"

"Yeah. Mrs. Harrison. She didn't have any family. She died alone."

"We all die alone," Big Ginny said. She told me this often.

"She kind of reminded me of you, actually."

Big Ginny stuck a hand on her hip and cocked her head to the side. "Yeah? In what way?"

I shrugged. "I don't know. Just her general energy, I guess. She was from Charleston."

The coffee pot buzzed, and I poured myself a cup. Big Ginny side-eyed me as I took a sip without adding cream or sugar. I poured a cup of coffee for her, too, and pushed the mug towards her. She pushed it back with a frown. "You best put some cream in there and quit playin'," she said.

I chuckled as I pulled the creamer from the refrigerator and poured until Big Ginny's café au lait was the color of a newborn camel. "What you about to do today?"

Big Ginny threw a glance at the clock on her microwave. "I been up since 7. I already been doing stuff."

"Humor me."

My grandmother sighed and fixed two plates of grits, bacon, and fried eggs with hot sauce, which she carried to the table. I joined her. "Got me some sewing patterns I might try to cut out after I finish watching my stories. Then maybe I'll go work in the garden for a little while."

Big Ginny had a secret crush on Ron Finley the so-called gangsta gardener, and as a result, she'd taken to turning the small patch of dirt behind the house into an organic garden. She actually had a knack for it: her raised beds were over-flowing with fat, red tomatoes, peppers of all colors and shapes, and an ungodly amount of squash. And every inch not growing vegetables was growing flowers. She didn't put as much effort into the flowers, though. Ron Finley didn't care so much about flowers.

"What about you? No hospital shift, so how you gone fill your day?"

"Going down to the bar to help Lamont today."

"That ain't till tonight. What you finna do with the daylight?"

I narrowed my eyes at my grandmother. "Why did you bring up Lola last night? You know that ain't nobody's business."

Big Ginny clucked her teeth. "Hush, chile, it ain't no kinda secret. When you lost your daughter, the whole church mourned with you."

I barked a bitter laugh. "No, they didn't. Half the church mourned with me. The other half turned against me. I don't know which side Ms. Peaches was on."

"It don't matter no way. The point was, you had to make your own choices, which you did. I wanted Peaches to catch some of your strength."

I grunted. "Choosing to give up your daughter ain't the same thing as choosing where to live, and you know that. Don't use me in your business. I don't like it."

But my grandmother waved away my objection with a frown. "It ain't about what you want. It's about what's right and wrong. When you was little and I had to take you out of school because you was killing your teachers and classmates, you think anybody asked me what I wanted? I'm barely educated myself, and they told me *I* had to homeschool you? Shit. You should know by now, life ain't about what you *want*."

I lowered my face, chastened. Big Ginny was usually very good about not making me feel guilty about my congenital defect—my necromantic affliction, devil's breath, witch's shadow, whatever you wanted to call it. All necromancers had it. My mere presence caused some people to get sick and die for no known medical reason, a malady cheekily referred to as "the blues." It didn't happen suddenly—a person needed to spend a considerable amount of time around me before they became listless and withered away. Problem was, "a considerable amount of time" could be anywhere from weeks to months. It varied a lot. And even then, most people were immune to it. But it was impossible to know whether a person was susceptible until they got sick. I was in fourth grade when my condition became apparent. My teacher died.

As a result, I stayed away from people the best I could. I worked night shifts at the hospice because it limited my contact with others, and I never worked more than a 5-hour shift, only three hours of which overlapped with others. I worked random days in my brother's bar, but never for long. He was immune. Didn't mean his regulars were.

"I'm just saying, I'd appreciate it if we didn't talk about Lola with outsiders. Please."

Big Ginny examined me a moment. "Why you so defensive about this? You made your choice. Why you shamed to own it?"

Appetite gone, I pushed away from the table, my chair scraping across the floor. "I'mma go run some errands," I said as I stood to carry my plate to the sink. "You need anything while I'm out?"

"Kezia—"

"Stop," I said, anger burning my cheeks red. "We not gonna talk about this. I mean it."

Big Ginny pressed her lips together. "Fine. What time you think you'll be home?"

I shrugged. "Don't know. Later. If you need something, text me."

Big Ginny said nothing as I left the kitchen, but I couldn't help noticing her expression as I left.

She looked regretful.

LATER THAT NIGHT, I arrived late for my shift at the bar. It was a little past nine o'clock, and things were already hopping. Lamont threw me a dirty look from behind the bar before returning a fake smile to the three women in front of him, each drunker than the last. I tried not to smile but I couldn't help it; Lamont wasn't attracted to older women, but they sure loved him. I cut through the crowds and slipped behind the bar and made hugely apologetic eyes at my brother, which he ignored.

I brushed my hands together and headed towards the end of the counter to take drink orders. Eventually, Lamont wandered over, scowling. "Why you late?" he asked.

I poured a bar spoon of maraschino liqueur into the Martinez I was mixing. "Would you believe me if I said I had a hot date?"

Lamont didn't even bother to answer. He just walked away.

I pushed the cocktail over to the woman who ordered it, and as I was preparing to refill the Luxardo cherries, I glimpsed someone gliding up to the bar. She snared my attention because, unlike our usual clientele, this woman looked like she'd stepped from the pages of Good House-keeping Magazine. Her long, straight, blonde hair hung in a sheet down her back and her heart-shaped face was mini-mally made up. She wore a crisp white blouse with a pearl necklace at her throat, and a pair of dark pedal pushers. When she slid into an empty stool, she folded her hands primly on the bar, waiting. Her nails were short, polished a pale pink.

She looked as out of place as a whore in church, but you'd never know it by the expression on her face. She looked for all the world like she believed she belonged.

"What can I get you?" I asked.

The woman removed her hands from the bar and placed them in her lap. "I need a corpse reviver," she said.

I nodded. "All right. You want the gin or the cognac version?"

The woman's expression did not change as she pushed a stray lock of hair behind an ear and answered, "I'm looking for the Kezia Bernard version."

I froze. She pronounced my name KEH-zee-uh, which I couldn't even be mad about, because it meant she learned it by reading it rather than hearing it. I pronounced it KEE-zee-uh. Over the years, I'd been called everything from Keisha to Kesha to Kelsey (which, what?) so when someone got even close to my name, I was pretty impressed.

But after I got over her close pronunciation of my name, the implications of what she had just said registered. She'd asked for a *corpse reviver*, and she didn't mean the cocktail. This woman knew something about me. That made me curious, but also wary. "Who's looking?"

The woman readjusted herself on the bar stool and cleared her throat. "My name is Brandy Carbajal," she said. "I got Miss Bernard's name from Dr. Adeyemo."

My heart screeched to a halt. "Dr. Adeyemo sent you here?"

A deep dimple appeared in her cheek. "So the name rings a

bell? In that case, I'm guessing you're the woman I'm looking for."

"Looks like it. It's *Kezia*," I said, correcting her pronunciation.

"Oh, my apologies," she said. "It's from the Bible, isn't it? One of Job's three daughters?"

I narrowed my eyes as my curiosity grew. Now that I was really looking at her, she seemed familiar, but I couldn't place her face. That was strange enough, since I didn't have many interactions with women like her. But her knowing the history of my name intrigued me. "I don't think I've ever met anyone who knew that right off the bat. I suppose I should be grateful I wasn't named Jemima or Keren-Happuch."

"Well, I'm a big fan of Job's," Brandy explained.

"Oh? That whole faithful-unto-the Lord thing appeals to you?"

Brandy shrugged. "What can I say; I have a soft spot for loyal people. Faithfulness is a rare trait to come by, don't you think?"

I glanced at another patron waiting to be served. "What can I do for you, Ms. Carbajal?"

Brandy's smile slipped away, a professional stoicism taking its place. "I need a necromancer," she said.

I smirked. "Uh huh. And what do you know about necromancy? We don't actually revive corpses, so if that's what you're looking for ... "

"I *know* you can't raise the dead," she said primly. "I'm not stupid."

"I never said you were. It's just that most people don't actually know very much about us. And most of what you think you know is wrong."

"I know that necromancy is considered almost holy to

those who practice. I also know that children with necromantic gifts are born only to Black communities in diaspora.
Your kind are born to those who have been cut off from their
history, land, and people through war, trafficking, slavery, or
other violence. Your ability to speak to and conjure the dead is
nature's way of rectifying that wrong. It lets you find your
ancestors so you can bridge the gap between the life you have
and the alternate life you could have had." She gave me a
precocious smile. "Do I have that right?"

I stammered, my cheeks hot with chagrin. "What do you
want?"

"As I said, I got your name from Dr. Adeyemo, whom I
corresponded with via email. What I'm about to say is going to
sound strange. But promise me you'll hear me out."

I almost laughed. "I don't make promises to anybody I
don't know. Hell, I barely make promises to people I do. But
you've got my attention, so I suggest you get to talking."

Brandy licked her lips and nodded. "I'm on the Board of
Directors for the Temple of the Inner Flame. Have you heard
of it?"

I stared. "Is this for real?"

The woman's lips stretched; it wasn't exactly a smile. "Oh,
I'm quite serious. So you have heard of it?"

Everybody who hadn't been living under a rock knew about
the Temple of the Inner Flame. They touted themselves as a
personal and professional enlightenment organization, but
really, they were a cult. A very well-known, very high-profile
cult in the habit of suing anybody who publicly dubbed them
as such. Still, I'd heard stories about these folks. They
recruited rich, powerful people and had a penchant for secrecy.
Well, as much of a penchant as you could have when you were

constantly in the news because some new celebrity had just been initiated.

"I've heard of it," I said, keeping my voice light and vague, "but I don't think I'm exactly the clientele you're looking for. My skin's not the right color for one, and for two, I definitely don't have the bank account to fund y'all's weekend intensives."

"We do have people of color in our congregation," she said with a slight wave of her hand as though dismissing my concerns. "Enlightenment knows no color. But I understand what you're saying about the bank account. I'm not here to recruit you. As I said, I was sent to you. It seems I need your help."

I pretended to wipe down the counter just to have something to do with my hands. I didn't want Lamont to look over and see me chatting up this White girl, thinking I was shirking my responsibilities. "You need my help with what?"

"Have you heard of the spiritual retreats we sponsor out at our property in the desert?"

I nodded. "I've heard of them."

"We just finished one up, and we're about to start a new one. The problem is, I'm not entirely convinced that we're in a good position to do so. Things are ... Well, I guess you could say *unsettled*." She gave me a piercing look, and a chill ran up my spine. "Recently, my personal assistant, Casey, encountered what she describes as a feeling of unwelcome in our temple— our most sacred house of worship. I went to investigate and what I found left me feeling ... uncomfortable."

I put my rag away and began mixing the corpse reviver Brandy had asked for. I placed it in front of her with a clink.

"Oh," she said, blinking. "No, thank you. I don't actually—"

I leaned forward, closing the distance between us and lowering my voice, even though no one was paying us any attention. "You want my time, you need to earn it. Talking's only part of the job if I'm serving drinks to go with the conversation. You ain't gotta drink it, but you do gotta pay for it. You feel me?"

The woman blushed and accepted the glass, wrapping her fingers around it. "I got it. Should I keep going?"

I shrugged. "If you want."

She was about to answer when she was jostled from the side by a man sliding into the stool next to her. He was too aggressive, smiling too broadly, and reeking of alcohol and drugstore cologne. We got our fair share of guys like him. I guess every bar does. And I guess every woman has her way of dealing with them. Brandy's way was to politely shift herself a bit to the left.

"Whatever she's drinking, give me one too. And might as well top hers off while you're at it," he said, winking in my direction. Brandy hadn't even touched her drink.

I leaned into my hands placed on the bar and gave the newcomer an exasperated look. "Something I can help you with?"

"You heard me," he said, speaking with exaggerated slowness. "I said, get the lady another drink and I'll have one as well. What, you fucking deaf or something?"

I didn't really need to gut check myself on this, but by this point in my life it was hardwired into my DNA to check on the ladies in the bar. I cast a sideways look at Brandy and, with her bewildered expression confirming my suspicions, took this one in my own hands. "Hey. Chad. We kinda busy here. If you want a drink, head down to the other end of the bar. My brother will be happy to assist you."

But "Chad" didn't move. "Oh, is that a Black thing? Is he your brother or your *brutha?*"

He laughed at his own joke and I gave Brandy a withering look, but she only stared back with wide-eyed anxiety. "Look, man, why don't you—"

"No, I like this seat," he interrupted, giving Brandy a once-over and a grin. "And I'm not interested in having your *brother* serve me." He scooted nearer to Brandy, who shrank back, her face gone ashen. He returned his gaze to me as his smile slipped away. "Why don't you do what you're told? You're the fucking bartender—tend bar."

Years of practiced restraint prevented me from tossing ice in Chad's face. "If you want a drink, pick your narrow White ass up and carry yourself *thataway*." I pointed to where Lamont was watching us, ready to jump into action if needed. But I had this under control. "I ain't tryna have your frat-boy lookin', Axe-body-spray smellin', no-moves-havin' ass disrespecting me in my own bar." It wasn't my own bar, but he didn't know that. "Now, you gonna play nice or do I need to call the cops?"

He smirked. "I thought your people didn't trust the cops," he said. "Or is that narrative only when it's convenient for you?" Chad staggered to his feet and rolled his eyes, making a huge show of obeying my wishes. He dragged his feet towards the other end of the bar, but not before turning his lecherous gaze on Brandy one more time. "You get tired of hearing this bitch blather at you, you come down here and chat with me."

With Chad out of our hair, Brandy let out an embarrassed sigh. "I'm really sorry about that," she said.

"Why are you sorry? I'm used to shitheads like him. However, when you leave here tonight, it might be a good idea if you had your mace ready. Some guys like him don't really take no for an answer."

Brandy's face went white as a sheet. "I don't have any mace," she said. "I don't really leave the preserve that frequently. I—"

I groaned and leaned my head back, staring up at the ceiling. "Girl. In this day and age, there is no reason for you to be defenseless. Shit. Okay, I want you to take mine." I reached under the bar and into my purse, pulling out my defense spray. I pushed it across the bar.

Brandy made no move to accept it, only staring at it like it was a snake. "Are you sure? I wouldn't want you—"

I waved her complaint away and shook my head. "I'll get my brother to walk me to my car. Don't worry about it. I want to make sure you're safe. Now. What were we talking about?"

Brandy tucked the mace into her purse. "Well, thank you. Right. So. The temple. I went to investigate, keeping an open mind, but to be honest, I expected a reasonable explanation for whatever Casey had been experiencing. She mentioned cold spots in the temple. And apparently, some attendees commented that they'd sensed people hiding in the shadows. Other people claimed they heard wailing and crying. A couple of people even said that they saw something. But it's hard to verify those claims because most of the people who come to our retreat are looking for a kind of spiritual awakening. Hallucinations and visions and things of this nature are part of the experience. They want to see the world through different eyes.

"But when I went to investigate the temple, it was very clear that something was wrong. The temple was unusually cold, but I don't necessarily mean the temperature. I mean when I stepped foot into the temple, it was like walking into my own grave. I felt this ... *pull* inside my chest, like my soul wanted to leave my body." She paused here, fingers unconsciously rubbing over her heart. "The longer I was there, the worse the feelings became. In some ways what I experienced there was not purely sensory. At least, not *physical*. But I do think Casey's right—there's something wrong there."

I pressed my lips into a line. "What do you think it is?" I asked.

"I think the temple is haunted."

I was silent a moment, preparing an answer. Finally, I said, "Look, it isn't that I don't want to help you. It's just that I don't know how to perform an exorcism. Banishing something from the plane of Earth is far beyond my ken. I—"

But Brandy held up a hand, stopping me mid-sentence. "I don't want you to exorcise it. I want you to get it to speak."

It was a simple reframing of the conversation, but it changed everything. Communicating with the dead was something I was very good at—my own mother notwithstanding. Still, the idea left me cold. "Damn, girl. That's a lot. I don't know. I don't want to offend you or anything, but going up to that ranch of yours is not really my idea of a good time."

For the first time since the beginning of our conversation, I saw Brandy freeze up a little. "We'll pay you well, of course. We just need you to investigate it first. If you determine that it's not a human entity or that it doesn't want to talk to you, we won't expect miracles. But I believe whatever is there has something to say. It wants something. And I also believe you're the best person to help me figure out what that is."

Brandy didn't wait for my response. She gathered herself together and pulled a pamphlet from her purse. She placed it and a $20 bill on the bar and pushed them toward me. "Please think about it. Don't decide now. But if you think you can help us, please give me a call. It would mean the world to us."

I accepted the pamphlet, folded it in half, and stuck it in my back pocket. I offered her what I hoped passed for a genuine smile and gave a small nod. "Yeah, okay. I'll think about it. If I decide to do it, I'll be in touch. But I probably won't call you just to say no. Catch my drift?"

Brandy nodded. "Yes. And thanks for the pepper spray. I hope I see you soon."

Brandy was barely out the door before a group of college students insinuated themselves into the empty barstools in front of me, laughing and clamoring for each other's attention, and before I even had a chance to mull over Brandy's request, I was already mixing a Sex on the Beach, the conversation swept neatly from my memory.

CHAPTER THREE

"HATE TO COUNT MY CHICKENS before they're hatched, but I'd say tonight was a pretty good take."

Lamont was wiping down the bar, the last of the patrons finally gone. He looked up long enough to drop me a wink and motion with his chin toward the center of the room. "You did good tonight. You rake up on tips?"

I dug a handful of cash out of my pocket and held up the wad for my brother's approval. He nodded in response. "You can take Big Ginny out for Olive Garden with that fat stack."

I rolled my eyes. "Please. Go out to eat? Never. Not on what you pay."

Lamont grunted. "What you need money for? House is paid for, and you ain't got kids—"

He snapped his mouth shut, aware too late of his mistake. The words hung dead in the air, and though we both tried to ignore it, what's said was said. I cleared my throat. "*Somebody's* still got to take care of Big Ginny," I said.

It wasn't intended as a slight, but Lamont's expression fell, and I immediately felt guilty for what I'd said. "I didn't mean anything by it. I'm just joking around like you are."

Lamont grunted again, his favorite form of communication. "You look like you've had enough for one night. Why don't you take off early? I can finish up here. Hell, I'm so tired I might just finish up in the morning."

I frowned, not wanting to leave things where they'd fallen. Lamont and I had never been close, and every attempt I'd made over the years to close the gap seemed only to worsen it. Tonight was no exception. "You sure?"

He nodded. "You did good tonight. You deserve it. Where you parked?"

I tilted my head in a random direction. "That little parking garage a couple blocks east of here. You know the one. By that new apartment complex."

"You want an escort?"

I shook my head. "Naw, I'm good. I've parked there plenty of times. Besides. You're letting me off early. Don't wanna look a gift horse in the mouth or ask for more favors than I've earned."

Lamont looked at me pointedly, failing to crack a smile. "You sure? I don't mind."

I pulled my purse out from underneath the bar and slung it over my shoulder, shaking my head as I hurried out the front door. "I'm good. Call Big Ginny tomorrow. And don't pretend like you forgot."

I didn't wait for my brother to respond as I headed into the night. The air was cool on my cheeks, and my skin prickled over with goosebumps as the night settled into my bones. The familiar smell of death and dying was somewhat lessened tonight; copal was wedged beneath baking asphalt, palo santo lost to exhaust. The faintness of the fragrances didn't mean anything. Definitely didn't mean that nobody was dying. Somebody was always dying. You just had to pay attention.

I was two blocks away from the bar when I sensed it. Somebody was following me, and they were gaining speed, closing the distance at a quick clip. I gritted my teeth and reached for my pepper spray, ready to turn on my heel and shout, "Can I help you with something?"

But as I spun around, my fingers closed over nothing but air. The pepper spray that I carried on my hip I'd given to that girl Brandy.

Shit.

The blow caught me across the left side of my face. Stars exploded like fireworks inside my head. No sooner had I registered what was happening than a second blow caught me square in the stomach, knocking the air out of me. I stumbled backwards, hitting the pavement, jarring my bones. And as I looked up, I saw my assailant and blinked.

I shouldn't have been surprised. It was Chad from the bar.

He registered my recognition, and something like a smirk passed across his lips but evaporated just as quickly. He was snarling, chewing and spitting his words, but I was in no position to register their meaning. He reached down and grabbed a fistful of my hair, yanking me to my knees. I shouted; I screamed. But the next thing I knew, another hand was clamped over my mouth, perilously close to my nose, and I was afraid that if I kept fighting his hand would move and I wouldn't be able to breathe. He dragged me only a few paces behind him before turning a corner. There was an alley there, poorly lit. Goddamnit.

Once we were safely out of sight from any passersby who might be wandering the main street, he spun me around and hit me again in the face. The blow landed awkwardly, missing my nose and catching the side of my cheek, but still the pain bowled me over. I swooned and crumbled to my knees. The next thing I knew, he was behind me, his hands in my hair, the force of his body slamming my head into the concrete.

Stars. Lightning. Blackness. Consciousness swam away from me as lights flickered on and off and sound ebbed. The scent of death that had been faint only minutes ago swirled thick and heavy in my nose, its scent cloying. This man intended to kill me. Reality slanted as though it had slipped on a patch of ice. I was certain I would pass out. I *should've* passed out. He lifted my head again and slammed it one more time into the ground. He was shouting something at me. Something about how I should mind my business. Something about how I needed to know my place. But the last thing I could do was make sense of words. My brain had shifted into pure animal survival mode. I was trying to hold on to my life.

Pinned beneath him, there was nothing my body could do to save itself from a violent death. And yet something inside me was fighting. Something inside me, the parts that weren't physical and bound to my flesh, were reaching out, scratching at every available surface, trying to hold on, to find purchase. Even as my consciousness faded and stars swam before my eyes, my soul or my energy or my aura or my *something* was reaching desperately beyond my body, clawing for shadows that offered nothing in their stillness.

I heard my own voice in my ears. *I can't go out like this. Somebody has to save me. Somebody has to know what happens to me tonight.*

I was scarcely conscious as my assailant rolled me over and pulled a glinting piece of metal from his pocket. He clicked a button, and a blade shot into view. My heart thundered in my ears so loudly I thought my head would explode.

But maybe that was the pain from being pounded repeatedly against the pavement. How many times had he done it? How many blows can a person take before their body gives out and their soul slips out to become one with the death current?

If I lost consciousness, I would die. Either because he would use that knife to slit my throat or because I would succumb to some kind of concussion or brain injury, I didn't know. But the overpowering scent of death that filled me and commanded my attention told no lies. I couldn't pass out. I had to survive.

Footfalls from around the corner. Voices. My attacker cursed, leaped to his feet. He kicked me once for good measure, and I groaned as he darted from the voices, away from the people who could save me. But even when he was gone, I couldn't find my voice. My throat was so raw, like razor blades had slashed my vocal cords to ribbons. I coughed, struggled to call out. But in the next moment, I blacked out.

I don't know how long I lay there in the street before finally coming to. Whoever had scared off my attacker didn't see me. Or if they had, they'd kept walking. Slowly, I pressed myself to sitting. Every part of my body was on fire. My muscles felt as though they had been stretched in every direction, every tendon ready to snap. My skin felt raw and ragged. I reached up to touch my forehead and found it slick with blood. Of course it was. Probably the entire side of my face, too, where he'd pounded my head into the pavement.

He hadn't taken my purse. It hadn't been a mugging, but then I knew that the moment I saw his face. It was personal. He wanted to kill me. And if those people hadn't shown up, I was certain he would have. I turned to the side and vomited onto the street. But maybe that wasn't because I was afraid.

Maybe that's just what happens when someone beats the shit out of you in the middle of the night.

Miraculously, I made it to my car. I slid into the driver's seat, locked all the doors, and rested the good side of my face on the steering wheel before I started the engine. I wasn't sure I could make it all the way home, but I sure as hell was gonna try. I couldn't handle some rideshare driver trying to get me to file a report or go to the hospital. I just wanted to get home.

Somehow, I managed to drive. Too slowly and my hands shook the entire time, but I made it home. I even managed to park close enough to the curb not to be an inconvenience.

I made it to the front door. I made it to the kitchen. I made it to my bedroom. I made it to my bed.

And then I shattered.

My face pressed into the pillow, I screamed until my screams became a cry. Until my crying became sobbing. Until my sobbing became hysterical release. I cried not only out of fear and pain but also relief. Relief that I was still alive. Relief that I was whole, that Big Ginny wouldn't have to worry and wonder what had happened to me. Relief that my assailant had failed, and I had been victorious. Yes, I was broken and bruised and bleeding. Yes, I was shaken to my core, and I didn't know how long it would take before I wasn't afraid of the dark. But I had my life.

I burrowed beneath my blankets, their weight an unspeakable comfort. I couldn't bring myself to remove my clothing. Everything hurt too much. Plus, I couldn't stand the thought of being nude and vulnerable. Underneath my blankets, where I shook and cried, I smelled the sour, salt smell of fear and sweat and raw determination. And yet I welcomed the smell, because it meant that I was alive.

I was *alive*.

Even as my eyelids grew heavy and I willed myself to fall into the arms of sleep, I couldn't ignore the irony. Just last night, I had reached into the veil seeking the comforting companionship of death. Tonight, death had reached back, seeking mine.

Perhaps we were destined for each other after all.

TWO DAYS PASSED before I got out of bed. Big Ginny tried to check on me several times, and I had a dozen missed calls from Lamont and the hospice. But I couldn't handle human interaction. Whether it was shock or horror or just plain survival, I knew my body needed solitude more than anything. And so, locked in my room, I gave myself what I needed.

Tenderly, I pulled myself to a sitting position, careful to test each set of muscles, my skin, even my mental health before making any grand gestures. Everything hurt, but I could function. I stifled a groan as I pulled myself to standing, avoiding the mirror at the other side of my bedroom. I'd have time enough to see the damage. As much as possible, I wanted to hold on to the light.

I trudged into the bathroom where I turned on the shower, making the water as hot as I could stand. I slipped out of my jacket, removed my blouse and my bra. But as I struggled out of my jeans, the sound of crinkling paper caught my attention. I reached into my back pocket and pulled out a glossy piece of paper. It was the pamphlet Brandy had given me, introducing the retreat that was about to start in a few days. She'd scrawled her name and cell phone number across the bottom.

I sank down onto the edge of the tub and smoothed the paper down in my lap. I stared long and hard at it as the steam from the shower grew thick. A few nights ago, I had no intention of helping Brandy with her ghost problem. A few nights ago, it hadn't interested me at all.

But after what happened to me in the alley, everything had changed.

I walked into my bedroom and found my cell phone. With trembling fingers, I dialed the number that I'd found on the pamphlet. After a few rings, a bright voice answered.

"Brandy Carbajal," she said.

"What do you think happens to the soul after death?" I asked.

The line was quiet for a moment. "That's an excellent question," she said. "I guess I don't have definitive answers."

"Of course you don't," I said, exasperated. "But I didn't ask you definitively. I asked you what you think."

"I think we go on to a better place," Brandy said, this time with no hesitation. "As beautiful as this world is, I think there has to be more to existence than just this. A place with no suffering. A place where we are always enveloped in the universe's love and protection. That's what I hope, anyway."

"Is that what your religion teaches?"

Brandy hrmmed on the other end. "Our religion focuses more on what happens in *this* world: finding satisfaction and joy and comfort here—to counteract all the suffering we otherwise experience. Ours is a religion of gratitude and abundance. We believe in manifesting our greatest desires here and now."

"And yet you personally think there's something else after this?"

Again, Brandy went silent. Then, "Isn't there?"

"There's something," I confirmed. "I've seen it. But I don't know if what I see is all there is. And I don't think it's the same for everyone."

"It's not?"

I shook my head, though Brandy couldn't see me. "When I visit the dead, I visit them in all kinds of places. Sometimes their homes, sometimes a forest or a field, sometimes a noisy cafe. I don't think the afterlife is absolute. I think it's something we choose. We make it what we want it to be. At least, that's been my experience." I paused, winding a lock of hair around a finger as I thought. "Whatever is out there is better than what we have here. So if there's something haunting your temple, I have to ask why. Why does it cling to this world when there is something better beyond?"

"I don't have an answer. That's part of the mystery I'm hoping you'll help me unravel."

I chewed the inside of my cheek as my eyes lifted toward the ceiling. Last night, as I scratched at reality to anchor myself here, I thought of the many reasons why I wanted to stay. Big Ginny. Lamont. The magic I so wanted to give my community. But if I had died in that alley, would I still have wanted to stay on Earth? Or would the same natural instinct that causes us to fight for life have allowed me to surrender and make the natural transition to the next part of my soul's adventure?

"I'll do it," I said finally. "I've never done anything like this before, so I need you to understand that it could be a huge failure. I don't want you to get your hopes up. It could be that we get in there and there's nothing I can do. Or we might find out that it's not a human spirit at all. You need to be prepared for that, too. It could be something else. A demon, an elemental, displaced astral energy ... So I'm just saying. I'm in. I'll do it. But I can't guarantee results. I can't even guarantee safety."

"I'm not asking for guarantees. I'm just asking for you to try. So thank you. When can you get here?"

"I have to make a few calls. I need someone to cover my shifts at work for the next few days. How far away is the preserve?"

"It's about an hour and 20 minutes outside of the city," she said. "I'll text you the address and you can Google map it. You shouldn't have any trouble finding us. But you didn't answer my question. When can I expect you?"

"I'll leave this afternoon," I said. "Before I come up there, though, there's a couple things I need to get. Some reagents we'll need for the ritual."

"All right. Sounds reasonable. If I may ask, what kind of stuff do you need?"

"Bones," I said. "We're gonna need some good quality bones."

CHAPTER FOUR

NECRO SIS WAS A MAGICAL supply shop on the other side of town owned by my friend and fellow necromancer, Opal. Opal sold good magic, but more than that, she sold an image of necromancy, too. She provided what the outside world believed us to be: Gothic, evil caricatures that cavorted with witches, mumbled incantations against our enemies, and dallied with things that go bump in the night. And in this way, Necro Sis didn't fail to deliver. The shop was a converted chapel in an older part of town, replete with steeple and keyhole windows. Opal had decorated the sanctuary to resemble a museum for the macabre and the strange. The walls were painted black, and electric flickering lanterns supplied a dim, shadowy light. Taxidermy owls, ravens, and birds of prey hung from the wood-plank ceiling. Skeletons peeked out from gloomy corners. Glass jars containing snakes and bats suspended in formaldehyde filled the shelves. Strange sigils lined her walls, and her shop offered everything from magical teas to cursed trinkets to ritual garb. Opal had it all.

She had to. Opal was on a mission to become independently wealthy for as little work as possible. If selling mostly harmless magical items to people with not an ounce of magic at their disposal was what it took, Opal was gonna capitalize.

My friend was standing in the corner of the store with her hands on a stranger's face. Her eyes were closed, and she was mumbling something I couldn't hear. The line to receive a gift was four people deep, meaning I had a few minutes to look around before it would be my turn. Assuming no one else showed up to receive their gifts.

I felt the familiar swell of jealousy in my gut as I glanced at the line. As a necromancer, I was supposed to do what Opal was doing now: drawing ancestral powers from the other side and granting them to individuals in our community. That ability was called a Godsend. Necromancers could lay hands on our people and bless them with a random psychic or magical ability. The gift only lasted a few weeks before fading away, but in that time the gifted might be able to read thoughts, detect lies, charm others, heal, or many other things. These small advantages were meant to help oppressed people gain equal footing with the majority and counteract the effects of hundreds of years of systemic racism, oppression, and poverty.

Opal could do it. I couldn't. I didn't have the Godsend and wouldn't until I found my mother on the other side.

While Opal performed her gift-giving, I shopped around for the items I knew I'd need to take to the preserve. I selected a bundle of raven bones, several black candles, and helped myself to scoops of Opal's famous loose-leaf tea. Today I chose her third-eye blend, which helped with psychic abilities. I tucked all these things into a basket and continued browsing. Opal's inventory never ceased to amaze me. All of the items she sold could be put to magical use by someone with talent; after all, the nature of magic was that it was flexible. But much of what Opal sold was nonsense on its face. I lifted a pair of enhancing candlesticks that promised to double the power of the candles that burned in them. I chuckled at the price tag before putting them back.

Finally, just when I was sliding a leather-bound grimoire back into its place, I felt someone sidle up beside me. I turned to find Opal beaming a smile that lit up her whole face. As usual, her platinum hair was arranged into bantu knots all over her head, her dark skin heavily rouged, her eyes lined in black kohl, and her lips colored a purple so dark they were nearly black. Today she was wearing a lacy, high-necked white Gunne Sax dress that made her look like an angel. Or maybe a ghost.

"Queen Kezia!" she cooed, leaning in for a kiss. I gave her both cheeks before offering my own greeting. She smelled of incense and musk. "It's so good to see you, girl. How you been?"

"Good! Busy with work and—"

"What happened to your face?"

I brushed my fingers along my cheekbone before snatching my hand away. "Nothing. Just a bar brawl. You know."

Opal didn't look convinced. "You been putting anything on it to help with healing?"

I shook my head. "No. What should I use?"

Opal guided me to her herb bar. She selected a small package and slipped it into my basket. "Arnica gel. Use it twice a day. It should help with inflammation and bruising."

"Thank you. Can you recommend anything for the pain?"

"Yes," she replied. "Ibuprofen and a stiff Martini."

I liked that about Opal. She was pragmatic.

The store was empty now, and Opal peered at me, her head cocked to one side. "Do you want a gift?"

I inclined my head. "Yes, please. If you don't mind."

My friend stepped nearer to me, placing the palms of her hands against my cheeks, avoiding my wounds. She closed her eyes and leaned her head backwards, her lips moving in a silent prayer. Warm, comfortable energy flowed between us, and a moment later, I noticed the world had shifted slightly. Colors were brighter. Sounds were sharper. I smiled, placing my own hands on Opal's. She opened her eyes expectantly. "What did you get?"

I grinned. "Super senses," I said.

"Ah, heightened physical sensations. Not one of the more exciting gifts, but useful, I guess?"

I shrugged. "I've never understood the point of this one, to be honest. If gifts are supposed to give us an advantage in the world to even the playing field, I'd rather have charm or mind reading any day."

"Don't always get what you want," Opal said. "Did you get anything else? A memory this time?"

I sniffed, pretending to cry. "I'll never get a genetic memory," I whined. "God don't love me enough."

"Maybe you don't want one," Opal said. "I had a guy in here last week who woke up a terrible memory. He was shaking and crying and carrying on. Not all of our people's memories are good ones, Kee. I don't know if I'd want to roll the dice on that."

"I guess you're right," I said. "Some things are best forgotten." Sometimes, when people received a gift, they also woke up genetic memories—mementos from our ancestors that hitched a ride in our DNA. We called this talent raising the dead. A necromancer once laid hands on my stepgrandmother and the next day she awoke knowing exactly how to cook a full-course, traditional Angolan meal. She'd never even eaten Angolan food before, but the blood of her ancestors remembered. Her forebears must have been amazing cooks.

But some people woke up memories of addiction, abuse, or worse. It was rare, but it did happen.

"Hey." Opal glanced around then. The store was empty, and I noted a change in her demeanor. Her eyes twinkled as she took my hand in hers. "You in a hurry to get home? Or do you have a minute?"

She didn't wait for an answer. She guided me to the back of her store through a door that led to her office. While the store itself was ostentatious and spooky, her office was dull, crammed, and dusty. She closed the door behind us. "I've been working on a new spell," she said.

Part of Opal's plan to retire a rich woman included crafting real spells that she sold to wealthy dabblers with more money than magical talent. While the items she sold in her store could be used in magic rituals, none of them contained an ounce of real magic. They were trinkets, mostly. But back here, Opal kept hidden the real deal. Spells, cantrips, incantations, amulets, you name it. One of the benefits of granting necromantic gifts to others was that it increased your own magical ability. Opal wasn't the best spell crafter I knew, but she was good.

"What is it?" I asked.

She lifted her chin, indicating a philodendron on her desk. "Watch this."

Opal lifted a hand, her fingers splayed. She whispered something I didn't hear and then quickly bent her fingers toward her palm—a summoning gesture. The moment she did, the plant shivered and then jerked toward her, landing on its side, the dirt from its planter spilling onto the floor.

I gaped, blinking in surprise. "Opal, did you just ... did you just move that plant with your mind?"

"With magic," she said, smiling widely. "More accurately, I called it to me."

I still couldn't believe what I had seen. "That's telekinesis," I breathed. "That's so fucking *rare*. I've never actually seen anyone do it in real life."

"I know," my friend said, pride lighting her up like a jack-o-lantern. "But I still have a long way to go. As you saw, the stupid plant didn't make it all the way to me—just a few feet. I want to be able to draw it into my hand. But for two, so far the spell only works on things with life energy, but not if they're sentient. For example, I couldn't make you move at all. A plant inside a container, sure. A tree? Maybe you could grab a few leaves. A wooden mug works really good," she said, her smile widening. "But a ceramic mug won't work at all. It's too dead. Wood at least has residual life on it."

"That's amazing, Opal," I said. "If you perfect this, you might actually become a for-real millionaire."

"Right?" My friend laughed and glided over to her desk where she opened a drawer, withdrawing a nondescript leather bracelet. "I enchanted this with the spell," she said, handing the bracelet to me. "I want you to try."

I accepted the bracelet, clasping it around my wrist. "Is it loaded?"

Opal sucked her teeth. "Girl, if I knew how to load that spell, I'da *been* sold it, okay?"

I chuckled. Loaded spells required absolutely no magical ability to use—they had all the necessary magic baked in. Unloaded spells like this bracelet were easier to create, though still difficult, and contained only the *potential* for magic—kind of like cake batter was only the potential for cake. You still had to put the thing in an oven. And in spellwork, the oven was magical energy. It was up to the user to summon whatever magical energy they could access to charge the spell and bring it to life.

For necromancers, that magical energy was the death current. Chaos mages accessed the chaos current, shamans and druids used the animate current, etc. There were more currents than I knew about, and while many spells could be empowered with any kind of current, specialized spells required specific magic.

"Is this a necro-only spell?" I asked.

Opal sighed. "So far. My girl Natalie was in here last week. You remember her— that Wiccan girl from Altadena. Anyway, she couldn't get it to work, but my other friend Two Top, that necro I met in Reseda last year? He got it to work no problem."

I groaned to myself. That didn't prove anything. Most Wiccans couldn't cast their way out of a paper bag, and even though Two Top had a stupid street name, the brother could actually do some pretty good magic.

"How do I activate it?"

Opal placed the plant back in its proper place. "Finger gestures," she said. She repeated the movement I'd seen her make earlier. "I also like to pray, but that's personal preference." She pointed to the philodendron. "Go ahead. See if you can bring it to you."

I took a deep breath, allowing myself to relax and sync with the death current. When I felt its energy moving through me, I reached out, palm up and fingers flat. I directed all my concentration on the philodendron. Then I curled my fingers toward my palm, just as I had seen Opal do.

Nothing happened.

"Try again," she said. "Try to be more fluid. But don't over-think it."

I centered myself, let my shoulders and jaw relax. I breathed in to a slow count of three, and exhaled similarly. Then, on my next inhale, I curled my fingers toward my palm.

The philodendron shuddered, jerking slightly toward me. Not enough to knock it over, but it definitely moved.

"Holy shit," I breathed. "It really works."

"Keep that," Opal instructed. "Practice with it. Tell me how I can improve it. I value your opinion."

"Are you sure?" I asked. "Even in its present state, I bet you could sell it for a good price."

But Opal shooed the suggestion away. "Naw, it ain't ready. But don't worry. When I get it right, *bam*! Ya girl gonna be on Oprah!"

I laughed. "Yeah, okay. Well, thanks. I'm headed out to the desert; plenty of opportunity to practice out there."

"Oh yeah? What's in the desert? Never pegged you for the camping kind."

I scoffed at the suggestion. "I ain't camping. You know that Temple of the Inner Flame? I'm actually headed out there to do some research."

Opal's eyes flew wide. "No shit? You gonna be up there with all them rich people?" She clucked her teeth again. "They gonna think you the help."

"You bet stop," I said, slapping her playfully on the arm. Reconsidering, I added, "You probably right, though."

Opal grew quiet, her lips drawing into a frown. "Listen, if you're heading out to the desert, you think you could do a favor for me?"

Again, Opal didn't wait for an answer. She ducked behind her desk and rummaged through a few dusty boxes before finally locating whatever she was looking for. She approached me, something cupped in her hands. I held out my own, and into my palm, Opal dropped a brass-colored disk.

I peered down at the object, cool against my skin. It looked like a coin, though it was too large—about two inches in diameter. On one side was the relief of a scarab. On the other, an alchemical symbol I didn't recognize. "What is this?" I asked.

"It's called Charon's Recall, named for the Greek ferryman that carries the dead across the river Styx. In the myths, the dead have to pay Charon for passage, so people buried their dead with a coin in their mouths as fare. This is sort of a fucked up take on that."

I frowned. "Fucked up how?"

"This coin is placed in the mouth of the dead also, but not to pay Charon to take the soul to the land of the dead. It's to bribe Charon to bring them *back*." When she saw the confusion on my face, she sighed. "You put that in a corpse's mouth, and it recalls their soul into the body." She frowned, shaking her head. "It doesn't animate the body or anything. Dead is dead; ain't no coming back from that. It just sort of ... traps the soul inside the rotting shell."

I grimaced. "Why would you ever want to do that?"

She shrugged. "Torture? I really don't know."

"Where did you get this?"

"Some jackass left it in my tip box," she said. "They're necro-only magic. People do that sometimes—leave me talismans they can't use or can't sell like I'm the goddamn occult Goodwill. But I do *not* want that. I was hoping you wouldn't mind getting rid of it for me."

"Get rid of it how?"

Opal crossed her arms over her chest, stepping away from

me. "I thought about throwing it into the ocean or something. But then I couldn't stop thinking of it washing up on the shore and someone finding it. I just don't think anyone should have it. It just feels wrong, you know? Something like that is unnatural."

Coming from Opal, who loved working weird magic more than anyone I knew, that was saying a lot. "So what do you want me to do with it?"

"Can you bury it out in the desert somewhere? Just—out in the middle of nowhere where nobody will find it. Please?"

Once again, I looked down at the coin. It didn't bother me as much as it bothered Opal, but it *did* weird me out a bit. Still, burying it somewhere in the desert seemed like something I could do, and it was an easy enough favor to bring my friend some peace of mind. "I'll take care of it," I agreed, sliding it into my purse.

"*Thank* you," she breathed. "That's a relief. Well, I don't want to keep you all day. You got everything you need?"

I nodded. "I'm ready to check out."

We left the office, heading to the cash register where I paid for my supplies and dropped the customary tip for my gift into the tip box. Necromancers never directly asked for payment for their services, but it was expected. To us, it wasn't different from tithing at church.

As I was leaving the shop, Opal called out to me one last time. "Queen Kee? Have fun up there. And call me later."

———————

ACCORDING TO THE PAMPHLET, the Temple of the Inner Flame Spiritual Preserve sat on over 300 acres of beautiful California desert in the hills outside of Los Angeles. The pamphlet was light on details about spiritual instruction: it mostly contained photos of people playing tennis, getting massages, taking walks, and doing yoga. In other words, it looked like a brochure for your run-of-the-mill relaxation spa. It listed noteworthy fauna like jackrabbits and roadrunners, and each page had a helpful *Did you know?* factoid illustrating some of the flora found on the premises. I had been expecting something a little more on the nose—maybe illustrations of naked people with their chakras lit up like Christmas trees or archaic drawings of alchemical rituals.

Another notable absence was any mention of price. Even a quick perusal of the website didn't tell me how much a three-week session at the Temple would set me back—not that I ever in a million years thought I could afford it. It also listed no schedule or suggestion of when or how often retreats took place. However, the website *did* inform me that currently, retreats were operating on a year-long waiting list and new reservations were by invitation only.

It seemed the cult was doing very well for itself.

The drive out of town was peaceful and put me in a good mood. The sum of money Brandy had promised for my efforts didn't hurt, either. It was more than enough for a month's worth of bills; longer if I was frugal, which I was. Living with Big Ginny meant nothing ever went to waste, and we were careful about our expenses. Had to be: even though Big Ginny's house was paid off, property taxes in Los Angeles were outrageous. Money was a constant concern.

I wasn't sure what I expected to find when I finally arrived in Oak Mission, California, but what I stumbled upon when I turned off the highway and pulled through iron gates emblazoned with a sign reading, "Temple of the Inner Flame Spiritual Preserve" was nothing I could ever have imagined.

A long, paved road edged on both sides with native plants and grasses wound through the desert, cutting elegantly through the terrain without looking out of place. I spied a few of the noteworthy fauna from the pamphlet as I followed the road through the preserve. Strategic lookouts along the way marked prime viewing for agave, yucca, and saguaro cactus. Humorous, cartoony signs instructed me to stick to the path and watch out for rattlesnakes. Turnoff points marked areas designated for camping.

The irony of that juxtaposition was not lost on me. White folks had more balls than I did. Camping with rattlesnakes? No ma'am.

Little by little, the desert gave way to more refined scenery. Oak and eucalyptus trees I recognized, but the smaller, flowering trees I couldn't name, probably because growing them was expensive, making them rare. Bushes blooming with flowers of every shape and color lined the road. I'd never seen such natural opulence. As the campus loomed nearer, the scenery became greener and lusher until it was impossible to believe I was still in the desert I had lived in my entire life.

The water bills alone would have bankrupted my family for generations.

Brandy was waiting for me when I finally arrived at the main building after parking my car. Today, she was dressed more casually than she'd been at the bar. A gauzy white dress was complemented with a pair of gold studs and sandals. She'd left her hair unbound and she wore no makeup. She'd been wearing a smile when she first came into view, but the nearer I drew to her, the darker her expression grew. When I was close enough to shake hands, her eyes were wide as saucers, a look of horror blooming over her face. "What happened to you? Are you okay?"

I tried to be nonchalant, but I knew what I looked like, and there was no way to be delicate about the situation. I offered a weary smile as Brandy gathered my hands in hers, squeezing my fingers lightly. "What happened?" she repeated.

I withdrew, wrapping my arms across my chest. "Remember that guy at the bar? Turns out I was right about his intentions. I was just wrong about the target."

Brandy's mouth dropped into a small *o* and her face blanched. As the color drained from her cheeks, she took a step forward and, before I knew what was happening, pulled me into a gentle hug. "And yet you came anyway," she whispered. "I don't know whether to apologize or thank you."

I peeled myself out of her embrace and shrugged. "You're paying me," I reminded her. "And this is business. Why don't we just leave it at that?"

Brandy stepped backward, putting a polite and comfortable distance between us. To her credit, she didn't look affronted. "In that case, why don't we go to my office? There's somebody here who would like to see you."

My eyes shot wide, perplexed. "Who?"

In retrospect, I should not have been surprised when she said, "Dr. Adeyemo."

My heart leaped into my throat as joy and nervousness thrummed throughout my body. I could practically feel my amygdala light up. It had been years since I'd seen my old mentor, Dr. Adeyemo. He'd been my professor when I was a biology grad student at the University of Southern California.

He'd been more than that, but I wasn't prepared to think about that now.

"Dr. Adeyemo is *here?*" I couldn't help the smile that broke over my face. "What's he doing here? Where is he?"

Brandy's smile widened. "You seem happy."

Again, I tried to affect nonchalance, but again, I failed. My cheeks reddened as I dropped my gaze to the ground. "It's just so unexpected. I haven't seen him in so long. I can't believe he really wants to see me."

Brandy tugged me forward, and we breezed through the front door, stale, conditioned air blasting me in the face. "Well, I'm glad to hear that you're excited to see him. He wasn't so sure you'd want to."

I frowned. "Really? The last time I saw him, he was the one who—"

A door opened, and a man stepped out. When my eyes caught his, my heart plummeted into my stomach, and my cheeks caught fire. Standing in the hallway barely ten feet away from me was not my grad school mentor, Dr. Adeyemo.

It was his son and my ex-husband, Marcus Adeyemo.

———

STUNNED, I blurted out the first thing that came to mind. "Marcus? What are you doing here?"

I didn't immediately understand the look of concern on his face until he took three sweeping steps toward me before stopping short, his eyes flowing over my entire body. "Dove? What happened to you?"

Dove. The nickname sliced like a knife through my ribs. Pain laced with longing twisted in my center as memories of my life with Marcus coursed through me, lighting up my hippocampus. The surge of emotions reignited the injuries I had sustained a few short nights ago, and I could have doubled over, awash with too many feelings both emotional and physical. I swallowed hard and closed my eyes, taking deep, steadying breaths. When I opened my eyes, my nerves had settled somewhat. "Don't call me that," I said, my voice barely above a whisper.

Marcus's nostrils flared, but he didn't argue. "Kezia. What happened to you?"

I squared my shoulders and tried to project indifference. "It's nothing. I was assaulted the other night walking back from my car, and no, I don't want to talk about it. So. What are you doing here?"

Marcus pursed his lips, a muscle in his temple spasming in response to my curt answer. I could almost feel the self-restraint it took for him not to press the matter. He gestured toward Brandy, who looked confused by our exchange. "Same as you. I'm here to investigate the ghost."

My vision swam, and I tried to fight against the current. Brandy must've noticed my dizziness, because she took me by the elbow and ushered me toward a couch where I sank down into the cushions, grateful to be off my feet. Marcus settled down next to me, close enough to offer comfort but not enough to invite intimacy. I appreciated that. "You're gonna have to explain this to me like I'm five," I said. "I guess let's start with ... *doctor* Adeyemo? I was expecting your father."

Marcus laughed, the sound ringing like a bell in my mind. I'd always had a Pavlovian response to Marcus's laughter, and I soon chuckled as well, as though I were in on the joke. It felt like old times, which was both comforting and cruel. "I should have guessed you'd make that assumption. I'm sorry to disappoint you. Brandy sought me out a couple of weeks ago, looking for an expert in hauntings. And while I'm no expert—"

I held up a hand to interrupt him. "She contacted *you*? Hold up. I just don't understand. Are you a doctor now? A doctor of what?"

Marcus crossed his arms over his chest as he leaned back

into the cushions, looking up at the ceiling as though searching for a memory. "I guess it was a few months after we got divorced? I went back to school. I got my PhD in metaphysical studies and arcane magics. Now, I'm an associate lecturer at UCLA in their Alternative Religions department. We don't have so-called haunting experts on staff. The paranormal has always been a throwaway discipline; most people who study it are quacks and charlatans. But a few of us do take the discipline seriously. Poltergeists, yokai, demons ... Kezia?"

"Sorry," I said, still reeling from the download. "But you're at *UCLA*? How did that happen? How did your father let you betray him—us!—like that?" My alma mater, USC, and UCLA had been rivals since the beginning of time.

Marcus grinned. "It was quite a shock to my pops, that's for sure! You know I never cared much about college rivalries, but I can tell you between the two, UCLA has the far better campus. You can't disagree with me there."

He was right about that. "So you're an associate lecturer at UCLA?"

Marcus shifted and nodded, offered a chagrined smile. "Yeah. I know. It's probably got to be a lot for you. I thought at least a dozen times about telling you. But you always made your boundaries clear, so I tried to honor that. If fate saw fit to bring us together again, I always assumed it would be you who reached out to us."

That casual use of "us" was what did it. A switch flipped in my brain, and this meeting was no longer business. I needed to know everything, and I needed to know now.

As though reading my thoughts, or perhaps just adept at reading a room, Brandy cleared her throat and got to her feet. "I've got some other business to attend to. Can I get you both some water or something else to drink? I should only be a moment."

Both Marcus and I shook our heads. "I'm good," I said. "Thank you. Is there someplace private Marcus and I can talk? I feel a little exposed sitting here in the lobby."

Brandy pointed to the same room Marcus had emerged from just a few minutes earlier. "Take all the time you need."

I followed Marcus into the office, where he closed the door with a soft click. He motioned toward the two comfy chairs in the room's corner. "Ladies first," he said.

We took our seats, staring at each other, hoping the other would speak first. I was the one who cracked. I gestured wildly at the space around me as I sputtered, "Is she here?"

Marcus shook his head as he leaned forward, placing the tips of his fingers on my leg. The intimacy was startling; I didn't know if I wanted it or not. He held my gaze as he said, "I didn't bring her, no. She's at home in Los Angeles with my mother. I'm still finding a nanny, and Mum's always been good with our daughter. Lola loves her very much."

Our daughter. The phrase was electrifying, igniting all my synapses, turning my whole body into a receptor. For the past four years I had refused to hear news of my daughter—*our daughter.* And while I believed it was the right choice, it was also the hardest thing I had ever done. Not a day went by that I didn't berate myself for abandoning the only thing in the world that truly mattered.

I gave a small nod, twisting the rings on my fingers, worrying a hole in my cheek with my tongue. I didn't know exactly what I wanted to say next or what I wanted to know. I pressed my palms against my cheeks as I chanced another glance at Marcus. Finally, swallowing down my pride, I asked, "How is she?"

Marcus gave me a soft smile as he settled into the conversation, making himself comfortable. "She's well. She's learning how to swim. She's like a fish; she never wants to get out of the pool. It's not true what they say about Black folks. She swims like a champ."

My heart fluttered at this new image of her, and fresh tears rose to my eyes. It was hopeless to blink them back, so I didn't try. The tears rolled down my cheeks and as soon as I tasted the salt on my lips, I began to shake with silent sobs.

"She knows about you," he murmured. "Recently, Mum decided it was time to tell her something. She doesn't really understand, of course. She's only five, after all. But she knows you are a necromancer and that being around you makes her sick. She understands that she can't see you, but it's really hard on a girl to not know even the sound of her mother's voice."

"I'm sure it's hard on her," I said. "It's hard on me, too."

Marcus blinked. "I know. Dove, I know. I didn't mean anything by it. I only meant—"

"It wasn't supposed to be like this," I said, burying my face in my hands.

Again, Marcus said, "I know."

We both grew quiet. Necromancers often couldn't carry babies to term, but when they did, the child was always immune to the blues. I myself lost a half dozen pregnancies in my years with Marcus before finally becoming pregnant with Lola and carrying her to term. I was too young and naïve to be cautious. If we'd made it that far, it must mean she wasn't susceptible! But it wasn't long after she was born that she'd shown signs. Listlessness. Unusual stillness. Refusal to nurse. At first, I refused to believe. I sat in the doctor's office screaming that she was just an infant, that there was no way to tell if her ailments were because of my affliction or her own failure to thrive. Eventually, gentle but stern admonishments from my husband and our pediatrician finally convinced me that if I was wrong, it meant my baby would die. And so I'd given in.

There was only one way through that scenario; Marcus and I had to live apart, and he needed to take sole care of our daughter.

At first, we pretended it wouldn't be forever; that ours was a temporary embarrassment that would eventually work itself out. But slowly I came to the sobering realization that both Marcus and Lola needed to get on with their lives—and that meant cutting them both loose. I filed for divorce, though Marcus begged me to reconsider. But I was stalwart in my resolve. Eventually he signed. We'd been divorced for four years now.

I'd wanted him to take Lola back to his family home in Nigeria and raise her there. I wanted her to grow up surrounded by people who looked like her, who spoke the language of her ancestors, who would never ask with ignorant, wide eyed awe to touch her hair. But Marcus said Lagos was too far. He wanted to stay in Los Angeles, hoping that proximity might make me change my mind about seeing her.

It didn't. It just made her absence in my life—*their* absence —hurt more.

While I searched for a way to end my affliction, I thought endlessly and tirelessly of Lola. Over the years, Marcus had offered to show me pictures, videos of my baby girl growing up. He said that we should Skype, that there was no reason we couldn't have a relationship just because we couldn't share the same physical space. But the heart wants what it wants, and my arms wanted to hold her. My breast wanted her little face crushed against it. I wanted to touch her, squeeze her, love her intimately and in person. And if I couldn't have that, it was best that I had nothing. Because the pain of losing her every time we hung up the phone or hit that disconnect button would have been too much for me. I had never been a strong woman. Even with all my powers, I wasn't superhuman. I couldn't lose my baby over and over again.

After a while, I shook myself free of the memories and sat up straight. "Is there anything else I should know?"

Marcus shook his head. "Is there anything else you *want* to know?"

Tossing my hair from my face, I said, "No, thank you," which was a lie. There was so much more I wanted to know. But I'd made my choices.

The only way I knew to deal with emotion was to ignore it, so I returned the conversation to the matter at hand. "So Brandy contacted you through UCLA to ask for your help with the haunting. If that's the case, why am I here?"

Marcus leaned forward, resting his elbows on his knees as he gazed at me with that soft, sly smile I used to love so well. "I don't have your talents," he said simply.

"Well, what is that supposed to mean?" I asked.

"I'm a scholar. But it turns out, understanding how things work and having the ability to do something with that understanding are two entirely different things." He laughed as he said this, but I sensed frustration there. "What's that old saying? Those who can, do? Those who can't, teach? Turns out when it comes to communicating with spirits, I don't have the chops. Turns out it takes an actual necromancer."

I licked my lips as I considered what Marcus had said. "So, does that mean that you've already seen the spirit? Is it a real haunting? Is it a ghost we're dealing with? Tell me something. Bring me up to speed."

Marcus shrugged. "There's nothing more to tell. I agree with Brandy that there's something off at the temple, but I can't suss out the cause. Hence, a necromancer."

I nodded. "Well, now that I'm here, I guess you'll be going back to the city?"

I didn't expect the look of surprise that colored Marcus's face. "Back to the city? No. I'm gonna stay."

I lifted my shoulders in confusion. "Why? You said yourself you couldn't talk to the spirit, so what's the point?"

Marcus made an irritated sound in the back of his throat and tilted his head to one side. "It'll be good for my career to see what you do here. There's a lot of academic material about how necromancers perform their rites and rituals, but not much on how they work with paranormal forces. And you're an interesting study, being both a hoodoo worker and a necromancer."

I frowned. "So you're suggesting you want to use this as a case study? Publish in some academic journal? You might not be able to get peer reviewed," I added with more than a little bitterness. "Necromancy isn't as fashionable as it used to be," I warned.

"It was never fashionable, and you know it better than most. I don't have any immediate plans to write a paper, but if it comes to that, I promise to keep you anonymous. But this would be ... it could be huge for my career," he finished.

"Well, if you promise to keep things professional between us," I relented, "then fine, you can stay and study. I'll teach you what I can. But there are some things that I know or feel that I won't be able to explain to you. So those things you have to pick up on your own. But I mean it, Marcus. This has to be about the spirit. Because if you're hoping for something else ...
"

"Don't be like that, Kezia. This isn't about you. This is, for once, about me." He smiled then, his gaze softening. "All right, maybe it's a *little* about you. After all, we are each other's *ayanmo*," he said, his smile growing wider. "You remember *ayanmo*?"

I couldn't help but blush as I suppressed a smile. *Ayanmo* was a tenet of the Yoruba religion, roughly translated as fate. Although Marcus and I were both Christians, we shared a tender affinity towards the Yoruba religion. Marcus's family was Nigerian, and I? Well, I was like any other Black American. Fascinated by a continent I had never seen, my soul clamored for a piece of my ancestors. I refused to give the government or any corporation my spit for a DNA test, so until I found my own ancestors on the other side or awakened a genetic memory, I'd likely never know what region of Africa they were taken from. Somewhere on the West Coast, I'm sure. That's where most of the slave trade happened. Still, it hurt my heart to not really know.

All of that aside, however, I didn't believe in fate. "Are we going to have this conversation again?" I asked, my voice light as a smile crept over my face. "If there is such a thing as fate, it's got some explaining to do."

Marcus laughed then, and the sound chimed throughout my body, even as I tried to ignore its effect. "You haven't really changed all, dove."

"Don't call me that," I said again as the smile slid from my face. Dove was the nickname Marcus had given me years ago. It was from the Bible. It was Marcus's way of assuring me that somewhere out there in that crazy world, I would eventually find my tree branch. I would eventually find my peace.

Marcus had always been full of childish ideas.

We stood then, and I was surprised when Marcus pulled

me into an awkward hug. Again, I wasn't sure I wanted this intimacy, but in the end, I melted into it. "It's good to see you," he said.

I nodded, not trusting my voice.

We left the office and returned to the lobby, pouring ourselves cups of cucumber water and chatting while we waited for Brandy to find us. It didn't take long for her to appear.

"Are we ready to go?" she asked.

I nodded and motioned for her to lead the way. "Let's get this party started," I said.

As we walked toward the temple, Brandy gave a miniature tour of the grounds, pointing out key buildings with a sprinkling of backstory for each. The preserve was extraordinary. It was so much bigger than I expected. Gleaming white buildings were nestled in the middle of emerald green lawns, something unheard of in the California desert. "This right here is one of three bathhouses," Brandy was saying when I diverted my attention from the greenery back to the tour. "They were all designed after traditional Japanese onsen. This one is the women's bath. Just ahead, there's a men's bath, and next to that, a coed bath. If you have time, you should check them out. The water is an absolute delight for your skin.

"Right up here is the yoga center. And that over there is just your average gym." She turned around and dropped me a wink. "Not everything has to be especially magical."

I tried to imagine having the money it would take to earn a vacation here. Even if my family worked our asses off for generations, we'd never accumulate the disposable income required to purchase one week in this place. "It's stunning," I said. "I don't know what I was expecting, but it sure wasn't this."

Brandy turned her brilliant smile on me, eyes wide as saucers and a pink glow in her cheeks. "I'm so glad you think so! We're constantly adding new features and accommodations to this place. Can you imagine? My husband bought this land almost 20 years ago. It's taken us this long to get it were we wanted. And even now, there are so many things we still want to add. I really want a traditional Native American hothouse, but my husband says that cultural appropriation is completely passé. He's probably right; but we do have the onsen. Is that not cultural appropriation? In for a penny, in for a pound, I always say."

I couldn't help but laugh at this. It was ridiculous. But then the relevance of what Brandy just said dawned on me. "Hold on. Who is your husband?"

Brandy blushed. "*Caleb* is my husband," she said. "Sorry. I thought I mentioned that."

I definitely would have remembered if she had mentioned that. Caleb Atwater was the Temple's self-proclaimed guru and leader. He was also at least twice the age of his bride. Brandy couldn't have been much over 25. So while it wasn't the strangest pairing I'd ever heard of, I couldn't help but wonder about this young woman's intentions. But looking at her, she didn't strike me as an opportunist. Nothing about her indicated that she was in it for money, or fame, or power. She truly seemed like a simple woman who just wanted to find spiritual enlightenment.

There was still innocence in the world, it seemed.

CHAPTER FIVE

WE HAD BARELY CRESTED a small hill when the temple came looming into view. I was expecting a typical church-style building or at least something relatively sedate. But this building was anything but that, and my breath caught at the sight of it. Jutting into the crystal blue sky, the temple was an octagonal spire of gleaming white stone and sparkling glass. I turned my gaze to Brandy, eyebrows arched. "Is this it?"

I expected Brandy to sweep her arms in a wide gesture beckoning me to enter. But instead, she became serious, almost withdrawn. The sobriety that overcame her was more than simple reverence. Something like anxiety colored the contours of her face, and I wasn't sure if it was the possible presence of a spirit or something more. Before those thoughts could really congeal in my mind, Brandy gathered my hands into hers. Her hands, feverishly warm, trembled. "This is the temple," she said, gesturing with her head. "We used to use a Presbyterian church that we purchased in the city for our sacred rites, but my husband wanted something more befitting our beliefs and values. We finished construction on this building about five years ago, and now it's the seat of our organization. Everything from wedding ceremonies to birthing dedications to funerals are held here. Under normal circumstances, we don't let the uninitiated enter. To maintain the temple's purity, we protect this space. Do you understand what I'm saying?"

I quirked an eyebrow. "Do you not want me to go in? I'm not sure how I'm supposed to help you if I can't go inside," I said.

Brandy shook her head, her brow furrowed. "I'm not saying that. I'm saying it's a sacred place. I need your reverence and respect. But mostly, I need your silence. The things you see in here, and the experiences you have, are for you and you alone. I request that you don't share them with anyone else: not family, not friends—*please* not social media. When they find out you've been here, newspapers and magazines will reach out to you, asking for quotes or for you to relay your experience so they can pedal their shady stories about the weirdos shacking up in Oak Mission, California. I don't have an NDA for you to sign. I'm not going to send a gaggle of lawyers after you if you go against my wishes. But from one spiritual woman to another, I'm requesting that you honor my request. Do you understand?"

I nodded. "I feel you. What happens in Vegas, stays in Vegas."

If my little quip eased her mind at all, her expression did not betray it. Instead, she gave my hands a gentle squeeze as she led me toward the temple's entrance. Now that I was free to gaze upon the building, I noticed that what I had previously mistaken for decorative carvings around the door was actually some language I didn't recognize. I paused at the entrance, squinting, trying to make out the letters. I wracked my brain but came up with nothing.

"What script is this?" I asked.

"That's Kaddare script," she said. "It's a rare alphabet used to transcribe certain Afro-Asiatic languages. That particular inscription is a prayer given to our initiates."

"What does it say?"

Brandy dropped me a rueful smile with a soft shake of her head. "I can't tell you that, as it's privileged information. But at its essence, it's a promise made of the flesh and of the spirit. In our religion, devotion is not just the mouthing of words; it's an act of the whole body. When our initiates pass through these doors, it's a renewal of the vows they took upon receiving the blessings of the flame."

It sounded like hocus-pocus to me, but I wasn't there for spiritual guidance; I had a job to do. I prepared to step past Brandy and into the temple when she stopped me, her hand on my shoulder. "One more thing," she said. "Once you go inside, don't pray."

I balked. "Don't pray?"

Brandy continued to give me a pointed look, and for a fleeting moment, she looked much older than her twenty-something years. But I blinked, and the sensation passed. Brandy said nothing more as she stepped aside, allowing me to enter. I threw a look to Marcus to see if he made more sense of this conversation than I did. But he looked like he always looked. Perhaps he'd already heard the same spiel from Brandy earlier.

Brushing past my escort, I stepped into the temple. I had been in many churches over the course of my lifetime, but this was nothing like any church I had ever been in. This was more like a cathedral. Above, blue sky clotted with pine trees shone through the temple's glass ceiling. It was almost like being inside a snow globe.

When I finally tore my eyes away from the sky, I took in the temple's interior. Each of the eight walls was adorned with murals made from a combination of paint and glass or maybe broken pieces of mosaic tile. On each panel were more words in Kaddare script encircling a central figure, an image that was both deeply familiar and beautifully alien. I paused, my mouth softly agape as I turned my attention to Brandy, eyes wide.

"Black Jesus?" I asked, gesturing toward the figure on each of the eight walls. I recognized the traditional depictions of Christ, replete with earth-toned robes and golden halo, but his ebony skin was new and as unexpected as it was beautiful. California was progressive, but not Black Jesus progressive. It made my heart swell to see it.

But Brandy only widened her grin and gestured to the images before us with a soft lift of her chin. "That's our prophet, Brother Zahi. He was the first in our time to bring the wisdom of the flame from Heaven to Earth. We honor him as a divinely inspired being, much like your Christ. The prophet is not himself a god, but he is the one who first opened the channel between this world and the next."

My initial reaction was to dismiss her words as more mumbo-jumbo, but now that she mentioned a channel between worlds, I *did* sense something different about this place. Something was here that felt like the death current, but unlike the death current, lay outside my grasp. I tried briefly to tap into it, to follow its trail to wherever it might lead, but I couldn't. Where the death current flowed through me like water through a faucet, this energy evaded my touch, dancing around my attempts to grab it almost playfully. Like it *knew* I wanted to engage, but it was sly and slick and unwilling.

Interesting, I thought. *Another current, one I can almost access. It's not the death current, though it's similar.* I filed this information away as something to ask Marcus about later. As a professor of arcane magic, he was likely to know more about magical currents than I did.

"What do these inscriptions say?"

Brandy offered me another of her mysterious smiles. "They come from a book of poems penned by Brother Zahi himself. We believe they are words gifted to him by the divine."

Moving on, I walked the length of the building, feeling, observing, admiring. The pews were polished to a high shine, and each was lined with thick velvet cushions. These people hadn't spared any expenses in creating this place of worship. There was no pulpit that I could see, but there was a small dais at the other end of the temple. Next to it were two basins: one filled with water, the other with ash. I assumed that second one to be a brazier. As I looked around, I didn't see any of the accouterments that often accompany Christian churches: there were no hymnals, no collection plates, no place on the wall for bulletins of any kind. This place was free of distractions, a sanctuary for the mind and spirit. Whatever they had done here, they had done it brilliantly. This didn't just feel like a sacred place. It felt like a place I never wanted to leave.

I took my time pacing around the building. I drew my fingers along the pews, even touching the gilded artwork that adorned the walls. But it wasn't until I came to the sixth wall that I felt something change.

The sense of peace that had enveloped me as soon as I entered the building evaporated in an instant. The fragrances hit me first: copal, palo santo, lemon furniture polish. Yes, death was here in abundance. Slow dread filled me as the hairs on my arms stood up, and a roiling unease settled in the base of my stomach. Curious, I turned my head to catch Brandy's gaze. Her expression was unreadable. I let my eyes flick to Marcus, who was similarly stoic. Fine: if they wanted to test me, I'd rise to the challenge.

The longer I stood in that spot, the greater the unease grew inside me until I felt physically ill. I took one step backward, and the anxiety lessened. Tentatively, I retraced my steps, entering that same small circle where the anxiety had clutched me. Once again, the cold despair circled its arms around me, threatening to pull me under. I removed myself from the circle and wrapped my arms around my torso. "You're not imagining things," I said. "There's definitely something here."

Brandy's expression remained painfully neutral as she asked, "Is it human?"

"I don't know," I said. "But we can find out. We'll need a few things first, though."

"I'll get anything you need," she said.

"First, we'll need a gas lantern. Like the kind you might take camping."

Brandy made a note in her phone. "What else?"

"Bones."

Brandy's eyes flicked up to meet my gaze. "Right; you mentioned that. Any particular kind?"

I had half a mind to say human bones just to see what she'd do. But Marcus answered for me, taking away my moment. "Bones that fit easily in her hands. She prefers the bones of ravens." He cleared his throat, apologetic. "Sorry."

I returned my attention to the cold spot in the temple where the spirit was undoubtedly waiting. "I already have the bones; I brought them up from the city. There's only one other reagent we'll need. Blood. *Your* blood."

At this, Brandy's expression finally shifted, betraying something like fear. "My blood? You didn't say anything about that on the phone."

I shrugged. "Whether I mentioned it or not doesn't change the fact that I need it."

Brandy swallowed hard a few times, reaching to finger a delicate gold chain at her neck. A nervous habit. "How much blood?"

I waved a hand dismissively. "Just a few drops. Not enough to paint over your doorway with." When she didn't smile, I sighed. "Brandy, it's only a few drops of blood. It's part of the ritual."

My host stammered. "Well ... I guess I can arrange that. So what do you think? Is this something you can work with? Do you think you'll be able to communicate with the spirit?"

My eyes wandered back to the empty patch of cold. "I can't promise anything. But if I had to guess, I'd agree that it's an earthbound human soul. When I stand close enough to it, I can feel its anguish. It feels like human suffering."

I ought to know.

I expected Brandy to launch into planning mode, assigning tasks and setting a timeline. But it was Marcus who spoke up. "Assuming we get all the materials you need, I think it's best if we perform the ritual tonight," he said. "The new session starts soon, and we don't want to draw any attention to ourselves. We won't be completely flying under the radar: one of the retreat attendees from the last session decided to stay another three weeks. She's still here, on campus. But one potential looky-loo is better than a full roster."

Brandy nodded. "Absolutely. We need to keep this hush-hush and have the temple back in good condition in time for the new session. So. Tonight, then?"

I heaved a little shrug. "As long as you can provide the blood and the lantern, we're good to go."

Brandy brushed her hands together, settling the matter. "Tonight then. It's a new moon, too, so we'll have the benefit of the cover of darkness. Let's meet here at 10 o'clock unless there's a better time, Kezia? Magically speaking?"

I hrmmed. "We should begin the ritual at midnight. But we may need some time to set up. How does 11 o'clock sound?"

Both Marcus and Brandy nodded. "I look forward to seeing you both then," Brandy said.

CHAPTER SIX

BRANDY SHOWED US to our rooms, which turned out to be individual, cottage-style houses. Rows of identical white buildings decorated with rose bushes and fountains lined the streets, looking like something out an episode of Real Housewives: Servant's Quarters edition. I don't mean that derisively; the bungalows were nicer than Big Ginny's house by a mile, and we took pride in our home.

Brandy instructed us on the kitchen's hours, where to find food between scheduled meals, and gave us keys to the facilities. We had access to everything the preserve offered, from hiking trails to saunas to tennis courts. "There's no wi-fi, but if you go down to Reception and speak to my assistant, Casey, she'll set you up with mobile wi-fi devices." She made a face as she said this, like she found the idea distasteful. "Service out here is abysmal, but that was by design. We prefer our participants disconnect as much as possible. But if you *want* to be connected, you have that option."

"I appreciate that," I said. "I have an elderly grandmother. I'll need to be reachable just in case."

"Of course. You don't need to explain your reasoning to me. You're our guest, after all, not our prisoner. I want you to be comfortable and only as immersed in the atmosphere as you want to be. Anyway. If you need anything, please let Casey know. Otherwise, I'll see both of you at 11."

Brandy took her leave, but just as he was about to disappear into his own bungalow, I caught Marcus by the wrist. "I hate to ask you this," I said, my voice wavering, "but do you think you could meet me here tonight?" Unconsciously, my hand went to my cheek, my fingertips brushing lightly against the abrasion. "I don't want to walk alone in the dark."

A flash of anger in Marcus's eyes let me know he was thinking about the asshole that turned the fierce warrior he married into a cowering damsel in distress. "Of course I will. Is that all you need? Are you all right to be alone?" he asked.

I nodded. "Yes. Really, I'm okay. I'd just appreciate an escort once it gets dark. If it's not too much trouble."

His eyes quickly traced the contours of my abraded face. "There's no such thing as too much trouble when it comes to my *ayanmo*," he said. "I'll see you at 11."

After Marcus left, I made my way back to Reception where I found Casey in a storeroom looking bewildered in the middle of a riot of open moving boxes.

I poked my head through the door, a bashful grin on my face. "You Casey?"

The woman looked up from the mess before her and dusted her hands off on her slacks. She was middle aged, with salt-and pepper hair, a dumpling figure, and a pleasant face marred by a slight frown. "That's me," she said with a pleasant midwestern accent. "What can I do ya for?"

"Brandy told me to come see you if I wanted a mobile wi-fi," I explained. "I'd like one."

"Oh, sure, I can get that for ya if ya like," she said, that frown trying to return to her face. "But are ya sure ya want it, honey? It's not every day ya get to put the entire world on mute and just focus on yourself for a little while."

I grinned and nodded. "I'm sure I want it but thank you."

Casey made a face like, "Well, I tried!" and motioned for me to follow her into a little office. She opened a drawer and began digging around. "You're not here for the session, are ya? Doesn't start till tomorrow. And if ya'd been here before, I'd recognize ya. You a friend of Brandy's? Cuz I know you're not a friend of Caleb's." She said this last part with a laugh.

"Oh? How do you know that?"

Casey chuckled as she pulled a wi-fi unit free, disentangling it from the others. "He's just a funny old coot, that's all. Very proper—highly educated. Despite the profile of the people that get invited here, he's actually very private. I'd even go so far as to call him a loner. More interested in books and scrolls than people. Although he is *very* dedicated to his people—don't get me wrong. Nothing brings as much joy to Caleb as sharing Brother Zahi's light with his initiates." She smiled absently, lost in her own thoughts. "Well, except maybe Brandy. Never saw two people so in love with each other. But the Temple—this is his life's work. You know he grew up in Somalia. His parents were missionaries. So I guess you could say his devotion to the divine is dyed in the wool."

The woman seemed to realize that she was rambling and promptly clamped her mouth shut as she handed me the electronics. "If ya have any trouble with that, ya come back here and let me know. Need anything else?"

"No, I don't think so. Well, actually," I said, reconsidering, "there is one thing. If you had just one day here, how would you spend it?"

At this, Casey's grin widened. "Aw, honey. Let me tell ya. You're in for a *treat*."

BACK IN MY ROOM, I unpacked and got settled. The cottage was far nicer than any hotel I had ever stayed in. It comprised several rooms: an eat-in kitchen, a living room, a small personal reflection room outfitted with yoga mats, rugs, and pillows, and a bedroom with an en suite. The bathroom contained a steam shower and a jetted tub large enough for two people. The other furnishings were just as lush, with real silk on the queen bed piled high with pillows.

There was a large television, a state-of-the-art sound system, and a shelf of old board games. But the only offered reading material was a map of the grounds and a slender, hard-bound book on the nightstand. The cover read, *Conversations with the Inner Flame* by Brother Zahi. I thumbed through it and saw that it was a book of poetry.

This must be the book of poems Brandy mentioned at the temple, I thought, flipping through the book. It reminded me of a Bible with its onion-skin pages and gold leafing around the edges. The inside cover was stamped with a note that read, "Please feel free to take this book home with you. If you already have a copy, please share with a friend." The signature beneath the stamp read, "Caleb Atwater".

I flipped it open to a random page. I wasn't fond of poetry, but with no particular plans for several hours, I began to read.

"This world is the beginning
But shall not be the end
A blueprint for frustration

And regrets we cannot mend
Free will a noble enterprise
But seeds of ill and woe
Ever tarnished the Creator's Plan
Laying the greatest creatures low
And so we shall
Another world seek!
Create it, if we must
For perfection lies
Beyond the pale
The lame, the low, the weak."

I flipped to another random location.

"My beloved is a vessel
Waiting to be filled
With the fire of a hundred stars
That fuel a precious will
My beloved is a concubine
Awaiting now my call
To sublimate and extricate
No victim to life's thrall
And so I shall
Possess you, my sweet!
Consume your very soul
And drink you down
And breathe you out
And then we both shall sleep."

I closed the book, returning it to the nightstand. I still had
no appetite for poetry.

When all my things were put away, I went out to explore

the grounds. I'd never been to a real sauna, and it was the first activity on my list. I walked in the direction indicated by my room's map, following a row of ivy-covered lattice walls. When I was nearing my turn, a small gap in the foliage caught my attention. I paused, peering into a small enclave. I checked my map, but this area wasn't marked.

It was a small rose garden. The ground was paved with mismatched stones etched with lichen, shards of grass shooting from the ground where the stone edges didn't quite meet. In the middle of the garden was a stone fountain sputtering rivulets of water gurgling from clogged spigots. The water smelled organic; I could almost taste the algae. Birds sat at the water's edge, dipping their bills and shaking droplets from their feathers.

Aside from the fountain, statues decorated the area. They'd fallen into disrepair, stained and eroded by years of acid rain. Their pedestals had sunk into the ground, leaving them upright but lopsided. Sparse tea rose bushes made up the garden's only other adornment, only a few of which were in bloom, and the blooms themselves were feeble. It was not the least impressive rose garden I'd ever seen, but it seemed remarkably shabby when compared with the opulence of the rest of the preserve.

I liked it immediately.

I stepped out of my shoes; the stone was cool against my skin. I sat on a bench facing a statue of a nude woman. Her arms were uplifted, and she was encircled by a halo of fire and stars. She reminded me of the Virgin of Guadalupe. Nestled in the crook of the statue's arm was a real, empty bird's nest.

"Looks like a vermilion flycatcher's nest," said a voice in my head.

I grinned. It was my patron, Papa Jinabbott. He'd been

dead long before I met him, and he rarely spoke to me unless I was in a trance or on the other side. But occasionally, he couldn't help himself. He had a special fondness for animals and would sometimes breech his silence to lecture me about them. In life, he was an animage—a witch doctor who could possess and control wildlife. In death, he was more of an obstinate encyclopedia. "How can you tell?" I wondered at him.

"They make unique nests. The lichen, the fur ... plus, they live round here. Bet you could practice on it."

I frowned. "Practice?"

"Opal's bracelet."

I glanced down to the homely bit of leather encircling my wrist. He was right; the bird's nest was a perfect target and the garden an ideal location. I stood, positioning myself a couple yards away from the nest. I focused on it before activating the death current, letting in flow through me. Then, I raised my hand as Opal had shown me and pulled my fingers back.

Nothing happened.

I tried again. I squared my shoulders and concentrated, imagining the bird nest moving toward me as I curled my fingers toward my palm. This time, it jerked slightly, just enough to give me encouragement. I grinned to myself and tried again. And again. After about a dozen tries, I had my first real success. The nest twisted, then floated from its perch, suspended for a moment in thin air. My eyes widened in amazement just as the nest fell to the ground a few feet away from where it started.

I practiced for another 10 minutes before my arm began to ache. Regretfully, I lowered my arm to my side and replaced the nest in the statue where I had found it. While I'd never pulled the nest directly to me, I'd gotten it so close that I only needed to take a step to snatch it from the air. For such small practice, it felt miraculous.

As I sat and rested my arm, I began to ponder the rose-bushes. What would it feel like to summon something that large? Part of me dismissed the thought out of hand. It seemed strange and unethical to try to summon something rooted to the ground. But it wasn't like rosebushes were sentient ...

My arm's soreness forgotten, I got to my feet and switched the bracelet to my other arm. I held my left hand out before me, palms up, fingers splayed. I focused my attention on the rosebush, using the concentration techniques I had improved with the bird nest. I opened myself to the death current and then with a quick flourish curled my fingers.

Something strange happened then. The smells of extinguished candles filled my nostrils and my hands begin to throb with cold. I recognize these sensations. They indicated the presence of mortic energy—that elusive energy that only appeared at the time of death, dissolving the vital spark that attached a soul to the body. When mortic energy appeared, death was imminent.

The rosebush, of course, didn't budge.

But that didn't mean nothing had happened.

I dropped my arm, and immediately the smells vanished, and my hands returned to normal. Perhaps I had imagined it? Raising my arm, I tried again. This time, I focused my attention not on the physical rosebush, but on the change in energy around me. As I curled my fingers, I sensed it again. Mortic energy bloomed around the rosebush, ready to dissolve its vital spark which would, of course, kill it. My breath caught. Under normal circumstances, I wasn't sharp enough to sense a plant's mortic energy—it was too small. But with my super senses, I had no problem.

With my fingers still curled, I drew back my entire arm, as though pulling on a rope. I felt resistance, like I was stretching a very tight rubber band. Color seeped from the bush, the pink petals fading to gray, green leaves losing their saturation. I felt that small life cry out as the plant's vital essence moved slightly out of sync with its shell.

Somehow, I wasn't moving the plant. I was tugging on its vital energy.

How am I doing this? I thought. I tried to pull harder, but my arms were growing weak. The plant didn't want to let go of its vital energy. That made sense; living things will fight tooth and nail to survive. Even plants. My small magic was no match for the plant's will to live, and so I relented, allowing the plant's vital energy to snap back into place.

Opal moved the philodendron without trouble, I thought. *Was the difference that her plant had been potted and mine was still in the ground?* It was possible, but seemed unlikely. I wanted to try again, but I had neither the desire to kill the rosebush nor, it seemed, the wherewithal. If I wanted to practice further, the nest would be a better target.

But I would be lying if I said the nest still intrigued me.

By now, both my arms were aching, and so, feeling more than a mild sense of satisfaction, I slipped my feet back into my shoes and exited the rose garden, resuming my hunt for the sauna.

AT A QUARTER TO 11, Marcus showed up at my doorstep carrying a gas lantern. I had changed into ritual garb—a thin, black shift with bell sleeves and a scoop neck, and a lace veil that hung to my waist. I wore a pair of black lace gloves and delicate earrings made of sparrow bones. There was nothing magical about the outfit, but there *was* power in presentation. When I felt like a death priestess, I worked more like a death priestess.

"You look stunning," Marcus said, stepping back to take in the ensemble. "I haven't ever seen you like this."

"The backpack kind of ruins the look," I joked, hitching the sack higher up on my shoulder. "Thank you for coming."

"This is for you," he said, handing me the light. "Probably don't need it right now, though." He turned his face skyward. Illuminated by moonlight, Marcus was even more beautiful than I remembered. "Stars are incredible out here."

He was right about that. Away from the ambient light of the city, I expected the preserve to be pitch black at night. But the night sky was brighter than I'd ever seen. "Makes you wonder how much the modern world has blotted from our eyes, doesn't it? I mean, all this," I said, waving my arm about indiscriminately, "all this is always here. We just can't see it."

When we arrived at the Temple, Brandy was already waiting for us, perched on a bench with a shawl draped over her shoulders. As we approached, she rose to greet us, donning that easygoing smile I'd come to expect from her. That impressed me; I half-expected her to shrink away from my outfit. It was almost enough to make me forget we were about to chit-chat with a spirit in a haunted temple.

"Did you enjoy your day?" she asked.

"I did," I said. "I visited the sauna and had a massage. Even with the limited staff, this place is incredible. Y'all could do better on the food, though," I said, only half joking. "Y'all ain't never heard of butter and salt?"

Brandy grinned, wagging a finger. "Cholesterol and blood pressure," she warned in a singsong voice. "But I'm glad you enjoyed the day. Hopefully, you're feeling refreshed enough to get started?"

"I'm ready if you are," I said.

We followed Brandy into the temple. At night, the sanctuary looked different—less holy, more eerie. Long shadows cast by the branches overhead lent a macabre feel to our already-ghastly mission. The dark images of Brother Zahi on the walls were scarcely visible in the starlight, but the artist's rendition of his golden, spiritual aura gleamed. The effect was ethereal and haunting, giving the impression that we were standing within a circle of otherworldly flames.

Brandy gestured for me to hand her the lantern. "Where do you want it?" she asked.

I motioned toward the dais. "Let's set it there. I think we'll have enough space between the lantern and the wall to do the work." Brandy did as I asked while I surveyed the temple, constructing the ritual in my head. When I was sure I understood how the rites would progress, I rubbed my hands together and blew out a breath.

"Okay. It's gonna go down like this," I said. "Like communicates with like. Our physical ears can't hear the words of a spirit, and a spirit can't properly speak, as it has no physical body. So we have to give it a mode for verbal communication. Mediums do this by channeling the dead through their bodies. I'm not willing to host an unknown entity in my body. I don't even know if I can." I shivered at the thought. "So we're gonna create a substitute puppet using a technique called shadow possession. For that, we'll use you, Brandy, and the lantern."

Brandy's eyes flew wide, and I gave my head a soft shake, smiling to ease her nerves. "Don't worry. It's not invasive. It may get a little uncomfortable though. I'll explain in a minute."

Now, I pulled the raven bones from the backpack. I unwrapped them carefully and set them aside. Next, I pulled a bottle of Florida Water from the backpack and anointed the bones. Brandy's voice was soft when she asked, "What are the bones for?"

I laid a finger against my lips and then pulled out a cone of frankincense. This I set in the brazier before lighting it. When the smoke was thick and fragrant, I ran the bones through it. I almost chanted a short prayer, but then recalled Brandy's warning. I kissed them instead.

I turned to my audience. "I grew up throwing bones with my grandmother at our kitchen table. Big Ginny is a Conjure woman—she practices hoodoo. You know, good old-fashioned magic from the American South. It's kind of an open secret in our neighborhood, and some ladies from round the block like to know if their husbands are faithful, if they're gonna get pregnant ... things like that. They ask questions, and we toss the bones and read the results. You might have heard of reading palms or tea leaves—it's all the same thing. Divination. Conjure women throw bones to receive messages from spirit, and we're gonna do the same."

Now, when Brandy looked at me, she couldn't hide the fear in her expression. "And the blood?"

"Think of it as an offering. We'll anoint the raven bones with it."

Brandy nodded. "All right. Anything else? How does the shadow possession work?"

I pointed to the wall behind the dais where the lantern threw the most light. "We'll cast your shadow along that wall. When your shadow is in place, we'll lay the bones as an offering and invite the spirit to possess the shadow. Only a human spirit can possess a human shadow—I think." I said this last part under my breath. "That should be enough to start the conversation. With a human shadow to give it form, the spirit can communicate. With the bones, we have a way to listen. Put the two together, and we've got a ghost telephone."

I grinned as I said this, hoping to ease the rising tension in the sanctuary, but when neither Marcus nor Brandy returned the expression, I let it fade from my lips. "All right. You ready to see what this spirit wants?"

Brandy's eyes flit momentarily to Marcus, who offered nothing but stony silence. I'd told him to stay out of my way, but his stoicism was becoming a little much. Even I was getting annoyed. I clapped my hands together. "Let's do this."

I settled onto the floor and arranged the raven bones before me. When they were in place, I beckoned for Brandy to come sit next to me. Marcus handed me the lancet and I motioned for Brandy to give me her hand. She gave it to me gingerly, trembling. I clasped her fingers and quickly broke the skin as Brandy winced. I dribbled the blood over each bone, smearing it with my fingers. Brandy wasn't a great bleeder—or I wasn't great at producing blood—and the preparations took longer than I'd expected. By the time the bones were properly anointed, Brandy was visibly shaking.

I helped her up and led her to the wall where we'd be casting her shadow. I linked her hand in mine, her skin hot even as she shivered. I closed my eyes and reached out with my consciousness toward the spirit, the spirit's death-smell wafting in and out. I sensed it there in the darkness, quivering. The death current swirled around it, but the spirit did not ride it through the veil. I wondered briefly if it *wouldn't* or *couldn't*. But that's what we were about to find out.

With Brandy's hand still clasped in my own, I raised my arms forward, the fingers of my free hand stretching toward the spirit. I felt mildly ridiculous doing this, like one of those charlatan preachers performing paid-for miracles at a revival. But it seemed disrespectful to lure a spirit into a shadow possession without assuring it of your intentions first. "You who dwell in the shelter of the Most High will rest in the shadow of the Almighty," I said, addressing the spirit with a recitation from the Book of Psalms. "No harm will befall you, and no disaster will come to you. In the breast of the Anointed One, you are welcome. A shadow by which to hold, and blooded bones with which to speak, I ask to know your name and understand your purpose."

I dropped Brandy's hand then and kneeled at her feet. I scooped up the bones and threw them the way I had hundreds of times. Something about how they fell tugged at my brain, but the actual landing of the bones didn't matter tonight. They were just an offering, not a fortune to be read.

I stood up and motioned for Brandy to stand between the lantern and the wall. "We have to show the spirit that your shadow is a true human form," I explained. "So stand with your limbs apart, making an X with your body. Let the spirit see the shape of your shadow."

Without speaking, Brandy did as I asked, spreading her legs and lifting her arms in a V over her head. The lantern cast a soft glow around her body, and the shadow she cast against the near wall was sharp and clean, a perfect form for possession.

I closed my eyes and reached for the spirit with my thoughts and my heart, but the being didn't reach back. It remained as it was, swirling and flowing, but not coming any closer than it had been a moment ago.

"It doesn't recognize your shadow," I said, frowning. "Probably needs more definition. Spread your fingers wide as you can."

Brandy obliged me, her shadow on the wall clearly depicting two human arms ending in perfect five-digit fingers. Yet the spirit still didn't respond.

I chewed the inside of my cheek and dropped my eyes toward the shadow's bottom. Brandy was wearing a dress, and the bottom half of the shadow was amorphous and ill-defined. I sucked air between my teeth. "I need more definition. I need you to take off your dress."

I expected Brandy to object, but it was Marcus's voice that cut through the darkness. "Is that really necessary? That seems—"

"You don't like it, you can go," I interrupted. "I'm not here for your opinion, Marcus."

Brandy's eyes flickered in the lamplight, her hands once again fingering her necklace. "It's just that I ... I'm not wearing a bra."

I gestured toward the shadow. "You see what I'm seeing? That doesn't look human enough. The spirit isn't engaging." Sensing Brandy's growing discomfort, I lowered my voice and stepped nearer to her. "If you want Marcus to leave, just say so. And I'll keep my eyes off you as much as I can. But if you want to talk to this spirit, you need to remove your dress."

Brandy's eyes flicked briefly between me and Marcus before returning her gaze to mine. Without saying anything more, she lifted the billowy garment from her body and dropped it, letting it puddle at her feet. As she stepped out of the dress, the light iridescent against her white skin, my breath caught in my throat. Her belly was round. I couldn't tell before because the shape of her dress had hidden this feature. Naked, Brandy was obviously pregnant.

Nude now and shivering, Brandy spread her legs wide, her fingers separating as she threw her head back and took a deep breath. Her shadow was as perfect a human form as anyone could muster. Two arms, two human hands. Two strong human legs and a head. If this didn't work, nothing would.

It only took a moment. Slowly, the shadow began to undulate. My eyes went wide and I gasped a little in the dark, turning my head to ensure that Brandy herself was standing still. She was frozen, eyes wide as saucers and full of fear. The three of us stared at the wall as the shadow began to turn, warping slightly before changing position altogether.

Then the wailing started.

At first it was one voice, an incoherent whispering that sounded like a snake slithering through the grass. But gradually, other voices joined in, becoming a chorus, a growing susurration that filled me with such dread that my blood ran cold. There were at least a dozen voices; no, two dozen. More. Some voices were crying. Others were shouting. Others were wailing. Amid the cacophony, one voice cut through the others. "Why is it so dark? Where's the light? There was supposed to be a light!"

I tried to swallow in a dry throat, my mouth opening and closing like a fish as I tried to find the right words to respond. What was happening? The voices were swirling in a vortex, coming from the right, then the left, above, then below. Female, male. Indistinguishable. Some voices seemed furious, others terrified. Their general moaning became screaming, followed by questions and accusations hurled from every direction at once. My ears were filled with their demands. "Why are we still here? Why can't I see anything? Where's my family? This wasn't what was supposed to happen. Am I trapped here? Why am I trapped? What's happening?"

I turned to Brandy, but it was Marcus I found in the darkness, his hands clasping mine, squeezing my hands, warm and comforting. I hadn't realized that I was trembling. It wasn't until I leaned into his strength that I found my voice. "Who are you? How many are you?"

At first there was no discernible answer. Just the voices trying to talk over each other. I closed my eyes to listen more carefully. There, slightly clearer than the others, were two competing monologues. One voice was saying something like, "It's so dark. Is this death? Where am I? Where are we? What happened? How did I get here?" Another voice, less frantic and more filled with fury: "That fucking shit-eating motherfucker's lies and promises I swear to God if I ever get out of here if I ever find him—"

It was all I needed to know. These were people—dead people. And for some reason, they hadn't crossed over to the other side.

Well, if there was *one* ability I was confident in, it was my ability to ride the death current. If I could take myself through the veil, surely I could help these poor souls cross over as well.

"I need to take them over," I announced to my companions. "They're too confused. We can't get information from them. We need to guide them through the veil. Brandy?"

"Do it," she said.

I took a deep breath, let my eyelids flutter closed. I reached out to the death current, activating it. It responded immediately to my call, lifting me up and out of my body as I expanded my consciousness, seeking the boundary between the worlds. I slipped my energy into the void, reaching out to part the veil. My astral fingers touched the partition separating our world from the next and—

Fire exploded all around me.

Blinding light seared my eyes, superheated and terrible, white-hot flame without form, stretching in every direction. The conflagration roared around me like an engine.

Inasmuch as I could think, I was certain my insides would boil and my skin would melt from my bones. My brain was on fire. Everything was exploding. In a panic, I tried to retreat, to pull my senses back and return to safety. But I *couldn't*. I was paralyzed. My necromancy was frozen. My psyche could not withdraw.

I was trapped, utterly at the mercy of a furious wall of fire.

Except it wasn't fire. Not exactly. It was *magic*—the strongest magic I had ever encountered in my life. Who could have cast a spell like this? And what was it doing in the *temple?* I tried to push myself away, to cut off any connection between myself and the preternatural fire closing in around me. But the more I fought, the hotter the magic grew. Suddenly, the power swelled and lashed out, striking me in the chest, searing my skin and knocking the wind from my lungs.

The walls closed in around me. I was drowning in a sorcery I couldn't even fathom. I opened my mouth to scream when suddenly, everything went blessedly dark.

Slowly, light began to bloom, edging in from the periphery of my vision and coalescing toward the center. It formed softly and gradually like daybreak. It was neither hot nor terrible, nothing like what had assaulted me. This light was rose gold and full of healing. It filled me up, pushing out every thought, every fear. Deep-seated serenity wrapped me in fuzzy numbness like a dose of nitrous at the dentist's office. Nothing mattered. Everything was okay. Everything was *perfect*. I could have stayed in that safe, quiet space forever. Slowly, languidly, I began to drift away.

But then, as my consciousness ebbed and my will waned to

nearly nothing, a familiar voice scratched at my ear, a benediction spoken in loving kindness.

The Lord bless you
and keep you.
The Lord make his face shine on you
and be gracious to you.
The Lord turn his face toward you
and give you peace.

An image swam before my mind's eye, watery and faint. Mrs. Harrison's rheumy eyes were liquid with tears as she smiled and patted my cheek with her old, soft hands. The blessing she had laid on me surged to life, emanating into my limbs, my heart, my lungs. I heard her voice, strong, steady and true. But it wasn't kind.

Mrs. Harrison was *mad.*

"*Fight. Kezia Antoinette Bernard, you will not surrender. You will not stay here in this void. You will fight. You will* fight *and you will* go back!"

I blinked in surprise, tried to rally my limbs to obey. But I was awestruck by the magic around me. More, I was powerless against it.

But Mrs. Harrison wasn't. With a snarl, the old woman grabbed me by the shoulders and threw me with superhuman strength, hurling me away from that strange power and out of the current. My consciousness snapped back into my body with a near audible crack.

When I came to, I was gasping. I rolled onto my side and heaved, but nothing came up. I swayed onto my knees, yanking the veil from my head and tugging off my gown, fighting my way out of it. I needed to see my chest. I wanted to see the damage.

Marcus appeared at my side. "Kezia, what are you doing? What happened? Dove? Are you—"

He stopped mid-sentence as I threw the gown off me and we all gazed on my naked body. A red gash like a wound from a whip marred my chest. It was clearly a burn—not life-threatening, but terrible to look at, and it hurt like a motherfucker. I laid down and curled up on my side, pressing myself against the stone floor, welcoming the coolness against my skin.

"There's something else here," I said.

The words hung naked in the darkness, no adornment necessary. The others couldn't have seen what I had. It hadn't happened here, but in that void reserved for necromancers like me. But they saw what it did to me. They saw my body thrown to the ground and the mark left on my chest. It was all the illustration they needed.

"Something *attacked* you?" Marcus asked, astonished.

Prone against the tile, I tried to shrug, even though my chest groaned in agony. "I don't know if *attacked* is the right word. When I tried to open the veil, some kind of magic ... *retaliated*. It didn't feel like ... " I searched for the right phrase, a way to convey what I had experienced. "It didn't feel like aggressive magic—the kind of thing you'd use to kill someone, for example. It felt more like a security spell. But instead of keeping people out, it's keeping human souls trapped inside this building."

Carefully, Marcus helped me to my feet. My head was throbbing, and I felt woozy. Brandy was at my side then, pulling my gown over my head as I shivered. She herself was still nude.

When I was clothed, I turned to my ex-husband and muttered, "I need to get out of here."

"Yeah, you got that right." As Marcus led me toward the

door, it was all I could do to keep my eyes open. Suddenly, I was so, so tired. Riding the death current always wore me out, but this was nothing I had experienced before. As the night's events began to fully sink in, my teeth began to clatter.

"She's going into shock," Brandy said. "Get her into bed and keep her warm. I—"

"Thank you, I have this," Marcus snarled. "I know my responsibilities. Do you know yours?" I heard no response from Brandy. "Close this temple," Marcus demanded as we stepped into the night air. "I don't know what the fuck just happened here, but we are not dragging anyone else into this until we know what's what. We good?"

Brandy grunted what I assumed was agreement. "I'll clean up here. Please take care of her. I'll check on you both in the morning." Brandy paused a moment before saying, "Will you stay? I mean ... are you still willing to help? I hate to ask, but ... "

"Now's not the time," Marcus growled as I pressed my face against his chest. "You can't expect her to commit to *anything* right now. We just—"

"Please stop," I said. I peeled myself away from Marcus, turning to Brandy. "I'll stay," I said, "but it's not for you. It's for the people trapped here, away from their loved ones on the other side."

Marcus's voice was tender when he asked, "You sure?"

"No," I said, adding a soft smile. "But I have to do this. I'd never be able to live with myself otherwise. Goddamnit."

Relief flooded Brandy's face as the conversation ended and Marcus led me shivering through the darkness, fighting for consciousness against exhaustion and fear. Underneath expanse of inky sky, the memory of my evening assault swelled loud and vibrant in my forebrain, an involuntary response to what my body now considered a dangerous environment: night. I squeezed my eyes shut, willing myself to forget, to swallow down the no-longer irrational fear of the dark. I had earned the fear that bloomed inside me like nightshade, threatening to consume me whole.

I couldn't walk home in the dark because a person—some insufferable, absolutely unremarkable dickhead—had attacked me like a coward under the cover of night. How could I leave those souls in the dark with no assurance they'd ever find someone to guide them across?

Like I said: Goddamnit.

CHAPTER SEVEN

I WAS STILL ASLEEP WHEN my phone buzzed at half past seven the next morning.

"Did I wake you?"

I grunted something incoherent as I pulled myself to a seated position, rubbing the sleep from my eyes. Under the best circumstances, I wasn't a morning person. I worked nights at the hospice and my brother's bar; a regular day for me usually began around noon. But to add insult to injury, I hadn't slept well; I'd had nightmares. I'd woken up drenched in sweat at least twice. I ached all over and smelled like a locker room. I needed a shower, coffee, ibuprofen, and another five hours of sleep.

If wishes were horses.

"It's fine," I said, clearing my throat. "I'm up now."

"I know it's early," Brandy said with apology, "but I have a lot to get done today. The new session is starting, and—"

"Yeah, no, I get it, it's fine. Really."

"Okay." The line was silent a moment. "How are you feeling today?"

"Scared," I admitted. "Tired. How are you feeling?"

"About the same," Brandy said, "but probably for different reasons." She paused. "Last night, I was asking you if you'd still be willing to help. At the time, you said—"

"I remember," I interrupted, glancing down at my chest. Although I had fallen asleep in my clothes, I'd had to peel them off the first time I'd awoken in a sweat, some time around 2:00am. Naked, I examined the wound on my chest that throbbed with my heartbeat. It didn't hurt as much as it had last night, which was strange. It should have hurt more. "I still want to help. But I think the first thing I need to do is talk to your husband."

Brandy was silent for a beat too long on the other end. "Brandy? You still there?"

"I'm here," she sighed. "It's just that I don't want Caleb to know about any of this. I don't want to distract him from his mission."

I snorted. "We're closing down the temple. That's gonna interrupt his mission pretty good, don't you think? I just want to ask him some questions. Sometimes when people practice magic they got no business doing, things go wrong. So I just want to know—"

"Caleb doesn't practice magic," Brandy interrupted. "He's not a mage of any kind."

That struck me as odd. Hadn't Casey said he was more interested in books and scrolls than people? I had assumed that meant he was a thaumaturgist—in other words, a mage. Someone who learned their magic academically as opposed to being born with it like me. Mages loved their scrolls. "Well, is it possible it's something he's been doing in secret? Something perhaps you don't know about?"

I heard Brandy sigh into the receiver. "If he's doing something in secret, of course I don't know. That's what secret means." She cleared her throat, sighing again. "But if he were practicing magic, wouldn't there be evidence? Stuff I'd find in our house? Potions, charms, scrolls, ritual tools, creepy reagents … I mean, can you be a magician powerful enough to cast the magic you encountered without anyone knowing? Especially your wife?"

She had a point. There were a lot of accouterments associated with being a mage. And there was no such thing as a solitary mage—they loved their councils. If Caleb were a mage, he'd have to attend conferences, dinners, fundraisers, etc. with other mages—especially his mentor. And for sure he'd have them over to the house. Thaumaturgy was really a fraternity for nerds.

"Plus," she continued, "it's not the kind of thing you would hide, is it? These days, being a thaumaturgist is no different from being, say, a Freemason."

That wasn't exactly true; there were still plenty of religious fanatics who shunned magic, but mostly, she was right. Most people saw thaumaturgy, like Masonry, as harmless—elitist and weird, true, but harmless. Mostly.

"Listen, we don't have a lot of other options here. It's possible your husband isn't a mage, but he knows someone. Or he participated in a ritual a long time ago—when he was a dumb kid in college. We've all done it," I joked. "But for real, though. Just let me talk to him. See if he can tell me anything that might shed some light on the situation. It'll be a tremendous help." I paused. "Brandy, this is important."

"Of course it is," she said too quickly, her words coming out in a whoosh. She must have been holding her breath. "I'll see what I can do, but I can't promise anything. Caleb is extremely busy as I'm sure you can imagine. In the meantime, let's keep brainstorming ideas that don't involve my husband."

I shrugged. "Don't know what ideas we'll come up with on our own, but okay."

"No ideas on how to get them across?"

"None yet," I admitted. "But I haven't even had my coffee."

"Go have your coffee then, and please take advantage of the grounds. If you need anything, let Casey at the front desk know. I'm sorry I can't attend to you myself, but—"

"I'll be fine. Thank you. Let's talk again tomorrow." I dropped the phone onto the bed and headed for the bathroom.

Gingerly, I pulled myself into the shower, letting the scalding water run over me, loosening the knots between my shoulder blades. The water was too warm and would probably dry out my skin, but to hell with it. I needed the healing only devil's-piss-hot water could provide.

After showering, I braided my hair into a protective style and covered it with a scarf. I dabbed the arnica gel Opal had given me on my face and applied a thin layer to my chest wound as well. As I dressed, my stomach rumbled, reminding me that I hadn't really eaten since yesterday's lunch. I perused the kitchen for a grab-and-go breakfast; I wasn't in the mood for whole grain cardboard from the cafeteria. The pantry was stocked with protein powder, apples, cream of wheat, and cold cereal. I considered the cereal but then quickly rejected it—I wanted something warm, and I hated cream of wheat. The kitchen did have an espresso machine, one of those nice ones that's connected to a water supply. I made myself a double shot took a sip; it was dark and acrid and wonderful. I finished the brew, rinsed the cup out, and reluctantly headed for the cafeteria.

Like yesterday, the menu was lackluster, featuring organic and tasteless dishes that we didn't even serve to the dying people in hospice. Still, my stomach rumbled again, so I searched for something that would take the edge off; maybe I'd leave the preserve tonight and drive into town for a proper dinner. The thought of burgers and fries made my stomach churn louder. I settled for whole grain toast, egg white omelet, and juice, and though I didn't especially enjoy it (well, the orange juice was good), at least I wasn't hungry anymore.

I lingered at my table longer than I needed to, and it took me a while to admit to myself that I was hoping for Marcus to show up. Every movement out of the corner of my eye caused my head to bob up expectantly, only for my heart to sink down again when it wasn't him. I was being ridiculous, so I scolded myself, bussed my table, and went back out into the sunshine.

I didn't know what to do with myself. I wasn't ready to go back to the temple, not that that was an option yet. I also didn't want to go back to my room, and I'd already gotten a massage, sat in a sauna, lounged in a jacuzzi, and perused the art gallery yesterday. Of course, this was a nature preserve, and I had run of the entire establishment. The one thing I hadn't bothered to do yesterday was get some exercise. And though I wasn't much of a gym rat, I never turned down a nice walk.

So I started walking.

In some ways, the Inner Flame grounds looked like a posh college campus. White stucco buildings with salmon red adobe tile roofs gleamed under an expanse of cloudless blue sky. There was signage aplenty: north would take me to the botanical gardens, the yoga studio, and the spa. Walking east would take me to the sculptor's studio, the temple, and the duck pond. South would take me back to the dormitories, cafeteria, and the parking area, and west would take me to the library and art galleries.

Of all those things, flowers sounded good. Flowers sounded easy. I walked north.

After a while, I noticed that the terrain had changed. The brick path I'd been on had faded away, and the pristine buildings were replaced by yucca and agave. Somehow, I'd wandered into the desert. Though that wasn't quite right either. I was on a hiking trail, though I didn't remember seeing signs for it. My sense of direction was garbage; I must have missed the turnoff for the botanical gardens. I was debating whether I should double back when I looked up to find a little rest area, currently occupied by the fiercest looking Asian woman I'd ever seen. She was sitting on a bench, legs crossed, eyeing me as she vaped.

I cursed inwardly but kept walking towards her. Even if I had wanted to turn back, it would've looked rude if I had stopped or turned around. Plus, when she saw me, her face lit up like she was genuinely happy to see me. Well, maybe not me, per se, but someone.

"Good morning," I said, forcing a lightness into my voice that I didn't really feel. I gestured toward the sky. "Gorgeous weather." Even after so many years as a bartender, I'd never mastered small talk.

The woman sitting on the bench readjusted her crossed legs and tilted her head away from me as she took a hit off her vape. Her eyes narrowed. "Try again," she said.

My eyebrows lifted as I approached. "Sorry?"

The woman exhaled like a dragon, and the smell of mint chocolate hit me in the face. "I said, try again. Something interesting this time."

Now that I was closer to her, she looked familiar. My

puzzlement must've shown in my face because the woman placed the flat of her palm on her chest and cracked a smile. "Eunice Cho," she said. "I don't usually drop my own name, but you looked like you were trying to piece it together."

I stopped dead in my tracks. My jaw probably dropped open a little. I knew that Temple of the Inner Flame attracted a certain clientele: rich, famous, or influential people. But actually seeing one up close was some shit. Ten or so years ago, Eunice Cho made her name—and most of her money—as the Chief Technical Officer of one of Silicon Valley's most prominent tech companies. But that's not why I knew of her. Today, Eunice Cho was the CEO of a biotech company, Sangrinos, that was slated to change the world by reinventing the blood testing industry. I'd inhaled several documentaries and an audiobook about her. She was the darling of Silicon Valley.

Turns out, her product didn't work. Never did, and word on the street was, she knew it. All along, she'd been selling hope and lies. Now, she was on trial for scamming her investors out of billions of dollars.

In real life, the woman before me still looked like TV Eunice Cho, but also different. In the flesh, she looked older and wiser. She was also far smaller than I imagined; if I sat on her, I could probably snap her like a twig. Up close, I saw the telltale lines around her eyes, the worry that tugged on the corners of her mouth. Her hair was frizzy. Her clothes were rumpled. The intensity in her eyes, though. That was the same.

"Kezia," I said, extending a hand. The woman shook it. "I agree, the weather thing was tired. I wasn't expecting to see anybody here. I was kind of in my head."

Although there was plenty of room on the bench as it was, Eunice scooted over and tapped the seat next to her, inviting me to sit. Up close, she smelled of Chanel No. 5 and mint chocolate. She handed me her pipe, but I declined. She took another drag. "Is this your first time here?"

"My first time," I said. "You?"

Eunice shook her head. "I was here for the last session, all three weeks. I was here last year, too. I try to come every year, but last year was the first time I really let myself transform." I tried to keep my face stoic, but she saw right through me. "No, I get it, you're not really convinced. You're here because it's the thing to do, right? I understand that. People sell their first-born to get into this place. What's the waitlist up to, now? Two years? Three?"

I didn't even have words. Were there really that many people in the world with enough money to come to a place like this? I vacillated between awe and anger, but if my internal struggle registered on my face, Eunice didn't notice. "It's a good place. Lots of workshops, lots of therapy if you're into that sort of thing. Plenty of prayer and meditation. For most people, I'm sure three weeks is enough. But with everything happening right now, I just wasn't ready to go back home. I didn't feel like I could face my investors, my colleagues, my friends. Well, what few of those I have left. One amazing thing about having all of your laundry aired in public? You find out who your tribe is. Everybody is just a goddamn hanger on."

This information was something I absolutely couldn't relate to, so I said nothing. I didn't have friends either, but it wasn't because I had trouble with ethics. In fact, just the opposite. I was overwhelmed with ethical considerations—spending time with me could get you killed. So I tended not to put anyone in that position.

Eunice continued to vape for a while, and I gazed out over the horizon, thinking about all the strange events that led me to this moment: Marcus getting a PhD in whatever the hell he'd studied, getting attacked in a parking lot, finding a haunted temple, being zapped by ruthless magic. And now, here I was sharing a park bench with Eunice Cho, one of the most infamous and hated women in the country. I guess it's true what they say. You just never know what you're gonna get.

Eunice's sharp intake of breath interrupted my thoughts. "So, can I say something completely rude? I have no idea who you are. I mean, I at least recognize most of the people that come to these things. How did you ... ?"

I grinned. "How did I rate an invitation to a retreat designed for the rich and famous? Yeah, I've kind of been asking myself the same thing." I blew out a breath and decided to tell her the truth. "I'm a necromancer."

Hearing this, Eunice whistled in appreciation. "No kidding? One of those heal-the-diaspora people?"

I nodded. "Yes, for all the good it's done me. I'm not very good at it."

Eunice lifted an eyebrow. "Still, Caleb has a soft spot for those with natural magic. It makes sense why he would invite you. You know Evangeline Morris?"

I chuckled under my breath. There wasn't a necromancer alive who didn't know of Evangeline Morris. She was one of the very few truly famous necros, renowned largely for being the first necromancer to heal herself of her affliction. She'd founded a church some ten-fifteen years ago. Early in my search for others like me, I'd written to her, hoping to start a discourse and maybe find some answers. She'd never written back.

"Not personally," I said, "though I know of her."

"I met her at a fundraiser about five years ago," Eunice said, staring off into the distance. "Absolutely amazing woman.

Brilliant. And kind? I heard that in the height of her career she was handing out a hundred gifts an hour."

I grinned. Eunice Cho must get her information from the same unreliable source as Opal.

"Do you do yoga?"

I sucked my teeth. "Nah. I tried it a couple times, but I found myself getting really angry. I wasn't tryna hold those poses forever. It seemed like it should be easy, but that shit actually hurt. Nothing pisses me off like something that seems easy actually being hard. I don't want to work for inner peace. I just want to find it."

Eunice laughed then, and it was contagious. Before long we were laughing and chatting together, sharing stories about other things we had tried that we hadn't liked. For me, it was yoga, pole dancing, and the Popeye's fried chicken sandwich. For Eunice, it was those painting and wine classes that all of her middle-aged friends were into. "Things people do for fun or relaxation usually fall flat with me anyway. Even when I was in elementary school, I was really intense. I couldn't just color or run around. I had to work on assignments. You know, *learn*. Study. Prove myself. Part of that was my upbringing," she said, a note of nostalgia underlying her words. "But part of it was just ... that's just who I am. Nobody liked me. They still don't." She exhaled a wall of vapor and flicked a stray lock of hair over a shoulder. "I don't really know what I'm looking for here," she admitted. "Everything has gotten so out of hand."

"If you don't mind my saying so," I began slowly, "you don't seem the type to come to one of these things. Maybe I'm naïve but I always figured these Inner Flame types were upscale hippies and New Agers."

Eunice smiled like I'd said something funny. "Yeah, my husband used to say the same thing, but twenty years and hundreds of millions of dollars later he's shut up about it." She narrowed her eyes and shifted her position as I swallowed around the lump that had just formed in my throat. This woman had hundreds of millions of dollars. That number made my head spin. "I knew Caleb way before he started Inner Flame. In fact, I was with him the day he bought the land for this place." She smiled at the memory, but it quickly faded. "His mother had just died, and he wanted off the crazy train: he was not into the dog-eat-dog stuff I was doing. We were both working in tech, though Caleb really had no stomach for it. He wanted to go off-grid; had these ideas about starting a commune, things like that. He was just done with the rat race.

"Anyway, I knew a guy who knew a guy who was selling some land, and I knew Caleb was looking to buy. He'd inherited a bit of money from his mom. So I called around and put him in touch with the seller. The two of us drove up here together to meet him. It turned out that Caleb already knew the guy, which was just grease for the wheels. Negotiations were easy. He gave Caleb this book of poetry called *Conversations with the Inner Flame* by Brother Zahi. Have you read it?"

I shook my head. "I found a copy in my room. I only glanced through it; I don't really care for poetry."

"You should give it a chance," Eunice said. "It's not all poetry. There's some stuff in there about reaching your potential and making the right choices. That, plus knowing when not to make a choice at all."

Again, Eunice offered me a hit of her vape, and again, I declined. "What do you mean not make a choice at all?" I asked.

"If all you have are bad choices, sometimes it's better not to choose," she explained. "Like, if someone held a gun to your head and told you to choose between blowing up 50,000 people in Cambodia or 50,000 people in Nepal but either way, someone was gonna die? You don't have to make a choice. You shouldn't. Force fate or the universe or whatever to do what it needs to do. But you don't have to be complicit. Choosing not to choose is also a choice."

I saw the sense in it, though I also knew it wasn't that easy. When Lola got sick, all I had were bad choices, but I chose. Maybe I hadn't chosen correctly, but I'd done it. "Well, my choices have been made," I said, almost to myself.

"Maybe," Eunice agreed, "but don't get caught up in sunk cost fallacies, either. Just because you chose something once doesn't mean you have to make the same choice forever. You *also* can choose to change your mind."

Somehow, that didn't make me feel better. I'd chosen to abandon my Lola, to let her grow up without me, hoping that maybe Marcus would marry again and give her a new mother who would love her and not make her sick. I'd thought that choice was forever until something changed.

But maybe that was a cop-out. Maybe every day that I didn't contact her was a new, awful choice I was making over and over again.

Could I really change my mind at any time and choose Lola?

I didn't want to think about it. "So, this poetry book. Is that what the Temple is based on?"

Eunice nodded. "Yeah, pretty much. The book, plus the dreams and visions Caleb had after reading it. It's all about self-actualization and ideas like that. Which was really what Caleb needed. Don't tell anybody I said this, but Caleb was ... an odd bird? Yeah, that's a nice way to put it. An odd bird." She shrugged then, her gaze once again shifting toward the horizon. "He was just really private. He didn't have friends. He never really talked to people at work except me. I think he felt like we had something in common because he grew up in Somalia with people who didn't look like him and I grew up in America with people who didn't look like me. I mean, you know what that's like."

I snorted. I knew.

"Anyway, Caleb started building out here at the same time he started doing the lecture circuit in the city. I helped with all of that because we were friends, but over time, I just ... I don't know, I started to drink the Kool-Aid. Everything Caleb was teaching me about my aura and about submitting to my higher self just sort of centered me in a way I hadn't been achieving on my own. And then the money and opportunities just started rolling in. The more invested I got with Inner Flame, the more success I had. I mean, you don't know how crazy my career has been. First Korean-American CEO at Permanente Health. First woman CEO. I was the CEO during our most profitable and innovative years. I attribute all that to Caleb. And the funny thing is, this belief system is all based on asking. Ask for what you want, and you'll get it. But I never asked for anything big. I didn't ask for money. I asked for a vision that people would relate to. I asked to be charming in meetings. Things like that. I never wanted my success handed to me—I wanted to know that I had earned it. Me. So I asked for small but meaningful things and the money just followed." She paused then, let out a huge sigh. "And then all this happened. Which is why I'm here now. This time, I need to ask for a miracle."

Eunice was looking at me through veiled eyes, and I could tell there was something more she wanted to say. She had that energy about her. I held my breath, waiting for her to continue. But the moment passed, and instead, she leaned forward, resting her elbows on her knees as she said, "Everybody out here has some intrinsic flaw they're trying to fix. Everybody has something that's broken. In a way, I'm jealous of people who know exactly what that flaw is. The 12-steppers who know they have a problem with alcohol. The religious people who are praying to God for guidance knowing that they need serenity. Me, the lying scam artist who snatched hope from the grasp of millions of sick people? You, the necromancer trying to heal her community? We're both broken. But neither one of us knows why. And the thing of it is, we're both broken in different ways. And yet we're both here looking for the same goddamn answers."

The smile she offered was sardonic, but I saw that she meant every word of what she said. I saw how the stress and anxiety sat in her shoulders, her neck, the tightness of her hips. She was coiled like a spring, ready to pounce or break. It seemed even hundreds of millions of dollars couldn't buy peace of mind. But perhaps a miracle from the Inner Flame could; who was I to say one way or another? "I hope you find what you're looking for," I said. It wasn't enough. But I didn't know what else to say.

"You, too. Unless what you want is my job. Then fuck you." The grin was wicked and intended to portray jest. But I recognized that look in her eyes. Eunice Cho was anything but kidding.

CHAPTER EIGHT

I
T WAS NOON WHEN my cell phone rang with Opal on the other end. "I didn't wake you, did I?" she asked. "I know what kind of schedule you keep."

"Nope," I lied, stifling a yawn as I crawled out of bed. "Okay, yes, but I was just napping. I was about to go find some lunch. How's everything?"

"Everything's fine. Big Ginny's fine. I'm calling to ask you about the bracelet. You tried it yet? It work?"

"I did try it," I said. "It works ... but maybe not as you intended."

Opal was quiet for a moment. Then, "What you mean?"

I recounted my story of how I'd managed to pull the nest toward me, but when I had tried to work with the rosebush, I seemed to pull its vital energy free instead of its physical self. "Did anything like that happen when you tried it?" I asked. "Or was that a surprise you were leaving for me to discover on my own?"

"Ain't no surprises in my magic," she objected. "I ain't like that. So, you tried it on a whole-ass rosebush? I'm surprised anything happened at all. I wouldn't have guessed that it would work on something planted in the ground."

"Well, that's just it, though," I said. "It didn't. At least, not how I expected."

"Huh." Opal grew quiet again on the other end. "I wonder if it's because you can ride the animate current."

I frowned, switching the phone to my other ear. "What now?"

"I can only ride the death current," she said, thinking aloud. "And the others who have tried it—Natalie and Two Top—they can only ride one current, too. But you can ride two currents—the death current because you're a necro, and the animate current because your patron is an animage."

I almost laughed. Of all people, Opal should know I had no affinity for anything but death. It was the only thing I was good at. "I can't ride the animate current," I said. "Maybe Papa Jinabbott can, but he's never gifted that ability to me."

"If he can, you can," she insisted. "That's how patrons work. He's part of you. I ain't saying you can possess a rottweiler, but I *am* saying that when you work magic, you access at least a tiny bit of the animate current."

I shook my head. "I see what you're saying, but I couldn't ride the animate current if I tried. I don't know how—"

"Queen Kee, you ain't hearing me. Just because you don't know how to consciously do it don't mean you ain't doing it. Shit, I don't know how to consciously make my heart beat, but there it go thumping away in my chest."

I hadn't thought of it that way before, but maybe she was right. Opal knew a lot more about magic than I did. "Well ... I guess it's a possibility," I conceded. "I can't promise I'll play with it more. Not on anything living, anyway. Seems wrong to pull something's vital spark out, even just a little bit."

"Agreed," Opal said. "When you get home, though, I might ask you to work with me some. I need to get this spell right if I'mma sell it. Which I am." She chuckled. "Hey. You get rid of that amulet yet?"

I groaned, squeezing my eyes shut. With everything else going on, I had forgotten about Charon's Recall. "Not yet, but I will. I promise."

"Thank you. Well, listen, I'll let you go. I just wanted to check in. You good? Everything okay out there?"

"Marcus is here," I said.

Silence. Then, "Hell, Kezia. Why?"

I sighed. "It's complicated, but it has nothing to do with me. Our marriage, anyway. We're both out here doing research. I'll explain later. I really do need to find something to eat."

Opal grunted on the other end. "Okay. Listen. Don't let him make you do something you ain't ready to do, you hear? You own your choices, Kee. Not him."

"Thank you, Opal. I won't forget. Talk soon." I thumbed the phone to disconnect.

───────

AFTER I HUNG up with Opal, I called Marcus.

"Dove. Good morning. How you feeling?"

"I'm okay," I said. "I just talked to Opal. Everything at home is good. You?"

"I've been better," he said. "I've been worried about you."

"Oh, don't be. Really, I'm fine," I repeated, assuring both of us. "Are you hungry? Have you eaten?"

"Not since breakfast," he said. "Dining hall in fifteen?"

"I'll head over now."

I found a table where I glanced briefly at the menu:

steamed salmon, gluten-free bread, lime sherbet. As I was sipping my water and deciding between the long grain wild rice and the rutabaga salad as a side, Marcus slid into the seat across from me. "So how are you feeling? You okay?"

I nodded, slid the menu in his direction. "Jesus, don't ask me again. I'm fine. Really."

Marcus narrowed his eyes. "You seem remarkably well-adjusted for someone who got bitch-slapped by protective magic last night." He tilted his head to one side. "What aren't you telling me?"

Unconsciously, my hand drifted to the wound on my chest. I fingered its edge and, finding it tender, withdrew my hand. "I'm not keeping anything from you. I don't know what to say. We both know that when it comes to the paranormal, nobody really has any answers. Least of all me. All I can tell you is that there's something keeping those souls in that temple. Keeping them from crossing over."

Marcus nodded. "And you think you can help them?"

I shrugged lamely. "I don't know. I just know I have to try."

"Even with that thing still there?"

"Marcus, trust me, I don't *want* to go back in there. Being attacked by a man in an alley was bad. Being attacked by something I can't even see?" I shook my head and looked down into my lap. "It's fucking terrifying, okay? But those people are trapped. We were all promised an afterlife. Salvation. *Peace.* Who would I be if I just let them rot there alone?"

Marcus nodded and folded his hands on the table. "I'm not gonna try to dissuade you, dove. I just want to make sure it's what you really want."

"What I want has nothing to do with it," I said wearily. After a long silence, I decided to change the subject. "You'll never believe who I ran into today."

Marcus lifted an eyebrow. "Who?"

"Eunice Cho."

Marcus's eyes went wide. "Eunice Cho? That woman who lied about her blood tech? She's here?"

I nodded "Yep. She was the leftover attendee from the last session, staying for another. Sounds to me like she's avoiding going home and facing up to all the shit that's going on in her professional life. Seems like a good lady, though. I know how that sounds, but really. I liked her. Not really what I expected. Although, I'm not sure what I expected from these people. Maybe more of the Hollywood-retail-guru types, I think."

Marcus chuckled. "You mean the kind of people who wear those magnetic bracelets to balance their chakras and stuff like that?"

I took a bite of salmon. For fish, it wasn't bad. "Yeah. Basic ladies who buy candles that supposedly smell like a vajayjay and think they're being slick."

Marcus offered a soft smile as he took a sip of his coffee, his demeanor growing quiet. I recognized that look. I steeled myself for an interrogation.

"So. You make any progress finding your mother?"

My skin flushed hot with embarrassment. I took a sip of water. "Not much. No," I said. "One of my patients died recently, and before she passed, I asked her for a blessing. I'd heard it could help. But I never got around to trying again after that. It's too late now," I added before Marcus got any ideas. "I used the blessing in the temple."

Marcus was quiet a moment before saying, "You know, dove, if it's a blessing you want, you could ask my mother."

I looked up too quickly. "Is she dying?"

Marcus laughed then, shaking his head. "No, thank you

very much. But you know she does that. Blessings, I mean. She and her church group."

My face fell, but I recovered quickly. "Thanks," I said, "but I don't think your father would approve."

"He's not the man you remember," Marcus said. "He's softened with age."

I tried to smile. "Not towards me, I'm sure."

My ex-husband did not respond as we both picked at our lunch, avoiding each other's eyes. After a while, he said, "He thought you were brilliant, you know. In the wrong field, yes, but brilliant. That connection you drew between apoptosis and your affliction? He still talks about that."

"He loved me as a scientist," I agreed. "He just wasn't so hot on me as his daughter-in-law."

Marcus cleared his throat. "So then, shall I ask her?"

Suddenly, I found myself without appetite. It brought me both pleasure and pain to know that Marcus's father still spoke of me. After all this time, I still thought of him often and fondly. I'd met Dr. Chuk "Call Me Chuck!" Adeyemo in college. I was a biology grad student, and he was my thesis advisor and primary investigator of our lab. I'd approached him about my hypothesis: that the necromantic affliction was not unlike apoptosis, or programmed cell death. He'd shined me on. "How so?"

"I'm thinking there's a corollary between the extrinsic pathway in caspase activation and the necromantic affliction."

He cocked an eyebrow. "I'm listening."

I swallowed. "Well, okay, in the extrinsic pathway, cells get the signal that it's time to suicide from other cells. This is a natural, normal part of life—every organism sheds cells daily this way. We understand that the death receptors on the cell's surface receive the ligands from other cells, initiating the death response, right? Well, this is what I'm thinking—that certain individuals have receptors designed to receive a necromancer's energy. Necromancers initiate the death response in certain people who have those death receptors. What I want to understand is why and if it can be stopped."

"That's outrageous," he'd said. "I love it."

The conversation took off from there. He accepted me into his lab, where I worked off-hours, sticking to a schedule that allowed me to be mostly alone in the lab so I wouldn't get anyone sick. And even under those less-than-ideal circumstances, I flourished for a while.

Until I didn't.

Getting my work peer reviewed was impossible. No one was doing similar research—necromancer biologists weren't exactly a dime a dozen. Worse, trying to get funding was hopeless, as my work affected so few people and captured the imaginations of even fewer. I tried so many avenues, but failure after failure took their toll on my mental and physical health. I stopped eating. I was hardly sleeping. I even—God forgive me—toyed with the idea of purposefully exposing someone to watch them die and document the process, though it never got further than the dark fantasizing phase.

One night when I had fallen asleep in the lab, I awoke to find Dr. Adeyemo standing over me, arms crossed over his chest, his brow furrowed in concern. He folded himself carefully into the chair next to mine, giving me a dour look. "Kezia," he began, his lips forming the gentle slope of a frown, "I think it might be time to consider abandoning this quest."

Groggily, I'd shaken my head. "Quest?"

"You have a spectacular mind, Kezia, and your determination is unparalleled. But let me ask you: what do you hope to accomplish in your research? What is all this for?"

I stared at him, my mouth agape. "To end it," I whispered. "To stop the cascade."

Dr. Adeyemo nodded. "And what if it isn't meant to be stopped?"

His words weren't making any sense. "What do you mean? Of course it can be stopped. Why would you say that?"

"In organisms, programmed cell death serves a purpose— an important purpose. When the fetus is forming in utero, the hands are webbed. In order for fingers to develop, the cells that form the webbing are programmed to die. We see this in every organism. Our bodies are not meant to reproduce cells indefinitely—some must die to make way for the new."

"I know all of this," I said, offended. "I'm not a fucking undergrad."

"Then you should also realize that if the falling away of the soul is similar to apoptosis, then perhaps it serves a greater purpose. Perhaps it is *necessary* for those sensitive to your trigger to die. Perhaps their death is part of the greater function of this organism we call Earth."

"Bullshit," I said. "Would you recommend I stop trying to find a cure for cancer if I were—"

"Cancer is something gone wrong," he corrected. "You have proposed that certain individuals are *designed* to receive your energy. That's not chaos. That's reason."

I set my jaw. "Then maybe I have it wrong. Maybe it's not programmed death. Maybe it's not like apoptosis at all."

"And if not," he countered, "what are you researching? Is your heart in your research or not? Do you believe you are on the right path or not? To be a great scientist, Kezia, you must follow your hypothesis all the way to its natural conclusion. But you must also know when your hypothesis cannot be salvaged. So either you're wrong, and you should abandon your research, or you're right, and you should abandon your research."

I was too shocked and appalled to speak. I stared into his eyes, searching for words to refute what he'd said. But I found nothing. His reasoning was sound. Either the soul was programmed to die like cells by necessity, which meant I shouldn't try to stop it, or souls were not programmed to die like cells, and my original hypothesis was just wrong. Either way, my research was pointless.

He wasn't wrong. I just didn't want to hear it.

"The scientific community needs the contributions you can make, Kezia. You have a talent for research and a tremendous creative mind. But a blind man can see that you're not well. And so I wonder: would you be better off in a different discipline? Perhaps someplace where you could enrich the death experience for both the living and the dying? I think you would flourish in the study of thanatology, for example."

I snorted, derision darkening my expression. "Thanatology isn't real science," I snapped.

Dr. Adeyemo narrowed his eyes at me. "What you are doing isn't science, Kezia. It's vendetta."

That conversation was the beginning of the end. I didn't exactly lose interest in my work, but I lost the passion driving me. I still wanted to understand the cascade. I still wanted to understand how and why I initiated this death response in certain people. I wanted to conquer it so I could hold on to relationships. Hold on to a full-time job. Live a normal life. But Dr. Adeyemo was right. I wasn't going to find any of that under a microscope. The answers to my questions weren't in the lab.

I was beginning to accept that it was time to move on when Big Ginny got cancer.

They found it in her stomach. I quit school to take care of her—at least, that's what I told myself. But it was an excuse; a way for me to drop out of the program while saving face. I went into Dr. Adeyemo's office to break the news.

Sitting across from my professor was a young man in a suit, skin so smooth it shone like tempered chocolate. Both pairs of eyes lifted at the interruption, and I stopped in my tracks, breath caught in my throat. "Sorry," I muttered, backing out of the room. "I didn't mean to interrupt."

"Come in, Kezia, you're not interrupting anything. This is my son, Marcus. Marcus, this is my grad student, Kezia Bernard."

"Pleasure," Marcus said, barely looking my way. "Anyway, I guess I'll be going. Mum canceled on me for lunch." He frowned down into his phone. "I don't suppose you'd like to join me?"

Dr. Adeyemo leaned back in his chair. "Wish I could. I—"

"Not you," Marcus said, looking up. "Her."

An electric shock ran through my body, my fingers and toes tingling. *Have lunch with this man?* I thought. *Hell yes I want to have lunch with you.* Aloud, I stammered, "Lunch? Uh, sure, that sounds—"

Dr. Adeyemo pulled himself to his feet. "I probably have time after all," he said, glancing quickly in my direction. "I can move some things around."

Marcus stood as well, and once again I tried to leave, but Marcus stopped me, his hand on my arm. The electricity between us was undeniable. "I have reservations for sushi. Do you eat fish?"

I disliked fish, but nodded mutely, keenly aware that Dr. Adeyemo was trying to insinuate himself between us to keep me from getting my necromantically afflicted claws into his son. The ominous look he gave Marcus was so clear even I could read it—*Not this woman; she isn't for you.* I understood that fatherly concern. I did. But hormones being what they are, in that moment, I didn't care.

And I didn't care the next time Marcus asked me out, either. Or the next. And though both his parents protested and prayed and tried their damnedest to keep us apart, Marcus and I became a couple. We started spending longer stretches of time together, each visit beginning and ending with my critical evaluation of him, looking for signs of illness. But he was healthy as an ox. Eventually we moved in together. And he never got sick. And he didn't die. And we were married, and I thought that was the end of it. Or the beginning. Depending on how you looked at it.

In a way, it was both those things. Just not in the way I had hoped.

In African families, descendants are everything. It's how Marcus's family embraced the notion of eternal life. We die, but our children live on. But Marcus and I quickly figured out that we couldn't have children. It took me longer than it should have to understand why: the babies just couldn't survive me. My body, so intimately connected to death, couldn't sustain life. The embryos couldn't persist.

Until one embryo could. Unimaginably, incomprehensibly, a pregnancy stuck. Lola was born, and Marcus and I couldn't have been happier.

Things were good for a while.

But then Lola got sick. The rest of that story is history.

I was so deep in my reverie that I had forgotten to answer Marcus's question. When I didn't answer, Marcus waved his hand and leaned back in his chair. "I'mma take your silence as an invitation to change the subject," he said. "Back to business, then. You got any idea how to get those souls across the veil?"

I shook myself, clearing my mind as I pressed a linen napkin to my lips. "Not a single, solitary clue. I need more data. If at least I knew what zapped me ... But until I can talk to Caleb, I just don't know what else to try."

Marcus steepled his fingers beneath his chin. "I have an idea."

I recognized the glimmer in his eye. "You better not say sex magic."

My ex-husband grinned. "You have to admit that the heightened sense of awareness could be beneficial in this situation. There's a reason that orgasms are called the little death, you know."

I bit down a smile. "I ain't playin' with you, Marcus."

"Not even a little?"

I grinned. "No. Ok, for real, though. What's your idea?"

He pretended to think. "Well, your sex magic idea is actually a million times better than what I was about to say."

I waited for him to continue, and when he didn't, I rolled my eyes and made a motion with my hand like he should get on with it. Marcus re-crossed his legs and stroked his chin, a favorite gesture he'd inherited from his father. "There's something in the temple that you cannot see, at least not with your physical eyes."

"I couldn't see it astrally, either," I clarified. "The souls were dim, but I could sort of see them. The magic, though, I couldn't see at all."

Marcus nodded. "Either way. I'm thinking that with a little help, you might see more clearly. Open up your third eye? Perhaps a little guided meditation?"

I cocked an eyebrow in his direction. "Are you for real? That sounds like some New Age shit again."

Marcus clucked his tongue and frowned at me. "Don't make it sound so pedestrian. You know better than that. I'm suggesting a shamanic journey. You ingest something like peyote to help you enter a higher plane of consciousness, and I, as your guide, could help you open certain gates that perhaps were not available to you on your own. Indigenous cultures have been doing this for generations."

I made a face and sank my chin into my hands. "I don't do drugs, but I do have Opal's third-eye tea. We could try it, I guess. Have you done anything like that before? This shamanic journey bullshit?"

Marcus nodded. "I have. In fact, I've done it several times, and it's not *bullshit*. I haven't spent the last years sitting on my ass twiddling my thumbs, you know. I've done several workshops with various established voices in the field. I've worked with more than a handful of Native American shamans. So while it's not exactly the crux of my purview ... " He let his voice trail, gave a soft lift of his shoulders. "Lemme lay it out like this. My teachers haven't been African. Africans ain't out here teaching just anybody how to access the spirit world. Our people keep that shit locked up *tight*. You know this. But I earned this information fair and square, and I didn't *appropriate* it from anyone, if that's what you're worried about." I blushed at being read so easily. "I don't see any problem using the skills I've gained through years of study if it's gonna help you get those souls across."

I shifted in my seat. "I guess it could work," I said warily. "I don't really like the idea of losing control, though."

Marcus gave a slow, thoughtful nod. "I feel that. But for this, would you make an exception?"

I sighed. "All right. It's the best idea we've got, anyway."

Marcus rubbed his palms together in excitement. "Great. I think we should practice first in a safe environment. Make sure you respond well to it and everything. I was thinking we could do a trial run tonight? I have some things I want to take care of first."

I didn't ask what things and Marcus didn't offer. "That sounds good," I said, standing. We cleaned up our plates and headed outside. "What time do you want to come by?"

"I'd rather do it at my place," Marcus said. "Is that all right?"

"Sure. Time?"

"Eight? Make sure you eat something first. And no alcohol."

I nodded. "All right. Well, I guess that means I have the rest of the day to kill, at least unless we hear from Brandy. You got any ideas?"

Marcus gave me his best shit-eating grin. "Could give that sex magic a try."

Say what you want about Marcus, but he sure didn't give up easily.

CHAPTER NINE

WITH OUR DATE SETTLED, Marcus and I parted ways. I had half a mind to hermit out in my room, but the better part of me scoffed at the idea, reminding me that I'd never have another opportunity to vacation in a place like this. So, after packing up a tote bag with a few necessities, I headed out to try the women's baths.

Pushing open the heavy door, I walked into a fetid, dim dressing room. Inside, I treated my hair to a healthy slather of coconut oil before loosely twisting it and covering it with my favorite silk cloth. I got naked, wrapped myself in a towel, and headed out.

The baths were outdoors, secluded by a perimeter of bamboo, eucalyptus, bottlebrush, and a thatch roof overhead. Dense steam rose in clouds from the water, and the air smelled of organic decay. Thin lighting filtered through the leaves, creating a relaxed and quiet atmosphere. When my eyes adjusted, I saw that I wasn't alone. Sitting in the bath were two figures partially obscured by the steam. But soon I determined that it was a woman and a man. Confused, I looked over my shoulder to double-check that I was in the women's only bath.

"You're in the right place," said a bored voice. I whipped my head around to find a young man frowning in my direction. "The ladies always have nicer facilities than the guys." He sighed and closed his eyes, easing his head back against the stone.

The woman waved me over. "Ignore him," she said. "Attitude aside, he's mostly harmless."

Mostly harmless or not, I wasn't exactly thrilled to disrobe in front of him. I was about to head back into the locker room when the woman spoke again. "You're a necromancer."

Hearing this, the man's eyes popped open but, seeing me still standing outside the bath, clothed, gave another exaggerated sigh as he closed them again. "I'm not going to sit here with my eyes closed all day," he warned. "Get in."

Blowing my cheeks out, I turned my back as I let the towel fall to my feet, kicking it out of the way. Quickly, before I lost my nerve, I turned toward the bath and lowered myself in.

When my nudity was safely obscured, the man opened his eyes, blinking at me warily. "So, is she right? Are you a necromancer?"

"She definitely is," the woman said through narrowed eyes. "Either that or she just has the weirdest energy in the world."

I frowned as I turned my attention to the woman. I thought I recognized her, but then again, it could just be that she wore the same line-free, artificially smooth complexion often boasted by the rich and famous. Her long, curly hair was colored a dusty pink and hung around her shoulders so that she looked like a mermaid. Curly tendrils framed a face that looked preserved. I guessed her to be mid-40s and aiming to look 30 with fillers. She wasn't an actress or singer or anybody of that caliber of fame. Still, I was sure I had seen her somewhere.

"Have we met before?" I asked, knowing damn well we hadn't.

She gave a vague wave of her fingers accompanied by a carefree shrug. "No. Vocational hazard," she said, by way of explanation.

It was then that I realized who she was. I was sitting in a bath with Andromeda Clark, medium and psychic to the stars. She had a reality show, hosted in her Bel Air mansion, where she read Tarot cards for celebrities or contacted their dearly departed. The show was beautifully produced and highly addictive, if you're into that sort of thing. But while it was wildly entertaining to watch these celebrities cry and melt down after their MeeMaw sent a message to them from the afterworld, I never took any of it seriously. I assumed that Andromeda Clark was a fraud.

And maybe she was. I couldn't discount the possibility that Brandy or Eunice had told her about me, though it seemed ridiculous that I would ever come up in conversation. But there was something in the way she held my stare, the confident set of her jaw and, hell, just an ineffable *je ne sais quoi* that told me she saw right through me. She was looking right into my soul—at all of the ghouls and goblins therein.

I decided to just go for it. "How did you know?" I asked, keeping my voice level, my eyes narrowed.

The man and the woman exchanged glances, causing heat to rise in my cheeks. The man looked at me and cocked his head to one side, a smile making his expression less bored, but more mocking. I wasn't sure which I preferred. "You don't have cable TV? *And* you're not on Twitter? What, necromancers live under rocks these days?"

"I know who she is," I said. Then, readjusting my attention, I turned to face Andromeda. "I know who you are," I repeated. "I just mean ... How did you know?"

Andromeda's face lit up with understanding as she dropped me a coy grin. "Well, it's obvious you're a magic worker. Your energy is very *plugged in*, if that makes sense. But you've also got these dark, cloudy tendrils surrounding you."

I lowered my chin into the water. The cloudy tendrils were my necromantic affliction. I myself couldn't see any of that, but aura readers could. She was offering a fairly textbook example of what it supposedly looked like.

"Plus," she continued, "you have this ... *haunted* look behind your eyes. Like you've seen some shit. Put all that together, and boom! Necromancer."

I shifted my gaze to her companion who was watching me now with curiosity, any contempt that used to be in his eyes having fled. When I said nothing, he offered an apologetic smile. "Sorry I was rude before. I'm Andromeda's manager, Ben Matheson." He offered me his hand. "It's nice to meet you."

"Kezia Bernard," I said, accepting the handshake. "It's nice to meet you both."

"So you're really a necromancer?" Ben came nearer to me until he was close enough that I could see tiny beads of water dripping from his lashes. I resisted easing away. "I've never met one before. Is it creepy? Do you just see dead people everywhere?"

I studied him, wondering if he was pulling my leg. But I found no jokes in his dark eyes. How strange to meet someone who had never met a necromancer before. But then, why would he? He was White; he couldn't receive necromantic gifts. He probably lived in a community of people just like himself, and there probably wasn't a necromancer within a thirty-minute drive of his house. None of that was his fault—wasn't even a *fault*. It just *was*.

But the knowledge that he had never met anyone like me before left me feeling vacant just the same.

"No, nothing like that. The dead don't actually hang around. They go on to a different place."

Ben and Andromeda exchanged looks. "Well, but what about ghosts?" Ben asked. "Are you saying there's no such thing?"

"Ghosts exist," I agreed, "but they're not dead people. Not really. They're more like the memories the living have of dead people. Like footprints. They're evidence that someone has lived, but little more than that. Their souls are in another place." I turned to Andromeda. "You're familiar with all this, right? Being a medium and everything."

"Obviously. But I admit I don't have much use for ghosts. I mostly channel the spirits of the dead into my body from the other side. I have no experience with dead things lingering around here."

I nodded. "It's the same with me." *Usually.*

"I figured as much," she said. "But even though I bring the dead across, the opposite isn't true. I haven't had the opportunity to study the afterlife, though I hope you won't think me simple for saying that I look forward to one day being reunited with my friends and family who have passed on."

I smiled at that. "I've been to the other side," I said. "Your ancestors are watching over you. They'll be glad to see you again."

"I've never doubted that," Andromeda said. "Though it is comforting to hear it from a necromancer." Her smile faded as her expression grew thoughtful. "I don't dwell on it too much, though. What happens when we die is determinate. I'm more interested in the choices we make on this plane. I guess you could say that's why I find Caleb's philosophy so attractive."

"What about it calls to you?"

Andromeda rolled her neck, lifting her wet mane of hair and readjusting it on her shoulders. "I've always known that I have a purpose. I'm a medium, for God's sake. My purpose is clear. But growing up, I was told you could be anything you want to be. The future is unknown and uncertain and nothing is carved in stone. I was taught that every one of us was free to will the life we wanted into existence. But Caleb teaches us that free will is a trick. It's a distraction. The point is to find your purpose and make choices that align with what the universe wants for you."

I frowned. "So you don't believe in free will?"

"It isn't that I don't believe in it. It's that I understand that it creates imbalance, and what is out of balance can't create. Too much rain, the garden drowns. Not enough, your tomatoes wither." She smiled as she said this, shrugging a shoulder. "I wouldn't *exactly* call it prosperity theology? But Caleb says the more you align yourself with your true purpose, the more the universe invests in you. I mean, it makes sense. If each of us is here for a reason, and we have the tools to manifest our purpose, it's kind of our *job* to do that."

I thought I was following, but the woo factor was high, and the heat from the baths was making me lightheaded. "Explain that," I said.

"Like, maybe you're supposed to bless those around you with your cooking skills, or your singing voice, or your exceptional ability to find tax loopholes. Or maybe it's necromancy," she said, her eyes glittering as she leaned into the narrative. "Those are all tools—things you use for some greater purpose.

But if you squander your time and tools and never fulfill your purpose, why would the universe bother to bless you with riches? Why should the universe care what happens to you? All of life is just one enormous ecosystem. And if any one piece of the ecosystem doesn't pull its weight, the rest of the ecosystem suffers. But if a piece does its job *well*, the whole system benefits and has more to offer that piece. It's all explained in *Conversations with the Inner Flame*. You should have a copy in your room."

A shiver ran down my spine. I recalled the poems I had read in my room, wishing I had looked over more than just the two. I had assumed I knew what the Temple of the Inner Flame was all about. But I was finding I was wrong. "I don't mean to be a negative Nancy but all that sits wrong with me. People *should* choose the course of their lives. I don't think God would punish them for making up their own minds."

Andromeda shrugged. "if you don't believe in the philosophy, why are you here?"

"Research," I replied, the lie coming easily. "What about you? Why are you here?"

The psychic grinned. "If I told you I had terrible luck with men and I just wanted that bad streak to end, would you believe me?"

I shrugged. "I've definitely heard worse reasons for personal improvement."

"Woman cannot live on spiritual enlightenment alone," she agreed. "She also needs some good—"

Ben groaned, speaking over his friend's words. "You are so crass," he complained. "I mean, you're not wrong, but you could be more ladylike about it." He gave Andromeda a disapproving look before turning his attention to me. "So tell me more about what it's like."

I lifted my chin. "Being a necromancer?"

"Obviously."

I answered before I could even think. "It's lonely."

"Because of your affliction?"

I nodded, my words catching in my throat.

At this, Ben leaned forward, sympathetic. "Yeah, I bet. So, what happened to you?"

I frowned. "How do you mean?"

He gestured toward me vaguely. "Your face and your chest. Those injuries look recent."

Andromeda elbowed him, throwing a dirty look. "What's wrong with you?"

"Oh, it's okay," I answered, my hand drifting to my cheek, caressing the wound with the tips of my fingers. The welt on my chest had already stopped hurting. "I was attacked on my way home from work."

Andromeda cocked her head to the side, eyes narrowing. "Really? That's surprising."

I grimaced. "Not really. I'm a bartender, and some of the patrons—"

"No, that's not what I mean," she interrupted. "When you sensed you were in danger, why didn't you just kill him? Just snatch his soul right out of his body?"

The question caught me off guard, and for a second all I could do was stare. "That's ... not really how it works," I said.

Andromeda blinked her huge, blue eyes at me, her expression all innocence and wonder. "Isn't it?"

"Well ... I mean, no? If you felt like you were in danger, would you just kill the person before they'd even done anything to you?"

Andromeda wasted no time in answering. "Yes."

Once again, Ben groaned a loud interruption. "*God*, you are so full of shit!" He ran a hand through his wet hair. "You are one of the most loving people on the planet, and you *absolutely would not* kill a person like that. I don't even know if you could kill a person who was *actually* attacking you."

Andromeda frowned, affronted. "I definitely could kill someone. *Especially* if they were attacking me."

Ben snorted. "Doubt it."

"I could."

Ben turned to me. "Go on, Kezia," he said. "Ignore Andromeda's hubris and bullshit. I'd actually like to hear what you have to say."

I hesitated, and in the pause, Andromeda tossed up her hands. "Okay, I probably couldn't kill a person like that," she admitted. "But if you were *truly* in danger and knew it ... " She shrugged. "Why *not* use necromancy in self-defense?"

"Well ... moral grayness aside, you *can't* just snatch people's souls from their bodies. And I don't mean you ethically *shouldn't* do it; I mean you actually *can't*."

Again, Andromeda's eyes went big and round. "Can't you?"

I pressed my lips into a hard line. "No. Souls actually have a deep affinity for their vehicles. So even if it were possible to lift a soul from its body, it would require tremendous will and energy. It would be nearly impossible to do against a person's will."

But even as I said these words, I wondered how true they were. My eyes darted briefly to the bracelet at my wrist. I still didn't know exactly what I had done with the rosebush, but I was certain I had pulled some of its essence from its physical being. The vital spark, however, wasn't the soul. It was merely the energy that anchored the soul to the body.

"You know, I tried it recently," I said, thoughtful. "Not on a person, obviously. On a rosebush. I used telekinesis to coax its vital spark free. It was brutal, and in the end, it didn't work. I pulled with every bit of magical force at my disposal and I couldn't completely dislodge it."

But just because I couldn't do it didn't make it impossible. With the right magical training or energy, *could* you snatch a person's life from his body?

Andromeda raised an eyebrow. "You have telekinesis?"

I shook my head, raising my hand to reveal my bracelet. "I borrowed it from a friend. She's working on a new spell that's supposed to bring things to you. You know, like using the Force." I chuckled. "But for some reason it doesn't exactly work as intended."

"That's not a bug, that's a feature," Ben grinned. "Can I try?"

I hesitated. "Can you do magic?"

His face fell. "No. It's not loaded?"

I shook my head. "Sorry."

Now, Andromeda's hand rose from the water. "How about me?"

Again, I dithered. "What currents do psychics ride?" I asked.

"Everyone's different, but I ride the animate current," she said. "My patron is the raven."

"A psychopomp," I said, unclasping the bracelet and handing it over. "Makes sense."

Andromeda donned the bracelet. "How does it work?"

I showed her the gestures I worked on in the rose garden. "Try it on the bottlebrush," I said.

But after five minutes of trying, Andromeda couldn't so much as wiggle a leaf. "Let's see you do it," she said, returning the bracelet.

I snapped it on and held out my hand, fingers stretched.

"One, two ... three!" I closed my fist and tugged, and the bottlebrush's color faded momentarily from red to salmon. The smell of extinguished candles filled my nose and my hands throbbed. More mortic energy.

"Are you fucking kidding me? That's wild," Andromeda breathed as I released the plant's life source. "Does it only work with the death current? Is that why I couldn't do it?"

"We don't know for sure. My patron is an animage. My friend suspects my magic is wonky because I ride the death *and* the animate currents."

The psychic made an impressed face. "That's cool."

"Yeah. But so far, just a party trick. Like I said. Taking a soul without permission is practically impossible."

Andromeda dismissed this objection. "Perhaps, but, there are people who do it. Steal souls, I mean."

"She's right," Ben said. "That's actually how Andromeda and I met. I came to her for a consultation to help me figure out why I couldn't leave a toxic relationship and she helped me realize that my partner was stealing my soul."

"It's not as rare as you might think," Andromeda said. "People don't realize it because it happens gradually. The soul is complex but also fragile. It breaks into pieces when we are overworked, stressed, abused, sick, whatever. If you're lucky, those fragments stay with you until you're able to reintegrate them. But some people are assholes. They'll snatch that shit right up. Lucky for Ben, I'm fantastic at what I do." She blew him a kiss, which he pointedly ignored.

I opened my mouth to ask another question when Ben suddenly jumped. "Oh, shit. I lost track of the time. Andromeda, we need to get going if we're going to make it to the drawing down."

The psychic groaned then, her lips drawing into a pout.

"Ugh, yeah, I forgot all about that. Would you hate me if I said I was gonna sit this out? I think I'd rather drink rosé and watch *Catfish* re-runs."

"Are you kidding me?" Ben cast the psychic a dour look. "You said you wanted to work on your bad luck with men. How are you going to do that drinking bad wine and watching ... okay, *Catfish* is a pretty solid choice," he conceded. "But still. We didn't come all this way—"

"Why don't you go with Kezia?"

I frowned. "Go where?"

Andromeda and Ben were already hauling themselves out of the water, so I followed suit, nudity forgotten. "To the drawing down ceremony in the temple." Ben slipped his feet into a pair of shower sandals as he wrapped a towel around his waist. "It's the big event that sets the whole retreat in motion."

"But the temple is closed," I said.

"Oh, it's definitely not," Andromeda said as she tugged on a silk caftan and wound her hair into a bun. "They were carrying in fresh flowers just this morning. You guys should go. I'm just not feeling up to it. My shields need strengthening," she frowned.

I wrapped my towel snuggly around my torso. "That can't be right about the temple. I could have sworn—"

"We're sure about the temple," Ben interrupted. Then, softening, he said, "It's definitely open. The drawing down is the whole *point* of being here. So do you want to come? Since Andromeda is ditching me?"

"Please go with him," Andromeda said. "I don't want to hear him whining about this later."

"You've got some nerve talking about someone whining when I have *at least* a hundred texts from the night what's-his-name broke up with you."

I tuned out the rest of their bickering as I followed Andromeda and Ben into the dressing room. My mind was racing. Brandy had promised to close the temple. She knew it wasn't safe. So why was it open?

I dressed quickly, and when the three of us were clothed and dry, Andromeda went back to her bungalow while Ben and I hurried to the temple.

BY THE TIME we got there, the festivities were already under-way. Two columns of attendants dressed in white donned leis around our necks as we plodded still dripping toward the entrance. *The leis are a bit much*, I thought, even as their soft scent wafted around me, gently nudging out the scents of copal and palo santo coming from the temple's open doors.

We paused at the doorway where Ben tilted his face upward, eyes closed as he mouthed something. I couldn't hear him, but I recognized the gesture. He was praying. When he finished, he opened his eyes, cheeks flushed when he turned to me and said, "I've been waiting for this ceremony for ages."

"It's too bad Andromeda couldn't be here with you," I said. "You do seem really excited."

Ben sighed. "Yeah, this happens to her sometimes. She poops out on big events because being around people is actu-ally really draining for her. One time, she was channeling the spirit of José Villalobos's uncle—do you know José? He won an Oscar last year for that sex robot movie? Anyway, she was channeling his uncle's spirit when she just passed the fuck out. We were at José's hacienda and the whole family was there—he had to have like thirty relatives. Her shields were weak, and all that energy just—pop!" He made a popping sound with his lips. "For a psychic, she's super bad at keeping her shields intact. You'd think she'd learn after all this time." He rolled his eyes.

"Well, the cobbler's children have no shoes," I muttered mostly to myself as we stepped through the doorway.

Even though I heard the voices outside, I wasn't prepared for what we found as we entered the temple. There were probably twenty people inside—more than I was expecting. I guess I figured the retreat would be more of a private affair. The energy in the room was wild and bright. If Andromeda wasn't good at protecting herself from swells of energy, then this definitely wasn't the place to be. You'd have to be a psychic zombie not to feel the currents in the room.

At the front of the temple, standing at the dais, was a face I recognized from the news—Caleb Atwater, guru and leader of the Temple of the Inner Flame. He smiled broadly with arms outstretched, palms facing upward, as he closed his eyes and leaned his head back, mouth moving in silent prayer. At least, it looked like prayer to me. Everyone was watching, tittering with nervous excitement. As soon as he began to speak, however, the room went quiet.

"Friends!" His voice was clear and deep and loud, the kind of voice that makes careers in Hollywood. "Thank you for being here in this sacred place today. How many of you have been here before? Show of hands."

A smattering of hands went up, and I craned my neck to look around. I recognized so many faces—a TV news anchor, a fashion designer, a prominent chef—but one profile in particular grabbed my attention. Eunice Cho was in the row ahead of me, hand up. She was glancing around as well, and when she caught my eye, she smiled.

"For those of you who are new, welcome. And for those of

you who have returned, it's wonderful to see you." *And your money*, I thought wryly. "Now, however, why don't we cut right to the heart of it? To begin our time together, and to set our transformation rolling, we will perform our drawing down ceremony!"

Applause erupted. Ben was clapping and smiling, his cheeks rosy with anticipation. I had no idea what a drawing down ceremony entailed, but despite myself, I was curious. Even enchanted.

"Friends, it's time to lift our voices to Heaven! It's time to unite our energies and fill this sacred space with our desires and our prayers and open ourselves to the gifts of the universe. Every one of you who has promised to align your drive with your destiny and the desires that the universe has set forth for you, open your hearts and chant your sacred words. *Now* is your time to draw on the power of the universe and use it to manifest your sacred dreams! And those of you who still harbor doubt, don't worry. You have time to find your faith." His smile grew impossibly wider. And though his gaze never met mine, I felt particularly called out.

"This is not an exercise for the meek. Friends, we must be *strong*. We must be *confident!* Lift your hearts! Lift your voices! Chant your truth and draw down the blessings of the universe into your being!"

All across the room, arms shot toward the sky, including Ben's. I felt somewhat like a jerk for not lifting my hands, and so I did what any self-conscious woman would do. I lifted my stupid hands and hoped I didn't look like too much of a jackass.

The chanting started off quietly. If these people were speaking a language known to mankind, it certainly wasn't known to me. It sounded both deranged and lyrical, beautiful and alien. My skin prickled over and beads of sweat broke out along my brow.

"Let the light flow through you. Let it carry your deepest and truest desires to Heaven. You are a child of the universe; there is nothing beyond your grasp! Fate *wants* to bless you. Your gifts *want* to be shared. Lift your voice! Lift your heart! Ask with pure mind and soul and you shall receive!"

The energy in the room was building now as the voices reached new heights. Some worshippers began to sway back and forth; others began dancing. At least, what passed for dancing among the melanin-free. Behind me, someone was singing. Others were reaching more of a fever pitch.

The energy was contagious; although I'd originally lifted my arms purely out of peer pressure, I found myself reaching up, up, up, fingers grasping at air, reaching for the divine. My eyes drifted closed as the energy swelled in my heart center, lifting my consciousness toward Heaven. Caleb's words were powerful; the spell he chanted wrapped around me and, despite my skepticism, I, too, was moved and inspired.

"What is your greatest desire? What can you manifest to bring light and love into the world? The universe spins your hopes and longings into reality—but you, each of you, must will your desire to life. Breathe it out! Speak it! What is it you were born to receive?"

I squeezed my lids shut as my ears filled with singing, chanting, and murmured prayers. I heard Ben's susurrations beside me; he, too, was deep in prayer.

"Sing praises, friends! Let your joy be known!"

The voices grew louder. The energy hummed powerfully; rivulets of sweat dripped down my temples. My heart raced, pulse thudding in my ears as something very like ecstasy threatened to overtake me. I fought against it only for a moment as wave after wave of euphoria crashed against the shore of my soul.

"Sing praises! Accept the universe's gifts! *Demand your blessings!*"

The swell of spirit was too great; I surrendered. I let the bliss swallow me down. My fingers stretched; my chest swelled and lifted as wildly, breathless with desire, my heart called out its solitary wish to the universe, "*Please help me find my family!*"

A row in front of me, a high-pitched voice rose above the others. I opened my eyes slowly, bleary and intoxicated. Everything was moving in slow motion. My eyes found the voice's owner: Eunice Cho was speaking in an unintelligible language, hands shaking as she stretched her arms higher over her head. The color was gone from her face; tears streamed from her eyes. It was impossible to tell if she cried from bliss or sorrow. But as I watched her, something happened. A sound like the rumbling of an on-coming earthquake filled the temple, and a wind blew, sweeping the room with warmth and the slight scent of ozone. Eunice's chanting became more fevered and rapid as her hair ruffled on the breeze and color returned to her face. But it wasn't the pink-red color of life and blood; her face was bathed in an aquamarine, flickering light.

I looked up to see the source of the illumination, and my heart skipped. A single flame had appeared above the woman's head, its color shifting from turquoise to amethyst to rose to gold. It looked like a prism, a fire burning every color simultaneously. In a moment, her neighbor received the same flame. In quick succession, identical flames appeared over the heads of other worshippers. Three people. Five. Eight.

The air shifted again. The change was palpable and familiar, but I couldn't quite put my finger on it, like seeing a face you know out of context. But then, recognition dawned. It was the strange current I'd felt the first time I visited the temple, except now, it was buzzing—the same way the death current buzzed every time I rode it into the veil.

The strange current in the temple was *activated*.

Instinctively, I raised my eyes skyward as I often did during praise services. But when my gaze lifted, what I saw made my heart stop, my breath catch in my throat. Floating above me like Christ rising from the tomb was Brother Zahi, larger than life, so real I could have touched him. He was smiling at me, hands pressed to his breast as he mouthed something I couldn't quite make out.

It was then that I noticed the second thing. A heated draft moved across my skin like the feverish breath of a lover on my cheek. And at the same time, I smelled it. The soft scent of Chanel No. 5 mingled with mint chocolate, copal, and lemon wax.

It was only then that my mind interpreted the words Brother Zahi had mouthed at me. He'd said, "Welcome home."

That's when I fainted.

THE FIRST THING I saw when I woke up was Ben's face looming over me. Worry lines creased his forehead and his mouth was drawn into a frown. I felt his hands on my face, caressing my cheeks. When my eyes fluttered completely open, a small smile broke out over his lips. "There you are," he said, relieved. "You gave me a good scare. You okay?"

I pushed myself up to seated, ignoring my dizziness. I chanced a glance around and noted that nobody was paying much attention to me. Good. On television, you see people pass out at revivals all the time. They receive the Holy Spirit, and the power of the Lord just knocks them on their ass. I had never put much stock in that phenomenon before. Now? Well, I wasn't exactly sure what I felt.

I tried to steady my breathing before answering. "I think I'm okay. Not sure what just happened."

"You fainted dead away. I heard that could happen to certain people—those who are especially receptive to spirit. You sure you're okay?"

Receptive to spirit? I supposed those words made sense, though I never would have described myself that way. The only sensitivity I had was to the death current, and yet, I *had* experienced something tremendous, hadn't I? Something that compelled me not to just go through the motions, but actually participate. But that experience had to be hallucination, right? Hypnotism? Brief reactive psychosis? A lot had happened to me in a very short amount of time: no one could blame me for having a temporary psychotic break. My rational brain, the scientific part of me that questioned everything and accepted nothing without evidence wanted to throw a tantrum and demand that I investigate the situation, but the human part of me refused. It felt so *real*.

But I *couldn't* have seen Brother Zahi, could I? He couldn't have materialized in the temple; that was impossible. Wasn't it? But even as I wondered this, I chastised myself. I believed in all kinds of things I'd never seen: spooks and demons and boo hags and haints. So why not a divine prophet?

That was just it, though. I believed in all kinds of things I couldn't see. It was another thing entirely to see a thing I didn't believe in.

And what about the scents? I hadn't imagined *those*.

I was readying my mouth to say that I was fine, when I

suddenly felt lightheaded and chilly, like I was developing a fever. "I think I need some fresh air," I said.

"Here, let me help you." He supported me as I struggled to my feet, the feverish feeling growing more intense when his skin touched mine. Ben didn't seem to notice.

Outside, with fresh air on my skin, I felt a little better. I took a few deep breaths of clean air and tried my best to smile at Ben, offering a brave face. "Thanks. Look, I don't want to drag you away from all that," I said, waving toward the door. "I'll be fine. Really."

Ben rolled his eyes, putting a hand on my shoulder as he shook his head. "I'm not leaving you to your own devices. I've seen this before. Used to happen to Andromeda all the time before she learned how to shield. Well, I mean, she's still shitty at it, but. Let me take you to her. I think she could help you feel better."

I tried to object, to insist that Ben not miss the rest of the ceremony on my account, but that sick feeling wouldn't quite loosen its grip on me. Being alone in my bedroom didn't sound wonderful, so I relented. "Yeah, okay. Maybe you're right. Thank you."

We walked in silence, keeping a slow pace as we made our way through the desert landscape toward the domiciles. After a while, I shot Ben a glance and asked, "Why did some people get the flame and others didn't?"

"Hmm?"

"At the temple," I said. "During the drawing down. I saw a handful of people get those flames over their heads. Eunice got one. Some others. You didn't. At least, if you did, I didn't see it. So why did some have a flame over their heads and not others? What does it mean?"

Ben cocked his head to the side, his brows drawn together. "Kezia? Are you feeling okay?"

I stopped, confused by Ben's blank stare. "Do you not know what I'm talking about? Didn't you see … ?" I raised a hand over my head, wriggling my fingers in a pantomime of flame flickering.

Ben shrugged and we continued walking. "I didn't see anything like that," he said. "But don't worry; it doesn't necessarily mean anything. You had a weird spiritual experience. Sometimes people hallucinate. It's perfectly normal," he said, his voice strangely flat.

I suddenly found it hard to think. Had I hallucinated the flames just as I had hallucinated the face of Brother Zahi? If I'd imagined one, I could have imagined the other. But if either vision had been real …

As I was gathering my thoughts to form a question, Ben stopped in front of one of the bungalows, his hand on the knob. He turned to me, probably to say this was it, when I gasped.

"What is it?"

I motioned toward the door. "Why—how is the door glowing?"

Ben's eyebrows shot high on his face. "You see a glow? On the door?"

I considered this question a moment before shaking my head. "Not *on* the door. More like … coming *through* the door?"

Ben gaped at me. "What color is it?"

I shrugged. "Pinkish? What—"

Ben's expression shifted as surprise elevated toward admiration. "You can *see* it?"

"What is it? What am I seeing?"

Ben indicated the door to Andromeda's bungalow. "She always casts protective circles around her when she's feeling vulnerable. But I've never met anybody—literally nobody, not ever, not even me—who could *see* one." His eyes narrowed slightly. "Yesterday at the hot spring. Did you notice a circle then?"

I shook my head. "No. I've *never* seen anything like this before."

Ben made thinking noises as he tapped a finger against his chin. "Weiiiiiiiiird," he said, drawing the word into two syllables. "She cast a circle yesterday, too. It was supposed to keep out anyone who didn't come in perfect love. That's how we knew you were okay. You know. One of us."

Whether I was one of them or not was up for debate, but I was familiar with the protective magic Ben spoke of—it wasn't unlike the brick dust that Big Ginny used to keep evildoers out of our home. Though I did think it a bit rich that she cast a circle like that in a semi-public space.

Though, really, given the Temple's clientele, I shouldn't have been surprised. Entitlement was everybody's middle name.

Ben rapped his knuckles on the door a couple times before turning the knob and pushing the door open. We found Andromeda lying on the couch with a cloth draped over her forehead.

At the sound of our entrance, she lifted the cloth from her eyes, mumbling, "You're back early." But when she saw me, her expression changed. Her eyes were large and round, face pale, jaw slack. She pulled herself to her feet and made her way to me in a couple quick strides. She gathered her hands in mine and squeezed my fingers. Her hands felt exceptionally cool against my overly warm flesh. The difference between our temperatures made me shiver.

"Are you okay?"

"I don't know," I admitted. "We were in the temple for the drawing down ceremony and all of a sudden I just felt … overwhelmed. I fainted. And then the next thing I knew I was waking up in Ben's arms."

Andromeda led me to the sofa where I tumbled into the cushions. Ben left the living room, returning with two glasses of water; he pressed one into my hands, which I accepted gratefully. The other he handed to Andromeda, who placed it absently on the table beside her as she continued to stare at me. "You're more than overwhelmed. You're absolutely filled with light."

I guzzled the water greedily, small rivulets escaping from the corner of my mouth. "What do you mean?" I asked in between gulps. Andromeda turned her attention momentarily to Ben. "Ben, can you bring me my mirror from the bathroom? The big cosmetic one?"

Ben said nothing as he left the room again, leaving me alone with Andromeda. She placed the flat of her palm on my cheek and then pulled her hand away with a nod. "And you're burning up."

I finished the water and placed the glass on the table. I still felt parched; the water seemed to arouse my thirst more than quench it. "I've had lots of strange things happen when I'm channeling the death current. I've heard voices, had flashbacks to lives I never lived, things like that. Sometimes the aftermath of working with that energy can linger for days like the world's worst hangover. But whatever happened today didn't feel like death energy. It felt more like … "

"Like what?" she asked.

I shook my head, unable to complete the thought. "I don't know. Like nothing I've ever experienced before."

"She says she saw people with flames over their heads," Ben said as he glided into the room with the mirror, handing it to me. "And when we were at the door, she saw your protective circle."

Andromeda hadn't taken her eyes off of me. "Is that true?"

I nodded. "Yes. People were chanting and praying and then a lick of flame appeared over the heads. *Some* of their heads." I sighed, dropping my face into my hands. "I don't know what I saw. I've never seen anything like that before."

"Not even yesterday at the baths?"

I shook my head. "This was the first time."

Andromeda lifted the mirror and handed it to me. "You need to see yourself. Look."

My hands were trembling as I accepted the mirror, and when I held it up to my face, my breath caught. She was right. There was something different about me. My skin seemed brighter and my cheeks rosier. I had a glimmer about me, like what some people refer to as a pregnancy glow.

That's when I noticed it. The light in my eyes. The same brown eyes I'd seen thousands of times now seemed foreign. The irises looked lit up from inside, flickering with a golden light.

Andromeda stood and went to her bookshelf, returning with the same slim volume I'd found in my room. She thumbed through the pages until she found the passage she was looking for. Clearing her throat, she began to read.

"My love is a flame upon your heart
Upon your bed
Upon your head
My love is a flame
My love is your flame
Our love is aflame.

My love is a fire beyond your chest
Beyond the womb
Beyond your tomb
My love is a fire
My love is your fire
Our love is afire.
My love is a blaze behind your breast
Behind your eyes
Between your thighs
And every blessing shall arise
Betwixt my fire and your sighs
And all the world shall be the wick
And you shall burn and light the skies."

She closed the book, her eyes soft and liquid. "He promised the flame from the beginning," she said. "But not everyone is fit to receive it. But this is what we seek. It's what we pray for," she cooed, smoothing my hair away from my face. "This is the love the prophet bestows on some of us. This is a *blessing*, Kezia. He chose you."

Although her words were soft and meant to be encouraging, I couldn't help but shudder. I'd been chosen once before, by my ancestors and death.

I wasn't as sure as Andromeda that it was any kind of blessing.

CHAPTER TEN

I SPENT THE REST of the day alone in my room, alternating between watching daytime television and staring at myself in the mirror. My poor face had seen a lot of change lately: the lacerations on my cheek and forehead were healing, but my lips and nose were still bruised and swollen. But much more concerning were the changes not caused by violence. My eyes glowed like embers, and my skin flushed like I had a fever. I didn't dislike what I saw, but neither did I understand it.

Not understanding bothered me. It bothered me a lot.

I was meeting Marcus soon, and since Opal's third-eye tea took some time to start working, I brewed myself a cup to drink while I dressed. I rejuvenated my curls and coated my lips with a fresh coat of tinted balm. I finished the look with a bit of blush and called it good. I wanted to look put together, but not like I was trying to look put together.

Being a woman was such bullshit sometimes.

The inside of Marcus's bungalow was more or less like

mine, except the lights were much dimmer and in the background there was music playing. Soft jazz? I found Marcus on the sofa poring over a scroll; he hadn't even heard me come inside. I waited a minute before clearing my throat to announce my presence, thumbing over my shoulder toward the speaker.

"Seduction music? Really?"

My ex-husband glanced up from his scroll and smiled. "Yo, this ain't seduction music," he drawled playfully. "I like to listen to this stuff when I'm studying. It relaxes me. Come on, Kee. If I wanted to seduce you, you know what I'd be playing."

I grinned. "Marky Mark and the Funky Bunch?"

Marcus mimed grinding his loins. "Feel it, feel it."

I relaxed at the joke, but I was still nervous about what we planned to do tonight. I glanced at the coffee table between us, lit with candles and incense. "And the mood lighting? Or is this for studying, too?"

"That's for the ritual," he said. "Don't tell me you don't put candles on your altar when you're doing your necromancy. I know better."

I couldn't argue, so I walked over to the couch and plopped down next to Marcus. I tapped the parchment open on his lap. "What are you looking at, anyway?"

Marcus shifted, giving me some space. "That is a replica of Khalid's Glamour, the archetype for all modern glamour spells. Khalid was one of the original High Mages of Illusion. Mages still use his glamours today to hide things in plain sight or hide a thing's true form." He paused. "Are you actually interested in thaumaturgy or are you just being polite?"

I grinned. "Well, I'm not interested in thaumaturgy."

Marcus stood, slipped the parchment onto a shelf before

returning, choosing an armchair across from me instead of the sofa. I tried not to take it personally. "I didn't think so," he said. "Well? Can I get you anything? Or do you just want to get started?"

I took a moment too long to answer. "Dove." Marcus's voice felt like velvet on my skin. "I promise you have nothing to worry about. I'm here with you, and I will not let anything happen to you."

"I know," I said. "I trust you. It's just ... " I cast about for the words to sum up my feelings, but I came up short. "It's nothing; I'm being ridiculous. Okay. Let's get this show on the road."

Marcus peered at me. "You drink the tea already?"

I nodded. "I did."

"I guess that means you're ready?"

"Ready as I'll ever be."

Marcus nodded and instructed me to lean back into the cushions. I did, closing my eyes and taking slow, even breaths to calm and center myself. My heart thumped against my ribs. Why was I so nervous?

"I'm going to guide you down an elevator," he said, his voice low and smooth and, goddamnit, sexy. "As I describe your descent, I want you to use all your senses to experience it. Hear the creak of the doors opening and closing. Smell the electricity. Feel the pull of gravity in your belly. Do you understand?"

I murmured an incoherent response, which Marcus took as affirmation. "We start on the top floor where everything is white. You are alone, but neither lonely nor afraid. You are comfortable. You are floating effortlessly in a cloud of white light. The doors close and the elevator descends slowly one floor, and the color shifts from a glowing white to a vibrant purple."

As he continued the meditation, my body relaxed, my thoughts slowing as my mind filled with the images he fed me. Long before my elevator reached the bottom floor, I no longer heard Marcus's voice, not consciously. I was on my own in a world that lived solely within my mind. It was disorienting. I was much more used to reaching outside of everything than I was to gazing within.

The further under I went, the more Marcus's voice devolved from words I could decipher to mere tones and vibrations, the steady beating of his tongue against his teeth. I fell into easy syncopation with his rhythm, I the upbeat to his down. I stepped out of the elevator into an open room, filled with black and darkness, but it wasn't cold. I wasn't afraid, and I didn't feel alone. All around me, I felt comfort. And then, I heard a familiar voice speak my name.

"Kiki."

The room shifted colors, becoming a warm gray, and as I turned, I saw Mama Fat, my other patron ancestor beside Papa Jinabbott, standing before me, hands folded in front of her, her head cocked to one side. She wore her hair in tight silver curls, the way I remembered her before she got sick and passed. Her small eyes gleaming in the darkness. She was working her lips, trying to say something. But for some reason, the words weren't coming out.

"Mama Fat? Are you supposed to be here?"

My patron stared daggers at me, ignoring my question. Eventually, her mouth moved, and her words found purchase. "What did the bones say?"

I blinked. "Bones?"

Mama Fat took one step toward me, eyes squinting

through the darkness. "I know Big Ginny done raised you better than this, Kiki. You don't throw the bones and then ignore what they got to say. You looked at them. I saw you look. But you didn't *see*. So you need to see it now. Tell me, sugar," she said, her voice growing more urgent. "Tell me what you saw. What did the bones say?"

I was about to object that I had no idea what she was talking about when suddenly I did. I had thrown the bones that night in the temple. I had tossed those bones at Brandy's feet to give the spirit a speaking voice, but I hadn't registered what the bones said. Something about the way they had fallen had prickled at my mind, but I'd ignored it. And here was Mama Fat telling me I needed to *see*.

Shame colored my cheeks. She was right. You didn't throw the bones and then ignore what they had to say.

In my mind's eye, I reconstructed the scene. I saw myself in the temple, standing in front of a bare wall next to Brandy's naked body. I looked down at the bones scattered at her feet, their bloody message shouting to be seen.

I didn't know how I missed it the first time. The message was unmistakable. Two warnings lay intertwined with each other. The first warning was fire. And the second was murder.

Now, ask any Conjure worker or even a tarot reader and they'll tell you that *death* in a reading rarely means actual physical death. It usually means transformation. But murder means murder; wasn't two ways about it. Mama Fat appeared in front of me again, erasing the scene from the temple. She grabbed both of my hands in hers, squeezing too tightly. Her nails dug into the backs of my hands. She was cold, and I trembled as she said, "Kiki. This ain't the time for games. You know what to do. Wake up. *Wake up*."

My eyes shot open, and I saw Marcus in the dim candlelight as he blinked back his surprise and I scrambled to my feet. I stood still for only a moment, trying to get my bearings. Then, I smelled it. Sharp and heady and strong. My stomach flipped.

"Do you smell that?" I asked.

Marcus rose, taking a step toward me. "Smell what?"

The usual fragrances were there: copal, palo santo, lemon furniture polish. But underneath those familiar death smells was something else, something that stood out and caused my skin to prickle over.

"Fire," I breathed.

I darted to the front door with Marcus only a few steps behind. He reached out, clasped his fingers around my wrist. "Kezia. There's no fire. It's probably part of your hallucination. You've been under about 15 minutes. Just give it a bit of time and it'll wear off."

But I knew damn well it wasn't the hallucination. Something was tugging me into action, a fear that rang in my mind like an alarm. I couldn't stay in that room anymore. I had to find the fire.

I threw open the front door, dashing into the night. I looked up and down the row of cottages, trying to discern where the smell was coming from. I didn't see any smoke. Eventually, I chose the right, racing barefoot with Marcus on my heels, shouting. "Kezia, I don't smell anything! No smoke, no nothing! Please, come back to the room. It's not real! It's in your head!"

I had already pushed Marcus's voice from my mind. I followed the scent as I dashed down the pathway and made a hard left at the next turn. I ran to the nearest house, banging on the door, calling out, "Open up! Open the goddamn door!"

When nobody answered, I gestured frantically at my ex-husband. "Marcus, break the door down."

He stared at me, his eyes going wide in the darkness. He held his hands out before him in a pleading gesture. "Are you crazy? We can't break the goddamn door down! Kezia. You need to calm down. You—"

I didn't have time to argue. My heart was thundering away in my chest. Sweat rolled off me in rivulets, dripping into my eyes, down the crevice between my breasts. Next to the door was a small window. I picked up a rock and hurled it through the glass, shattering the pane. I reached through the jagged pieces, angling my arm for the door lock. Broken glass sliced into my shoulder; blood and sweat poured down my arm as I finally got the door unlocked. I jumped to my feet, withdrew from the window, and went for the door.

The door swung open, and I ran into the house with Marcus behind me. The front room was empty. Still, something was tugging on my heart.

The bedroom.

All the bungalows shared the same design, so I bolted down the short corridor to where I knew the bedroom to be. As soon as I stepped through the doorway, I drew up short, hands flying to my mouth.

In the center of the bed, a person was on fire.

"Jesus Christ!" Marcus howled. He pushed me aside, scrambling bedside. "Kezia, fire extinguisher! Go, now!"

But I didn't move. I was rooted to the spot, and not just because finding a body burning in a bedroom paralyzed me. It was because of how the fire looked. It was all wrong.

A human body should burn bright red-yellow or orange, owing to large amounts of sodium and hot, unoxidized carbon particles emitting red-yellow light. But these flames didn't glow with colors from the low-frequency end of the light spectrum; they were bright cobalt blue. All flame, no smoke.

"*Kezia!*"

At the second screech of my name, my feet unglued, and I ran to the kitchen, throwing open cabinets until I found a fire extinguisher. I hurried back into the bedroom where I thrust the device at Marcus. He fumbled with it only a moment before aiming the nozzle at the burning body and pulling the trigger. A cloud of potassium bicarbonate burst forth, covering the victim in a mountain of suds. The flames went out. Marcus dropped the canister as he turned his shaking body to face me. He was coughing and moaning as the ruined body on the bed hissed. Still, no smoke rose from the body. And yet, the corpse was nothing more than a charred lump.

Trembling, I stepped toward the bed and reached out my hand. But before I could touch the corpse, Marcus grabbed me by the shoulder and pulled me back. A stab of fresh pain sent me reeling, shocking me into the moment, and I crashed to my knees. My shoulder screamed in agony. But it wasn't even the pain that stopped me. It was the fragrance.

Under normal circumstances, I'd never have been able to smell it beneath the charred skin and hair and everything else.

But thanks to Opal's gift, I had super senses.

And I smelled mint chocolate and Chanel No. 5.

"Jesus," I said. "That's Eunice Cho. What do we do? Do I call 911?"

Marcus, however, was hardly listening. "How did this happen? The front door was locked. Nobody else was here."

"Should we call the police?" I asked again.

"Police," Marcus repeated, still not listening. "That was a *magical* fire. Someone cast this spell at a distance."

"Yes," I agreed, "but that's not really helpful at all. Magically speaking, death by fire isn't uncommon."

"Every baby mage thinks he can control fire," Marcus agreed, "and ends up getting someone hurt in the process."

I nodded. Every mage who had tried to tame wild natural forces had dallied with fire and lost. Because it was so chaotic, it made for a great personal harm spell. Such spells were illegal, of course, but easy to come by on the black market if you knew where to look.

"Maybe it was an accident," Marcus said. "Maybe she did this to herself? Is Eunice a baby mage?"

I looked down at the floor, imagining the bones lying there. "The bones said fire and murder," I said. "This wasn't an accident. Someone used magic to kill this woman intentionally."

Marcus nodded in dumb agreement right before he turned and staggered into the hallway where I heard him vomit onto the floor.

No, hell no, I wasn't gonna be the one to manage this crisis. This was beyond my paygrade. Instead, I texted Brandy an urgent message and waited.

When she arrived, she took one look around and, unlike us, didn't freak out or start screaming. She placed her palms on what remained of Eunice's hands and kneeled by the side of the bed, pressing her forehead against the mattress. When she looked up, our eyes locked, and we both gasped.

"Oh," she whispered, fingering the chain at her neck. "You have it."

I didn't need to ask what she meant. She meant the light in my eyes.

I hadn't noticed before, but now it was clear as day. She had it, too.

I blinked and shook myself, forcing my mind to stay on the present matter. "Should we call the cops?"

Brandy exhaled and shook her head. "No. Thank God you called me instead of them. I can't even imagine what would happen if this got leaked to the press." She paused, took a breath. "I'll get my people to handle it."

I narrowed my eyes at her and took a step forward. "You seem remarkably calm given the fact that there is a corpse burned to a crisp on your property."

It was a long moment before Brandy answered. "This has happened before."

My heart stopped. "Brandy," I drawled, "what are you talking about?"

She fingered the gold chain at her throat and closed her eyes. "There have been others. Perhaps five. That I know of."

I opened my mouth to respond but Marcus beat me to it, his voice preceding him as he came in from the other room. "You need to start talking," he said. "I mean like yesterday."

"I'm trying, but I hardly know where to begin. We have tens of thousands of adherents. But a few of them—like I said, less than a dozen that I know of—"

"You said *five* just a second—"

"—have perished by burning," Brandy continued, ignoring my interruption. "That's all I know. Really. I don't know the details of the fires or anything like that."

"But you know who they were. You know their names."

Brandy swallowed, lifted her chin. "I do."

"I want those names," I said.

Brandy made a sound of disgust in the back of her throat. "I can't give you that," she said. "You don't know the hoops we had to jump through to keep the names out of the media, the money we had to pay the families ... I trust you, Kezia, I do, but ... I won't do anything to jeopardize this enterprise. What we do is *important*. Surely you understand that."

I narrowed my eyes and try to make myself as menacing as possible; difficult to do when you're the same height and build as the person you're trying to intimidate. "I ain't playing with you, Brandy. I need the names of the other people who burned up. I need them now."

Brandy took a slight step backward, holding up her hands, exasperated. "Why?"

I stared at her, incredulous. "You brought me here because you have souls trapped in your temple—and you never thought to make the connection between those souls and people who have mysteriously burned to death?"

"I never said it was mysterious," Brandy said, her voice small.

"What the hell does *that* mean? I saw the fire that consumed Eunice. It wasn't natural! If that same fire killed your other followers, don't you want to know who did it? Or why? Don't you want to know what the hell you're dealing with?"

Brandy's nostrils flared, the tendons in her jaw straining. "Yes! Of course I do! But not at the risk of everything my husband has worked for blowing up in the media! Not at the risk of ridicule and lawsuits and agony! If I give you those names, and you draw attention and someone links those deaths with this place ... " Brandy let her voice trail, her head shaking. "There has to be another way."

"If there is, I don't see it," I said, working to bring myself under control. "I need to understand these deaths, and that means I must understand any connection between them. Something they all have in common. A *reason* someone targeted them. And I can't find that link unless I know who they are. Please."

My words were getting through to her, but not fast enough. I needed her to stop wasting time. "If you don't give them to me, I'll just go get them myself," I said. "I'll take Marcus to the temple and we'll perform the same ritual we performed that first night, and I'll ask the souls myself. I'll ask every single one of them to tell me their names. And that will probably take a while. And in that time, somebody will probably notice something strange going on." I watched as understanding dawned on her, and her skin paled. "So we can do this easy or hard; it's your choice. You gonna give me those names or do I need to go stir up some shit?"

Brandy shook her head, taking another step away from me. "It might not even be the same list," she said.

"You can't possibly believe this is a coincidence," I said, anger rising like mercury in a thermometer. "Quit. Playing."

I watched as her resolve melted and resignation settled into her shoulders, pressing them low. She let her breath out slowly, nodding once. "Fine. I'll send you what I know. Right now, though, I have to take care of this," she said, gesturing to Eunice.

"Brandy—"

"I said I'd get it to you," she interrupted, anger flashing across her face, cheeks going ruddy. "You have my word. Now please, go. We have a doctor on staff; I'll send her to your room to clean up your shoulder. You probably need stitches." She ran a hand through her hair, shoulders slumping. "Go. Be careful. And don't breathe a word of this to anyone."

I opened my mouth to retort, but Marcus hauled me away gently, steering me into the dark, cool night. The chill desert air felt good against my skin, and it was only then that I realized how hot I was from anger and adrenaline. I let Marcus lead me back home, my mind racing.

The secrets I had promised to keep in ignorance now felt like treachery. As we walked home, I wept and prayed for forgiveness.

But I was not sure I would receive absolution.

CHAPTER ELEVEN

MOST OF THE NEXT MORNING had passed by the time I received Brandy's email. When the necrology arrived, Marcus and I met at my bungalow to research the names. There were fifteen. I sucked my teeth, shaking my head. "She goddamn lied to us," I swore. "Is this some kind of fucking game to her?"

"There's no telling what's on her mind. How do you want to do this? What are we looking for?"

That was the million-dollar question; I didn't know. I was familiar enough with most of the names on the list—an actor, a senator with a sex scandal, a megalomaniac inventor, and a shockingly unfunny comedian. A few here and there I didn't recognize. What was their connection? Money? Clout? Yes, but that described most of the registry for Inner Flame, far more than the fifteen people who were dead.

"Just start reading up on these people, I guess. Make note of anything interesting or unusual; things that could be connective tissue. Maybe they all went to the same Catholic school, or they all have the same psychiatrist, or they all pissed off a magically-talented mafioso. I don't know, really. We'll peruse that list for similarities at the end."

Saying the words out loud made me realize how impossible this was. We would never get to the bottom of it.

"You take the first seven and I'll take the bottom eight," I said. "If you find something interesting ... "

I wished I had brought my laptop with me to the retreat, as poring over celebrity websites on my phone was less than ideal. There were hundreds of news articles on the first dead celebrity alone. Eventually, I started searching for the celebrity names plus the word "weird". That wasn't helpful. I combined the names with "scandal", "inheritance", "religion", "birth". But nothing I found was noteworthy—at least not obviously so.

The articles on their deaths I found peculiar, however. They were strangely light on details. No mention of having burned to death—or any cause of death at all, for that matter. Just that they had passed peacefully in their sleep. Even TMZ's reporting was squeaky clean.

Just as I was thinking that the entire endeavor was futile, Marcus whistled. "Kezia. Have you seen the news?"

I frowned. "You know I don't watch the news."

"No, but you read Twitter," Marcus said, rolling his eyes. "Did you see that Eunice Cho is trending?"

I shrugged. "Doesn't that always happen when a celebrity dies?"

"Sure, but I actually haven't read a single mention of her death. Not sure anyone but us even knows about that yet. The stories are about her trial. Turn on the news."

Brow furrowed, I turned on the television and switched it over to CNN to see what Marcus was talking about. Someone I didn't recognize was giving a press conference; that part wasn't interesting. What *was* noteworthy was the ticker in the lower third. It read, *Biotech mogul Eunice Cho exonerated of all charges.* I turned up the volume.

" ... yesterday, when lawyers for the investment firm noted anomalies in the Sanguinos signatures. Upon further investigation, experts discovered that Ms. Cho's signatures on the fraudulent disclosure to investors were forged. Recent video footage anonymously submitted to the SEC shows Sanguinos Chief Financial Officer, Karl Eubanks, signing the documents with Ms. Cho's name while alone in his office." Footage of a White man being arrested, microphones thrust in his face, rolled on screen. The lower-third read, "Karl Eubanks arrested for forgery and fraud." "I didn't do anything wrong," Eubanks was saying as police officers led him away from the courthouse through a crowd of reporters. "Everything in that document would have been true by next quarter. We would have all been rich. Now nobody gets rich, and more sick people die. Congratulations, social justice assholes. You're all pathetic.'"

I leaned forward onto my elbows, my eyes glued to the screen. "You gotta be fucking kidding me," I breathed. "So she *didn't* lie to her investors? Her CFO forged her signature on the disclosure documents? What the fuck, man! They ruined that woman's life. Absolutely dragged her through the mud. You should have seen her, Marcus. She was hanging on by a thread. She was wrung dry."

Marcus grunted, shaking his head. "It's a crazy, fucked up world. Can you imagine? If she had lived just a little longer, she could have looked her accusers and detractors in the face and told them to go fuck themselves. She could have saved her reputation. And now?"

I sank back into the couch. And now. Would there even be a funeral? Or would a funeral under these circumstances be too high profile for the cult's executives? In my research, I didn't come across any mention of funerals or wakes or even memorial services. Every celebrity death had been very hush-hush. Was that what would happen to Eunice Cho? Was her legacy just going to fade away instead of burn out?

I didn't intend that to be a pun.

"I have a thought," Marcus said.

I switched the TV off. "What is it?"

"We've been going through this list looking up life details for these celebrities, but we're not finding anything because there's so *much* information. What if we start with some of these names we *don't* recognize? Maybe they're less newsworthy and won't have as many articles online? What do you think?"

I shrugged. "Can't hurt. I'm not finding anything otherwise."

I skimmed my list for the least recognizable name: Erica Bowman. A cursory Google search returned typical results: several Facebook pages, a Twitter profile, a handful of different LinkedIn bios. Any of these women could have been the Erica Bowman I was looking for, but something told me none of them were. The Erica I was looking for was a Temple member, which meant she was either famous, wealthy, a notable freak (like me), or influential.

Something in the back of my mind perked up at the thought of influence. On a hunch, I added +influencer to my Google search and scanned results until I found something promising.

It was an article in the student-run Stanford Daily. The article featured a student named Erica Bowman, a junior who founded a local organization to rescue young women and girls from sex trafficking. According to the article, Erica was also a cheerleader, A student, the daughter of a Hollywood executive

(*Ah, there's the money*) and an Instagram influencer. I scrolled through the article until I found a link to her Instagram page. I clicked on it.

When it loaded, I gasped.

My hand went to my throat and then my mouth as I scrolled through her pictures. Barely daring to breathe, I glanced up from the phone to find Marcus looking at me expectantly. "You find something?"

I scrolled back to the top of the page and handed the phone to him. "What do you notice?"

Marcus glanced at the screen for no more than a few seconds before he started scrolling. I sucked my teeth and shook my head. "No," I said, taking the phone and returning to the top of her profile. "Go back to the top. Look at that very first picture. What do you notice?"

Marcus stared at the photo for a good fifteen seconds before shoving the phone in my direction. "It's just a selfie. Nothing special."

I gaped, incredulous. "Really?"

"It's just some White girl," he said.

I narrowed my eyes at him. "Look harder. Look at her eyes."

He looked, but again, shook his head. "Okay? I don't see anything weird about her eyes. You like the filter she used or something?"

Frustrated, I tapped the phone with my forefinger. "Yo, I know guys don't notice shit like when we get our hair done, but damn, even a blind man can see this. Right?"

But the pure look of bewilderment on his face answered that question. "Kiki, what are you *talking* about?"

My heart dropped into my stomach like a rock. "You don't see that *light* in her eyes? It's bright as hell. And then if you scroll through some of her older pictures, you can see how that light is dimmer and dimmer until it's not there at all. You don't see what I'm talking about?"

Marcus handed the phone back to me. "Just looks like some White girl," he repeated.

As I took the phone back into my hands, I was trembling. This wasn't just male obliviousness. Even the most unobservant husband could tell his wife had gotten colored contacts once you pointed it out to him. But while the light was obvious to me, Marcus could not see it. Which meant he also couldn't see that in these photos, the light in her eyes dimmed the further back you scrolled until it disappeared altogether. It was only in her most recent photo that her eyes were nearly incandescent. Like she was practically ...

Practically on fire.

That wasn't a light in her eyes. That was *flame.*

"*Jesus Christ,*" I muttered to myself, my heartbeat racing. "I think I know ... "

Now that I knew what to look for, I went back to the beginning of the list, pulling up each celebrity's Instagram page—a chronological gallery. I hadn't realized I'd been holding my breath until I let it out in a warm, fetid whoosh.

All the celebrities on my list followed the same pattern as Erica Bowman. Each one had a preternatural brightness in their eyes that dimmed the further back I scrolled until it was gone altogether. It was most evident in the images from Camilla Stevenson's Instagram, because she took a lot of close-ups of her face. On February 27th, she was just a model smiling beautifully into the camera. But by March 17th, she'd changed. She'd acquired an inner fire.

Her most recent photo was dated June 10th. A quick search revealed that she died June 12th.

"Marcus," I said, my brow furrowed, "go to the Temple of the Inner Flame retreat archive page and tell me if they held a retreat between the end of February and the middle of March of this year. I have a theory."

I heard Marcus tapping on his laptop. "They did," he confirmed, his curiosity piqued. "March 5th. Why?"

I moved quickly to the next celebrity's Instagram page. "Between August 8th last year and August 24th?"

Marcus grunted. "Yes. Damn. How are you doing this?"

We did this twice more, comparing the dates that a celebrity's Instagram page showed a change in their eyes with Temple retreat dates. They matched up each time.

So I was right. Each person had developed a flame at the same time the Temple had held a retreat. They'd gotten them here. Just like I did.

And then they'd died.

I pushed that thought to the back of my mind as I explained my theory to Marcus. "In the most recent pictures, they all have a bright flame in their eyes. I went back to earlier pictures until I found a photo where there was no light. Think about it this way: at some point in the past, they *acquired* the inner fire. And you helped me prove that they all acquired the flame at the same time the Temple held one of their retreats. And then it grew brighter and brighter until ... well, until they burned to death."

He was quiet a moment. "Dove, it's just that I don't see any light. I truly don't know what you're talking about."

"Well, maybe it's because I have super senses on me," I mused.

Marcus looked doubtful. "Maybe, but super senses is a very common gift. *Somebody* on Black Twitter would have mentioned seeing folks with lights in their eyes. So how is it that no one—not a manager, not a fan, not a paparazzo—*no one* noticed or commented that these people looked different upon their return from the retreat? Seems like the kind of thing that might eventually make its way to TMZ."

"Because they couldn't see it," I said.

"What are you talking about?"

"Before I fainted in the temple, I saw people with flames appearing over their heads," I said, puzzling it out aloud. "I asked this guy Ben why some people received a flame, and others didn't. He didn't know what I was talking about. But then Andromeda read me a poem from that book of theirs. It was all about flame and fire and love and Andromeda said I had been chosen. It was only afterward that I saw the fire in Brandy."

Marcus balked. "So Brandy has it, too?"

"Yes."

"I didn't see it," he asserted.

"I know. *Because you can only see the flame if you have it, too.*"

At this, Marcus chuckled under his breath. "Flame recognize flame."

I jabbed him in the ribs with my elbow. "You think this is funny? Maybe you're not getting me. Whatever these people have, I have it, too."

That wiped the smirk off Marcus's face. "What are you talking about?"

"Look at me. You don't see anything strange about me, do you?"

Marcus squinted. "Strange how? You look like you always look."

I closed my eyes, sure now. He couldn't see. Of course he couldn't. Marcus didn't have the flame. "I went to the temple for the drawing down ceremony," I began. "I participated. I didn't mean to, but I did. And then I saw the flames, and now, I have the light in my eyes." I paused, letting my words sink in. "That same fire is inside me, too. Which means whatever killed these people could take me, as well."

Marcus's eyes widened. "Whoa, whoa, whoa. Dove, let's not jump to conclusions. You don't know for sure. Did you see a flame in Eunice Cho's eyes?"

I shook my head. "No, but I didn't have it then, so I wouldn't have seen it even if it was there. Then again ... "

"What?"

I turned my attention to Marcus, head cocked to one side. "Andromeda noticed it. She said I was filled with light. And she doesn't have it."

Marcus made a face. "Andromeda? Andromeda *Clark*? The psychic? She's here? You met her?"

I stared. "Marcus, please. *Focus.*"

He nodded, abashed. "You're right. Sorry. But, look. Andromeda is a psychic. I have no doubt she could see your light without having any of her own. I mean, that's part of what psychics do. See auras and shields and magic."

"Huh." I recalled that day at the bath, when Andromeda had described my aura to me. "She said she could tell I was a necromancer based on my aura. You think it's the same kind of thing?"

"We need a control," Marcus said. "Maybe *all* members of the Temple have this flame. Who else is a member?"

We perused the Instagram profiles of a dozen other people: actors, moguls, politicians, YouTubers. None had the fire in their eyes.

None but the people who had died.

And Brandy.

And me.

My ex-husband clenched his jaw, severity settling into the lines of his face. "Dove, this is *serious.*"

I frowned, eyes wide. "Who you tellin'? It gets worse the more we find out. But what I want to know now is why *I'm* a target. There's absolutely no reason to target me for murder. I don't have money or influence or anything like that. There must be another explanation."

"Of course there is," Marcus groaned, scrubbing his face with his palms. "How did I not see it before?"

"See *what* before?"

"This isn't run-of-the-mill magic, Kezia. We've been thinking about this all wrong."

I rolled my eyes, my nerves fraying. "For God's sake, Marcus, *what is it?*"

He paused. "It's possession."

Marcus was on his feet now, pacing. "In grad school, I read a paper about a tribe in Angola in the 1930s. This anthropologist, Torabi, heard about a community that was plagued by an evil spirit. Torabi recorded it as 'fire demon' but there was a footnote indicating that some translators found this language inaccurate. Supposedly, a closer translation would be divine illumination—like in the Bible when God presents himself to Moses as a burning bush. But anyway, somehow, people who became possessed with this demonic energy—this *divine illumination*—went mad before bursting into flames."

I blinked. "Spontaneous combustion?"

"Not exactly spontaneous," he said, "though I'm sure it looked that way to an onlooker. But for the possessed, it was more of a slow burn until..." He mimed an explosion with puffed out cheeks and gestures.

I thought about this a moment. "But these celebrities didn't go mad."

Marcus quirked an eyebrow. "Can you be sure?"

I opened my mouth, but closed it again. No, I couldn't. I hadn't been there when they'd died. Who knew what state of mind they'd been in?

I leaned back into the sofa, pulling my knees to my chest. "Okay. So you're thinking maybe we're dealing with ... a fire demon? Inaccurate translations aside," I interjected before Marcus could correct me.

He offered the barest of shrugs. "It's possible," he said. "That could be what attacked you in the temple. It adds up."

"And the point of entry is the drawing down ritual in the temple." I clucked my tongue against the roof of my mouth. "That tracks. You know what this means."

Marcus nodded. "Time to see the wizard."

CHAPTER TWELVE

"A PRIVATE INTERVIEW WITH Caleb is absolutely out of the question."

We were standing in Casey's office, arms folded across our chests as we tried to intimidate Brandy's assistant into giving us our way. But as meek a person as she appeared on the outside, her insides were all steel. She would not budge.

"Casey, this is a *life or death* situation," I repeated. "If he knew what we knew, he'd be breaking down our door to get our help. All we need is an hour with him. Just to ask questions."

"You're welcome to hand your questions over to me, and you have my word that I'll relay them to him. If he wants to answer—"

"I can't give the questions to you," I groaned, clenching my fists at my side. I didn't know how much Casey knew, and I would not be the one to tell her a fire demon possibly possessed her beloved temple. "Where's Brandy? I'd rather just speak to her."

Casey sighed. "Brandy is indisposed at the moment. I'm sure I can help you."

"I'm sure you can't," I retorted. "I need to speak to Caleb myself. If I—"

"Ms. Bernard, if I had the ability to create more hours in a day, I would, but I can't. Caleb would love to speak with each of his people one-on-one, but that's simply not possible. There isn't enough *time*. These retreats are everything to Caleb. He sinks everything he has into them. He simply doesn't have free time in his schedule to meet with every seeker who requests his attention."

I turned to Marcus, helpless. He squared his shoulders and narrowed his eyes. "Casey, we're not seekers looking for spiritual guidance. We're not groupies or apostles, either. What we want to discuss with him is a legal matter."

That wasn't precisely true, though I suppose it could be, depending how you looked at it. Like, if you tilted your head and squinted. But it was as good an angle as any other. But Casey only looked tired when she said, "I'd be happy to give you the name and number of the Temple's legal firm." She picked a business card from a holder on her desk and scribbled on the back of it before handing it to me. I slipped the card into a pocket without looking at it.

"Listen, I—"

"Kezia? Marcus? Everything okay in here?"

Brandy breezed through the door looking fresh as a daisy and not at all indisposed. She slipped into a chair at Casey's desk, beckoning for us to do the same. We remained standing. "We need to speak with your husband," Marcus said.

Brandy sighed. "We've been over this already." The weariness in her voice belied her fresh appearance. "Caleb isn't available. If every single person wanted time with him, he'd never—"

Marcus dipped his chin, flicked his eyes impatiently in Casey's direction. "Brandy."

The younger woman breathed out a heavy sigh and ran a hand through her hair. "Jesus. All right. Casey, I hate to do this to you in your own office, but would you mind ... ?"

Casey got to her feet wordlessly, closing the door behind her as she left. Only now did Marcus and I take our seats.

"We think we know what's in the temple," I said. "I don't want to scare you, but we think it's a demon. A *fire* demon; a living intelligence that's holding the souls captive. There have been documented cases of similar situations in Africa, but there're no records of anything like this in America. Marcus?" I turned to my ex-husband for corroboration. "Is that right?"

"That's about the size of it," he confirmed.

"What we need to understand is how it *got* here. And the only person I can think of who might hold those answers is your husband. Once we understand how it got here, we might better understand what it wants and how we can free those souls. And," I added, my voice dipping low, "how you and I can break free before we meet the same fate."

Brandy broke my gaze, her eyes going liquid. "I warned you not to pray in the temple," she whispered.

I glowered at her. "So you knew," I said. "You knew, and you did nothing. Did you warn the others? I saw other people with flames over their heads. What if they—"

"They don't have it," Brandy said. "I spoke to everyone after the ceremony. The flame doesn't always take. But it took with you."

"We told you to close the temple," I growled. "You *knew* and you put those people at risk."

"This is our religion," she snapped. "I didn't put them at risk. I gave them the opportunity to be *blessed.*" Now, Brandy's hand went to her belly, caressing her unborn child absently. "And anyway, I didn't *know*. I suspected that something was happening in the temple, and I traced my own fire to the day I asked for—"

She cut off then, fidgeting with her necklace. "It doesn't matter. So you think it's a fire demon," she repeated. I couldn't read any emotion in her voice. "Well, I admit I didn't see that coming. And you want to go to my husband with this? Now?"

I lifted my eyebrows in surprise. "Is there a better time?"

"A better time to tell my husband that everything he's built —his entire life's work—is about to be destroyed because you allege there's a *fire demon* in his temple? No, I'd say there will never be a good time for that."

Real anger gripped me by the throat. "Brandy, are you out of your mind? I don't have time for this shit anymore! You brought me here. You put me in danger. You *withheld vital information* and now *I* have this fucking fire inside me waiting to destroy me from the inside. Do you think this is a game?"

She remained so stoic that I could have slapped her, but I used every drop of grace I had cultivated as a Black woman in America to hold myself together. "Whatever light we have inside, it's gonna burn us to death just like it did Eunice Cho, and Camilla Stevenson, and Erica Bowman and all those other people." I let my eyes drop to Brandy's midsection. "You willing to put your baby at risk for all this?" I saw my arrow hit its bullseye. "Brandy," I said, letting my voice grow soft, "what are you so afraid of? Why are you so afraid of your husband?"

Incredulity flashed to anger in Brandy's eyes. "I'm not afraid of my husband! Jesus; are you that stupid? I'm afraid *for* him!" Brandy stood now, threw her arms about her stomach and began pacing steadily around the room. "You don't understand the sacrifices he made for this place. For all these people. To bring them truth and light and satisfaction. You don't know how hard his early years were for him, before he found success. He lived out of his car. He was completely alone. He had nothing—no friends, no family. He built this from conviction, hard work, and the singular belief that the world needed a light only he and Brother Zahi could provide! If you let this shit about fire demons get out, it would ruin him. It would ruin *us,*" she said.

"It doesn't have to get out," I said, softened by an image of Caleb as a lonely man without friends or family. I related too well to that. "Not if we *take care of it.* So help me help you, Brandy. Let me talk to Caleb. Let's bring this fucking horror story to an end."

She was silent a moment. Finally, she sighed, exasperated. "Fine. Come to the house at 7." She stood, showing us the door. "I'll make sure you receive directions."

We shuffled out of Casey's office with an interview time secured under our belts, but it didn't feel like victory. It felt more like an expiration date.

I WASN'T sure what to expect after everything else I had seen on the preserve, but when we pulled up to Brandy and Caleb's house, envy nibbled at my insides. It was exactly the kind of California dream house I'd wanted as a child, the kind of home that would have been equally welcome on the beach or nestled in the desert. Eggshell stucco with an adobe shingled roof, the home was large but not overtly ostentatious. A xeriscaped yard encircled it, yucca and sagebrush surrounded by pearly white gravel. A stone fountain out front housed frogs and koi fish, lily pads floating on the surface. I raised my eyebrow at Marcus. "Do you feel underdressed?"

It was supposed to be a joke, but Marcus's expression was somber. "Let's just get this over with," he muttered as we climbed out of the car.

We had scarcely ascended the steps when the front door opened and a woman appeared, leading us silently to a living room where Brandy was already waiting for us. She looked different: wrapped in a silk kimono and barefoot, she exuded none of the professionalism I had come to associate with her. In that moment, she was just a wife trying to protect her husband.

She didn't stand to meet us but indicated that we should have a seat, which we did. The same woman that greeted us at the door poured glasses of wine for both Marcus and me. Neither of us reached for our glasses.

"Caleb will be down in a minute," Brandy said, twirling her wedding ring around her finger with her thumb. "I'm sorry, but I won't be staying for the conversation. I hope you don't mind. I'm not feeling well, and I'd like to lie down. But I thought greeting you was at least proper."

"It's no problem," I said. "Thank you for having us."

Brandy didn't acknowledge this; instead she rose, clutching the edges of her robe tight against her chest. "Be careful what you say to my husband," she said. "I know he doesn't come off this way, but he's extremely vulnerable. Whatever you do, please don't lay the guilt of what has become of our temple at his feet. I don't think he could handle it."

I didn't have time to respond. Brandy exited the room just

as a man's voice boomed what I thought was supposed to pass for a greeting.

"Well! You must be the two newcomers that Brandy hasn't stopped talking about."

Caleb smiled as he entered the room, a glass of whiskey in his hand. When we made motions to stand, Caleb waved the intention away with a frown. "Don't get up, please. We're all friends here, I hope." He eased himself into the armchair across from us with a small grunt, and I realized for the first time that he was no spring chicken. Still, he crossed his legs elegantly and took a small sip from his glass. "My wife made you comfortable, yes? Can I get you something other than wine? Bourbon? Water?" Neither of us had a chance to answer before Caleb leaned forward, his eyes glittering. "I recognize you. You're the girl that fainted at the ceremony the other day. Are you feeling all right, sweetheart?" He indicated the side of his face with a finger. "You didn't get that here, did you?"

My fingers drifted to my cheek where the abrasion was still visible from my attack. I shook my head. "No, this happened before I got here. I feel fine now. Thank you for asking."

Caleb narrowed his eyes, pursing his lips. "That's a lie, but I understand why you told it. My wife says you want to discuss some disturbances in my temple. Is that right?"

Up close and without the splendor imparted by ceremony, Caleb bore nothing of the radiance he emitted just days ago. Nothing about him seemed otherworldly. He was small in stature, with salt and pepper hair gone mostly to gray, slightly wrinkled eyes and a mouth that liked to smile. His movements were slow and ponderous, and in that moment, the reality of his and Brandy's May-December union was brought into stark relief. Caleb would be nearing eighty when their child blossomed into adulthood. Would he live to see his grandchildren? Would he be spry enough to play catch in the backyard?

But then I chastised myself, color burning in my cheeks. Youth alone wouldn't guarantee him a relationship with his child, anyway. I knew that much better than anyone.

But perhaps strangest of all, his dark eyes contained none of the fire I saw in his wife's.

How could that be? If praying in the temple was enough to fill someone with the inner flame, why didn't Caleb have it? Was I supposed to believe he'd never prayed in his own temple?

That could be, I reasoned. *Especially if he's a charlatan.*

My stomach twisted. I didn't believe Caleb was a fake. And anyway, I'd seen Ben pray in the temple, and nothing had happened to him.

For whatever reason, Caleb simply hadn't been chosen.

"Brandy contacted me because she suspected the temple might be haunted," I explained. "I'm a necromancer. I assume she told you." When Caleb didn't respond, I pressed on. "What I discovered is that several members of your church have died by spontaneous combustion. And I've reason to believe the souls of the people who died in those fires are now trapped in your temple."

Caleb sucked in a deep, noisy breath through his nose. "This much, my wife has told me," he said. "I would have rather she spoke to me about this *before* she invited outsiders into our sacred space, but what's done is done." He took another sip of his whiskey and gestured toward our untouched glasses. "If you're not a fan of wine, I'd be happy to pour you something more to your taste. Scotch?"

I demurred, but Marcus accepted. While Caleb stood and fiddled with a decanter at his bar, I continued. "When we went to investigate," I said, weighing my words carefully, "I tried to guide the souls over to the other side. But something stopped me. I think it was a security spell. Something holding the souls captive."

Caleb handed the scotch to Marcus and returned to his seat. "I feel like there's a question in there somewhere. Care to lead me to it?"

"Are you a magician? Thaumaturgist? Shaman? Wizard? A spellworker of any kind?"

At this, Caleb chuckled, a mirthless sound. "Would that I were, but, no." He flicked a hand in my direction. "If you're a necromancer, you've far more ability than I do." He sighed then, resignation settling over his face. "My parents were social workers in Somalia. That's where I grew up. I returned to America as a young adult to pursue a degree in arcane studies. I applied everywhere, but the only school that gave me an interview was UCLA, which is how I ended up here in Los Angeles. Unfortunately, however, I failed the aptitude tests. Profoundly failed them. UCLA turned me away. And as you both must know, you can't study thaumaturgy on your own. Every mage requires a teacher."

"That's true," Marcus said, nodding. "But we don't do aptitude tests anymore. We accept all kinds of students, even those with no real talent for magic. Myself included," he added with a wry grin.

At this, Caleb's brows lifted. "Is that so? You're a mage?"

Marcus shook his head. "No. Associate Lecturer in alternative religions. I got my doctorate in metaphysical studies and arcane magics a few years ago, though, after the aptitude requirement was lifted." Marcus shrugged. "Seems magic can be taught even by those of us who are bad at it."

"Well, times've changed, it seems," Caleb said mostly to

himself. "But I suppose things would have worked out very differently if I'd taken that path. I don't think I would have founded this church, for example, or met my wife. So I can't really complain about the course life has taken me."

We nodded in silent agreement. Then, I tried a different tack. "Caleb, do you know anyone who can cast powerful magic? I mean, I understand that you can't, but how about someone close to you? Family, friends, business associates?"

The guru shrugged, head leaning sideways in thought. "Now? Not really. I knew someone a long time ago, when I was a child. There was a man who frequently came to pray with my parents; his name was Abdi. I wasn't supposed to speak to him because my parents discovered a scroll hidden among his belongings one night—an enchantment by the scholar Khalid.

"Of course, everything taboo is more enticing, and soon Abdi and I became friends. He was my only friend, really. One night, I asked him about the scroll my parents had discovered, and he got very angry and told me to mind my own business. But then I think he felt guilty when he saw my face—I didn't mean to hurt Abdi. I was just a curious boy. And that's when he confided in me that the scroll was a glamour—a spell of illusion. Abdi explained that he had been horrifically burned in his youth, and his ruined face scared people away. He used the glamour to hide his deformity. It was his way of drawing people to him. Making them like him."

Caleb's face was drawn at the memory. "I asked if he could use the spell to give me black skin. Maybe then the other children would like me." He cleared his throat and shifted in his seat. "He said he couldn't do that, because then my own parents wouldn't know me, and he would never hurt them or me. But he did give me something. A scroll—the only real piece of magic I've ever owned. It was a minor incantation of friend-ship; the sort of thing you might give to a shy child without many playmates. As I understood it, it was supposed to ensure a connection between the giver and receiver that lasts the test of time. But I think now he was just pulling my leg."

I wrinkled my brow. "Why?"

Caleb shrugged. "Because I read the incantation and never saw Abdi again."

There was something buried in those words—sadness? No, it was something heavier. The grief of betrayal. Suddenly, I felt deep sympathy for Caleb Atwater. He must have been profoundly lonely as a missionary's child in Somalia. Had he ever fit in anywhere? Was that how he came to form a cult—just to surround himself with people who loved him?

If he did, I almost couldn't blame him.

"Listen," Marcus said. "I don't know how or who, but someone who has access to your temple has been working magic behind your back."

Caleb scoffed. "Behind my back? In my own temple? Impossible."

I shook my head. "No, it's true. Because what we've discov-ered ... well, what we suspect ... "

"We suspect a demon," Marcus said, finishing for me when I couldn't quite get the words out. "We believe there's a fire demon in your temple, and when Kezia tried to get those souls across the veil, it attacked her. So what we need to know is how it got there. And we'd appreciate it if you spared us more of these fucking stories."

With a sigh, Caleb finished the last of his drink. "There's no need to be crude," he said. "I take your passion and inten-sity without all that sort of language." He leaned back, pressed his eyes closed. "What you're saying really is impossible, though. It can't have happened."

His voice was so thin, so weary, that once again I found myself filled with sympathy. He shouldn't be here, answering questions about evil entities taking over his temple. He should be upstairs with his wife, planning a baby shower or a vacation or choosing baby names.

The man before me was an utter mystery. He was so unlike the vibrant salesman who had moved me to prayer just a few short days ago.

"Why is it impossible?" I asked.

"Everyone who comes through here is thoroughly vetted. Everyone except the two of you," he said, more than a hint of irritation underlining his words. "My parishioners are very prominent individuals who live their entire lives on the world stage. They don't have a private life to speak of. If there were some nefarious personality running around casting evil spells and summoning demons into my temple, I would know about that proclivity long before they ever got here."

"Unless they used a glamour to hide their abilities," Marcus said. "Like the one your friend Abdi used."

At this, Caleb barked a laugh. "You're not suggesting Abdi had anything to do with this. My God, man, I knew Abdi on a different continent nearly a half-century ago! Besides, does a glamour that powerful even exist? Magic that can hide from cameras, aura readers, fortunetellers, psychics, mages—"

"He's right," I interrupted. "There's no magic that can hide from *everything*. Every glamour has its chinks. And I'm guessing," I said, returning my attention to Caleb, "that your vetting process includes multiple levels and types of magical investigation."

"That's right," Caleb said, nodding. "We aren't running a circus. This is a *church*. Our mission —"

"What about your staff?" It was Marcus who asked, leaning forward on his elbows. "Are they thoroughly vetted as well?"

"Even more so," Caleb asserted. "Do you really think that I'm just some buffoon who lucked into a multimillion-dollar enterprise? I know what the hell I'm doing. Everyone I associate with gets a thorough background check. I know every single person who works here personally. I've had spiritual counseling sessions with each of them. Everyone who works here is a member of the church."

"Why did you name your church Temple of the Inner Flame?"

Marcus's second interruption caught us both off guard, but as soon as the question was asked, I felt both a chill in the air and the flame in my breast blaze to life. I understood what he was getting at: it couldn't be coincidence. Caleb, too, sensed the trap. His eyes narrowed; his nostrils flared. "I got it from a book of poems."

"*Conversations with the Inner Flame*," I supplied.

"That's right. Given to me by the gentleman who sold me this property," Caleb said. "I was young, then. Poetry and song lyrics were powerful ... What is it?"

I must have been making a face as I'd already heard this origin story from Eunice. I curled my head into my lap and pressed my fingertips into my eye sockets. "God, I'm so stupid," I mumbled. "All that shit about flames and possession —it's right there in that book. Which was written before you ever bought this property."

Marcus frowned. "What are you saying?"

"None of this is a coincidence. The poems, the magic,

everything was already in motion before the property changed hands. The demon was already here," I said.

Caleb's eyebrow quirked. "How's that?"

"We've been assuming that whatever is in your temple is a recent introduction, but it's not. What's happening here is described in the poetry book. *I will possess you my love. I'll put flames in your breast,*" I said, offering a poor recitation of the poems I'd encountered. "Sound familiar?"

"Yes, I see your point," Caleb said. "But it's *poetry*. It isn't meant to be taken literally."

I rolled my eyes. "Caleb. Open your eyes."

The guru looked abashed. "Fine. But that doesn't guarantee a demon was already here when I bought the land."

"It's not a guarantee," Marcus admitted, "but Kezia's right; it's a damn good assumption at this point."

"And the gentleman who sold you this property for a song probably knew it," I said. "He's the key. He's the one we're looking for."

Caleb blinked. "But I bought this land ages ago. That would mean the demon's been here for twenty years."

"Caleb, who sold you this property? Where can I find him?"

The guru chuckled, shaking his head. "I hope you're not expecting me to remember the *name* of the person I bought land from decades ago. I'm sorry; I have no idea."

"That's okay," Marcus said, facing me. "That's public record. We can get that information from the county tax assessor. Jesus, dove, you're a genius."

My phone rang, interrupting our moment. Irritated, I glanced at the screen, but when I read the name that appeared, a lump formed in my throat. My brother never called me unless I was running late for work. Or something was wrong.

I picked up immediately. "Lamont?"

"Kezia." His voice was raw. "It's Big Ginny. Wherever you are, you need to come home."

"Why, what happened?"

"I'll explain when you get here." He hung up.

My eyes found Marcus's. "Something's happened to Big Ginny," I croaked, my words creaking from a dry throat.

Marcus stood and pulled me to my feet. "I'll drive."

CHAPTER THIRTEEN

W E WERE ON THE ROAD within minutes. While Marcus drove, I furiously tapped out a message to Brandy, explaining I had to take some time to go back home, but I'd be back. Then I messaged Casey, asking her to find out who had sold Caleb the land. When that was through, I leaned back into my seat and gave in to my fatigue, thankful that Marcus gave me silence and space.

When we were about 15 minutes away from home, I received another text from my brother. "Big Ginny is at Queen of Angels hospital," I said. "You know where it is?"

Marcus pushed a couple of buttons and the car's infotainment center pulled up a map, directing us to the hospital.

Twenty minutes later, I entered Big Ginny's room to find Lamont standing at my grandmother's side, holding her hand. Big Ginny was tucked into the hospital bed, sitting up with a light blanket draped over her lower body. When she saw me, her eyes lit up. When she saw Marcus, her entire body came alive.

"Marcus!" she exclaimed, removing her hand from Lamont's

and opening her arms toward my ex-husband. "The hell you doing here, baby? When you get back in town? How long you here for? Come here and give me some sugar," she said.

Marcus was all smiles as he strode over to Big Ginny and enveloped her in a hug, kissing her noisily on the cheek. The sight of my grandmother and my daughter's father together stung at the back of my eyes but I refused to cry. My gaze flipped towards Lamont who, to his credit, remained indifferent. He offered nothing, and I felt no need to explain.

When Big Ginny and Marcus disentangled themselves, Marcus settled himself on the edge of the bed, taking her hand in his own just as Lamont had been doing when we first arrived. "I never really left town," he explained. "I went back to Lagos only for about six months. Been here ever since. I took a job at UCLA. I've been helping Kezia with a little investigation outside of town."

Big Ginny looked like a child on Christmas morning. "Is Lola with you?"

Marcus shook his head. "Naw, she's at home with my mum."

"Home where? In Los Angeles?"

Marcus nodded. "Yes, that's right."

"When can I see her?"

Now, Marcus turned slightly to catch my gaze. "That's up to Kezia," he said.

Taking that as invitation to escape this line of conversation, I pulled Lamont into the hallway, eyebrows raised. "What happened to her? She seems fine."

Lamont took me by the arm and pulled me further down the hall, away from the door. He kept his voice low when he said, "She had an episode."

"Episode? What kind of episode?"

Lamont exhaled heavily out his nose. "Neighbors found her stumbling around the street half-dressed and talking to herself. They called me and I brought her in—had to close down early," he added, his voice dripping with reproach. "She had a temperature and irregular heart patterns. They want to keep her for a few days because at her age, nothing is just nothing, you know what I'm saying?"

I nodded and leaned against the wall, the weight of the day's events pressing the air from my lungs. I felt so tired. "Thanks for calling me. And sorry I wasn't there."

"Is everything okay? What happened to you? You get mugged?" He gestured to my busted face and the shoulder bandage that peeked through the neck of my t-shirt.

I considered the various ways of answering this question. "I'll be fine," I said, opting for something I hoped might eventually be true.

Lamont sniffed and flicked his eyes toward Big Ginny's room. "Anything you want to tell me about?"

I knew he meant Marcus, which I didn't want to talk about. I peeled myself away from the wall and padded toward the room. "Nope."

Inside, Marcus took one look at me and made his farewells to Big Ginny. "Kee's had a long day," he said by way of explanation, "and I should probably get her home. You want us to bring you anything tomorrow? You got your Kindle and whatnot?"

"Bring me my bones and my Florida water," she said, tugging the blanket up under her armpits. "This place ain't seen a good cleaning since Moses parted the damn Red Sea."

I kissed Big Ginny on the cheek and promised to be back

after I'd gotten some rest. Marcus took me home, where he dropped me off on the porch. "You be okay by yourself?"

I shrugged. "Am I any safer from the demons if I have company?"

Marcus hung his head and rubbed the back of his neck. "Naw, probably not. But listen ... "

"No, I'll be fine," I said, lowering my voice and removing the sass. "You've done enough already. And thank you, by the way. For everything. I mean it."

"You're welcome. I'll give you a call tomorrow. If you need anything, anything at all ... "

"I know where to find you," I said. I resisted the urge to hug him, to kiss him on the cheek. Kissing Marcus, even just on the cheek, couldn't take me anywhere good. "Good night."

I SLEPT until noon the next day. I hadn't slept well; my dreams were awash with screaming dead people, fiery emanations that wanted to devour my soul, and the image of Big Ginny lying small in a large hospital bed, muttering nonsense and tearing the clothes from her body. I'd woken several times in a deep sweat, my nightclothes clinging to my skin and my hair scarf damp. I must've drunk a gallon of water, but nothing satisfied the deep-seated thirst I awoke with.

Without Big Ginny around, the house seemed too big, too quiet, and too empty. I went into the kitchen and was greeted by the lingering smell of bacon grease, pulling an unwilling smile faintly to my lips. I brewed some coffee and made myself some grits and scrambled eggs. I knew I needed to eat, even if I didn't feel like it. Whatever was going on with Big Ginny wouldn't resolve overnight. Nothing in this world or in the world beyond was ever that easy. I needed to keep up my strength.

When I finally looked at my phone, I saw that I had four missed calls from Marcus, but no return text yet from Casey. I sighed as I poured my coffee and dialed Marcus back. He answered on the first ring. "How's your shoulder?"

I moved my shoulder in gentle circles, feeling it out. It still hurt. "It's fine. Why did you call me so many times? Everything okay?"

"Oh. Yes." I could almost see Marcus straightening up, returning his attention to things that mattered. My physical injuries were the least of our concerns. "I have some information for you. Actually, it's less information and more an introduction. I got in touch with an old colleague of mine. I think she might be able to help us."

As much as I didn't want to involve anyone else in this nightmare, my interest piqued. "How? Who?"

"She's a demonologist. She's made some time in her schedule this afternoon if you'd like to go over to her place. She's considered one of the foremost experts in the field. If anybody can help us with the situation, it's her."

I glanced at the clock above the microwave and did some quick calculations. "Okay. What time were you thinking? I'll need at least two, maybe three hours this afternoon. I have to get dressed, go down and see Big Ginny, probably catch a couple of lectures from Lamont. But after that ... ?"

"Let's say 5 o'clock. There's an Ethiopian place not too far from where she lives; we can stop by there and pick up some dinner. From what I remember, Theodetta's not much of a cook."

There was something in how he said this, a playfulness in the timbre of his voice that made me wonder how close he and this Theodetta actually were. My pulse quickened, and my heart squeezed, but I was quick to chastise myself for this reaction. Isn't this what I had wanted all along? Did I not always say I wanted Marcus to move on, find a mother for our daughter, and make himself a home and a life? I had always said that. But maybe I'd been a liar all along.

"Yeah, that sounds good. Do you want to just pick me up? We can go together."

"You got it. Give Big Ginny my love."

I grunted an affirmative and disconnected.

MARCUS PICKED me up promptly at 5 o'clock, the car already smelling deliciously of Ethiopian food. After the past several days of chewing nothing but alfalfa and whole grains, the smell of roasted meat with actual spices had me salivating like a dog. I threw a quick glance at the food over my shoulder. "You went without me?"

Marcus grinned. "I decided not to subject you to the management. They can be a bit rude."

I chortled under my breath. "That's how you know the food gonna slap." We both shared a chuckle at that. He knew.

As we got on the highway and found a comfortable speed, a bothersome question formed in my mind. I cleared my throat and turned sideways in my seat, facing Marcus. "If you already know a demonologist, why did you have me come out to the preserve? Why not just bring in your colleague?"

Marcus kept his eyes on the road. "Well, for one thing, we didn't know at the time that it was demon related. We *still* don't know that for certain. But for two and this is the big one, Brandy wanted to keep the situation at the preserve on the

DL. And Theodetta is ... " He twirled a hand in the air as though trying to summon an appropriate description from the ether. "Well, she's not exactly a flying-under-the-radar sort of person. She stands out. Besides that, she's a director for the American Council of Demonologists. They have very strict rules for engagement, kind of like the Catholic Church. You can't just call on a priest and could get him to come do an exorcism for you. The same is true of the ACD. They investigate every claim of demonic presence before they send out a specialist. Brandy didn't have that kind of time, nor did she want to bring that scrutiny on the church. She reached out to the university—and by proxy, to me—as her most expeditious option. And you, dove, fit our needs precisely."

What he was saying made sense, but I couldn't help but feeling that the real reason remained unspoken. Marcus had reached out specifically to me because he wanted me. His ex-wife. His daughter's mother. It wasn't any coincidence that of all the resources he had available, he called upon the woman that he claimed was his fate.

Or maybe I was getting too big for my britches.

"So did you used to work with this woman, or ... ?"

Marcus shrugged. "Not exactly. She did a stint as a visiting scholar a couple-three years ago. I was still a grad student at the time. I took one of her classes—Ethics in Demon Conjuring and Summoning. But that's not how I got to know her. I first met her at a Mommy and Me class."

I smothered a grin. "With your mother?"

Now, Marcus barked a laugh, bright and full of life. "Of course not! With Lola."

I snapped my mouth shut, unexpected tears stinging my eyes, the back of my throat closing up. Of course Marcus took our daughter to a Mommy and Me class. It was exactly the sort of thing he would do. Especially since Daddy and Me classes were probably a lot harder to find.

"So she has kids, then?" I asked, struggling to move past the visions that swam before my eyes of Marcus and Lola crafting together, making pottery, art, finger painting. The images were so real I could almost smell them: the paste on Lola's fingers, the paint smeared across a cheek. I stifled a sob and turned to look out the window.

"No, she doesn't have kids. She was the ceramics instructor. She's not the marrying type."

I sucked in my breath, digging my nails into my palms. Not the marrying type. I wished he hadn't told me that. It begged so many questions: why did he know that? Was it a discussion they'd had? Was there history there? Had they been lovers? How well does she know my daughter? Did Lola's face light up when she saw her? Did Lola have a cute nickname for her? Do they still see each other?

When I was sure I wouldn't cry, I returned my attention to Marcus, studying his profile. I knew that face so well; its lines and curves, its color, its texture. There was a time when that face was mine to touch, to stroke, to playfully pinch. But not anymore. Worse, he wasn't my confidante, my better half, my keeper. I couldn't tell him how it cracked me wide open to hear that my daughter was so near but that I couldn't see her. I couldn't tell him how much it meant that he hadn't replaced me in her life, especially because I had claimed for so long that it was what I wanted. But everything was laid bare now. If I ever thought I knew what I wanted, the past few days had proven that I was wrong. I was as ignorant now as I had ever been. And now, Lola's mere accessibility made me feel like so much more was at stake.

I turned away again, looked down into my lap. He didn't

need to know how much I was suffering. Divorce meant my internal world no longer had anything to do with him.

Why couldn't I make my heart believe that?

We pulled up to the apartment complex about 20 minutes later. I carried the bags of food while Marcus led the way to his colleague's apartment. He rapped a few times at the door, which instantly flew open.

I boggled. I couldn't help it. I hadn't expected the door to be answered by a goddess.

The woman standing in the doorway was supermodel tall, all legs. Her skin was a deep, dark brown with plum undertones; slanted eyes glittered above chiseled cheekbones. A full mouth opened to even, white teeth. She was dressed in a pants suit made of bright yellow and purple Ankara fabric. The suit fit her like she had been poured into it. On her head, she wore a traditional Nigerian *gele.* A pair of oversized gold hoop earrings completed the outfit. I'd never seen anybody like her before. Not in real life.

I was in love with her instantly.

"Marcus!" The woman pulled my ex-husband into an enthusiastic embrace. She squeezed her eyes shut as she held him, her smile making her cheeks high and round, her face impossibly more beautiful. When they pulled away, she placed the flat of her palm upon her cheek. "Happy to see you, ha? You look good."

Marcus motioned for me and I took a tentative step forward. I couldn't tear my eyes off of her. I hoped she was used to that sort of reception. "Kezia, meet my friend and colleague Theodetta Watley. Theodetta, please meet Kezia Bernard."

The woman extended a hand, which I accepted gladly, even though the introduction stung. Did he purposefully omit the nature of our relationship? And if so, for whose benefit? But I didn't have time to dwell on this. "Theo," she said with a smile, giving my hand a few good pumps. "Only my family and Marcus call me Theodetta. Please, come in. What you got there? That food smell *good*."

We followed her into the apartment, which was just as elaborately and deliberately dressed as she was. "Please, have a seat," she said, gesturing toward the overstuffed sofa in the center of her living room. "Here, give me that food, and I'll get us some plates. We can take our meal out here."

When she returned, she handed around the plates which she had piled high with meat and vegetables. She disappeared one more time into the kitchen, returning with a plate for herself. She nestled into an armchair, her legs tucked delicately beneath her. She was in better shape than I. My knees hadn't been that flexible since high school.

"So what seems to be going on?" she asked as she took a bite of her kitfo, her eyes rolling back in their sockets as she danced in her seat, the universal sign that a Black person was enjoying their food. "On *God* Marcus, you know the best places to eat."

"That ain't never gone change," he said, dropping her a wink and digging in.

For a good ten minutes, the only sounds were chewing, the smacking of lips, and the occasional, "Ooh, Lawd!" When we were finally sated, Theo took our plates into the kitchen, and when she returned, she was all business. "All right. Let's talk. What y'all need?"

Marcus cleared his throat and then launched into a monologue about the events that led us to Theo's living room. He told her about the temple and the preserve — leaving the identities as vague as he could — and about the trapped souls that couldn't pass through the veil. He told her about the charred corpse and finished with my run-in with what we deemed to be fire demons.

Theo took all of this in silently, occasionally punctuating Marcus's tale with murmurs of agreement or understanding just to show she was still listening. When he was finished, she folded her hands in her lap and looked to me, her expression solemn, calculating. It was the look of someone absorbed in their professional work. I knew that look well. I saw it often when I studied under Dr. Adeyemo.

"Well, let me begin with the obvious," she said, her tone sliding into a lecturer's cadence with grace and ease. If I were her student, I'd have been transfixed. "It's very unlikely that you're dealing with a demon. You see, demons *are* intelligent beings, but they're not complex. They're not like people. With rare exception, they're not conniving, and they don't play the long game. They exist for the moment. So the timeline alone would exclude demonic activity. Twenty years?" She rolled her eyes and screwed up her nose. "Nah. Demon'd be bored in less than a quarter of that time."

"Is it just the timeline you have trouble with?" Marcus asked.

"No. It's also the method of torment. While a fire demon absolutely could possess a living person, there's no reason for it to trap a soul that has already left the body. They have no *use* for a soul without a body. In fact, they have no use for souls at all. The entire point, the entire interest of most demonic entities, is to *spoil the flesh*. And so, if what you're saying is accurate, these souls are either being tormented by something that exists for the torment of the *spirit*, or torment has nothing to do with it, and the captor has other motives. Either way, that's not what demons do."

Marcus took all of this information in while he steepled his fingers beneath his chin. "Okay, I see what you're saying. But what about that tribe in Angola? I can't recall the name."

Theo lifted an eyebrow. I'd always been jealous of people who could lift just one eyebrow. "What tribe in Angola?"

"That tribe that Dr. Hassan Torabi was investigating back in—"

Theo's laugh was sharp and quick and completely devoid of mirth. She sucked her teeth and waved her hand in front of her face, shaking her head vigorously. Her hoop earrings jangled. "I know you not about to drop that charlatan's name up in here. You can't take any of the reports that Torabi submitted seriously. He's known for falsifying his exploits. First of all, the people he studied were not in Angola. They were in Somalia."

Marcus frowned. "Somalia? Are you sure? I thought—"

Theo stood and walked toward a cart in the corner of the room. She lifted a bottle of brandy and held it out, a silent invitation. Both Marcus and I nodded, and she poured. "Torabi was a liar. He claimed to have traveled to Angola to obfuscate the fact that he was studying his own people, which of course is frowned upon in academic circles. Anyway, he didn't travel to Angola; he stayed in his home country of Somalia. The people he reported on were in Hargeisa, for Pete's sake."

I accepted the tumbler of brandy and took a sip. It wasn't my preferred drink, and it burned on my tongue, but I felt my muscles relax. "That doesn't make sense, though," I said. "According to Marcus, Torabi was studying a tribe that was worshipping fire demons. Somalis are Muslim."

Theo smiled from around the rim of her crystal glass. "Angolans aren't demon worshippers, either." When she saw me blush, she lightened her tone and continued. "Let me disabuse you of the notion that in academia, everyone is honest. Torabi wanted to make a name for himself. And you're right. Somalis are Muslim. The people that he studied were also Muslim, and they certainly weren't worshipping fire demons. In fact, every incident of fire demon possession started *after* Torabi got there. Not before. Outside of his own, there isn't a single account of demonic possession before Torabi arrives in Hargeisa in 1937. However, we can't completely call Torabi a phony, because his accounts of the demonic possessions are corroborated by one of his colleagues, Dr. Martin Van den Berg. Van den Berg was very vocal about what he saw: he claims he saw multiple individuals burst into a smokeless, blue flame, burning to death. There were at least a dozen of these burnings, and eventually, Torabi and Van den Berg were forced to flee. Van den Berg returned to his home in the Netherlands, but Torabi was arrested and accused of possessing those young people. The penalty for which is, of course, death."

Marcus frowned. "They claimed *he* was possessing them? How? What were the allegations?"

Theo winked. "They accused him of being an ifrit."

Marcus gave a low whistle, so this information obviously meant something to him. But to me, it meant nothing. My gaze bounced from Theo to Marcus and back again. Finally, I asked, "What's an ifrit?"

It was Theo who answered. "A fire jinni."

I stared in disbelief. "A *genie?*"

Marcus threw me a reproachful look. "We don't use that word, but yes." He returned his attention to Theo. "So *after* he went to study these people in Hargeisa, they started bursting into flame? And the locals blamed Torabi?"

Theo nodded. "Yes. Several local religious leaders launched their own investigation and found some questionable incidents in Torabi's past. At first, they thought he couldn't be to blame, because how can a corporeal being possess another? But his human appearance was just a glamour. Jinn are made of fire composed of infinite flames. And all it takes to possess a human is one flame." She smiled like this was clever. "After that realization, they all came to the same conclusion: Torabi was a bona fide ifrit. Once word got out, it was over for him."

I stammered, my gaze shifting between Marcus and Theo. "Hold on. Y'all are telling me ifrit exist?"

Marcus frowned in my direction. "Of course they exist. Why would you ask that?"

"You have to forgive her, Marcus," Theo answered. "We live in a world where people disbelieve in a round Earth. They scoff at global warming. They shun science completely. Why shouldn't she express disbelief in something she's never seen?"

"I'm not expressing disbelief," I replied, affronted. "I'm expressing *ignorance.*"

"Well, ignorance we can work with," Theo said, smiling.

I settled back into my chair, taking a deep sip from my drink. "So, what happened next? Did he ever get out of Somalia?"

Theo finished her drink and stood to pour another. "His colleague Dr. Van den Berg got him out, eventually. Governments the world over are susceptible to bribery. Torabi relocated to the Netherlands, reinvented himself and, rumor has it, started writing poetry that he peddled to spiritually vacuous Europeans. He even took a new name." She clucked her tongue and shook her head. "Had the audacity to start calling himself The Resplendent Brother Zahi."

CHAPTER FOURTEEN

MARCUS AND I LOCKED gazes, and in his face I saw the same surprise that I was certain colored mine. "Brother Zahi?" I repeated, my voice barely above a whisper. "That's ... that's their prophet."

As soon as I said the words, I snapped my mouth shut, realizing my mistake. I wasn't supposed to be talking about the inner workings of the church, but I suddenly didn't care anymore. Secrecy had gotten me into this shit. It was time to dig myself out.

"So it's a jinni," I said to Marcus. "A jinni has those souls trapped in the temple, and some kind of jinn magic is what slapped me down when I tried to cross the veil."

"It seems so," Marcus said. "But now the question is, *why?*"

Theo tilted her head to one side. "Remember how I said that demons are not complex? The same is not true of jinn. They are as complex and varied as we are. Their motives are vast. The same things that move humans to perform atrocious acts move jinn—greed, fear, anger, mental depravity. But they can also be moved by love, hope, passion, and faith. In short:

there's no telling why. I know that's not the answer you want to hear. I'm sorry for that." She adjusted her seat, a small frown beginning to creep over her face. "If it *is* a jinni ... you know you're in very deep, right? You didn't make a wish, did you?"

"A wish?"

"Jinn trade in wishes. It's almost a currency. They will grant wishes, but at some expense to the wisher."

I frowned. "How do you mean?"

"Well, you can ask a jinni for nearly anything, and it will do its best to grant your request, but it always takes something in return—often more than the supplicant expected. The greater the wish, the more the jinni takes. But if you didn't make a wish, you should be fine."

I opened my mouth to reply but closed it again as a lump formed in my throat. I hadn't made a wish.

Had I?

Was praying in the temple a form of wishing?

I thought of Caleb, standing on the dais, shouting to the congregation. "Ask with pure mind and soul and you shall receive! Demand your blessings!" And then I thought of myself, hands stretched to Heaven, sincerely begging to find my family.

Maybe not exactly begging. Maybe it was more like wishing.

I closed my eyes, mentally kicking myself. I'd been so stupid. So goddamn careless. I clutched at my breast, carefully avoiding the wound the magic had left behind when an idea struck me. Theo said a wish *granted* came at a cost. I hadn't found my family; my wish had not been granted.

But even that was small relief. Finding my family was the only thing I wanted in life. It was my reason for existing. But if

I ever found them, would my body go up in a bright blue flame? Would the jinni take my soul and lock it in a temple?

I had to rid myself of the fire inside me. I had to. Now, that was the only thing that mattered.

"Another thing about jinn," Theo continued after a moment, "is that they don't operate without contracts and they're very clever with them. I bet when this jinni sold the land, it came with some unconventional terms."

"Wait," Marcus said. "You think the jinni *himself* sold the land to Caleb? Couldn't the land seller just be a hapless victim like us?"

"Could be a hapless fool," Theo agreed. "But I doubt it. It sounds exactly like an elegant jinni trick. If this jinni is still connected to this property after 20 years, it's by design. He made a deal with Caleb in that land transaction. I'd bet money on it."

Marcus scrubbed his face with his hands. "Christ, this just gets worse the deeper we go. Theo ... I hate to ask you for a favor, but we're impotent here. If a jinni has its fire inside Kezia, our demands to release her might get ugly."

Theo held up a hand and tucked her chin to her chest. "Let me save you from verbalizing this request, since as a member of the ACD you know I can't grant it. That said." She pulled herself to her feet and gestured with a tilt of her head toward another room. "Why don't y'all come with me."

Marcus and I followed Theo into a little room at the back of her apartment. As soon as I stepped through the door, a wave of unease washed over me. The walls were covered with strange sigils like those painted on the walls at Necro Sis. Stacks of papers littered a well-used desk. The walls were lined with filing cabinets. Aside from the art on the walls, the room didn't *look* strange. But the feeling I got was undeniable—

there was power in this room, and not necessarily the good kind.

Theo moved to the far wall and, with a key she removed from a chain around her neck, unlocked one of her filing cabinets. She rifled through the papers briefly before pulling out a single sheet of paper.

A single *glowing* sheet of paper.

But no, that wasn't right either. The paper itself wasn't glowing; it was the ink that pulsated with the colors of twilight. This, she handed to Marcus.

"If anyone knew you had that—worse, if anyone knew I gave it to you—it would be your ass. Both our asses. But under the circumstances, I don't think I'd be a very good friend if I didn't give you *something*."

"What is it?" I asked.

"That's a one-time use conjuration spell I stole from a greater imp several years ago. It's fully loaded. I can't vouch for its effectiveness, but it should allow you to evoke a small number of lesser imps that will attack on command. How small a number, I couldn't say." She sighed and shook her head. "I wish I could give you something reusable. Something you could control yourself. You're a non-magic user about to go up against a possible—damn son, a *likely*—fire jinni. I can't let you go in there unarmed, but neither can I teach you to become something you're not. All the other spells I have are activated by the chaos current alone." She looked to me. "Can you ride chaos?"

I shook my head. "Not even a little."

"Then that will have to do," she said, gesturing to the paper.

Marcus folded it and slipped it into a pocket. "Thank you,"

he said, his voice wavering. "This is more than I could have asked for."

"Don't mention it," Theo said. She gave both of us a pointed look. "Seriously. Don't."

"Thanks for the *hospitality*," Marcus said with a smile. He motioned me toward the front door. "I'll be in touch soon. You've helped more than I can say. Pray for us."

Theo's expression was serene as she replied, "I always do."

CHAPTER FIFTEEN

"SO, WHAT'S YOUR TAKE on this?" I asked after we were on the freeway heading back to the preserve. "Do you think Brandy and Caleb know?"

"I think somebody knows more than they're saying," he said through clenched teeth. "Though I don't know who or how much. I think Brandy knows something's up, but she's not quite able to put the pieces together herself. That, or she just doesn't want to be the one to go against her husband."

He was white-knuckling the steering wheel, his foot like lead on the gas. Cars whizzed by us faster than I was comfortable with, but I shared his urgency. Beads of sweat popped out along my brow, the heat under my collar threatening to overwhelm me. I closed my eyes so I wouldn't have to see how fast we were zooming past the cars in the other lane. Marcus was a good driver. I just kept telling myself that.

Silence wedged between us. I wanted to say more but didn't know where to begin. What did the jinni want with me? With the others? If jinn needed contracts, how had I ended up in this mess? I hadn't signed anything. I knew we were getting closer to the truth, but each new piece of data felt like two steps forward, one step back.

Just then, my cell phone buzzed. Glancing down, I saw that I had a message from Casey. When I opened it, the message confirmed what we already knew. "Casey says Caleb purchased the land from a man named—"

"Hassan Torabi," Marcus finished.

I nodded. "You got it. Our jinni in anthropologist clothing." I put the phone away and looked out the window.

By the time we arrived at Caleb and Brandy's mansion, I was practically rabid for answers. I bounded out of the car and headed straight for the front door, pounding and shouting demands to be let in. Marcus caught up with me and took my free hand in his to calm me down. I didn't pull away. I gave his hand a squeeze, a silent thanks, and only then did I slip my fingers free.

When no one answered, I started pounding again. "Brandy! Caleb! Open up; we need to talk! Now!"

Marcus peered through a window. "I don't see anyone inside," he said. "Perhaps we should call?"

I pulled out my phone and dialed Brandy. I walked around to the side of the house, straining to see through the windows. In the back of the house, a glass sliding door looked into the kitchen. All the lights were out, but my intuition told me someone was home. And if I'd learned anything in the past few days, it was that I needed to start trusting my intuition.

I went back around to the front of the house and this time I tried the doorknob. The door swung open, and I stepped inside. I heard Marcus dithering behind me. "You sure you want to do this? Did you forget you're Black?"

"I ain't forget shit," I hissed over my shoulder. "They're

here, Marcus. People are dead. We need them to answer some questions."

We checked all the rooms on the first floor, but they weren't there. I checked my phone, but Brandy hadn't responded. I slipped the phone into my back pocket as I made my way upstairs.

We checked every room before finally coming to the end of the hallway. "This has to be the master bedroom," I said. I pounded on the door, but no one answered. Finally, I barged in.

"Brandy? I—"

I stood in the entry of the room with my hands pressed to my mouth, my eyes wide as the blood drained from my cheeks and the fire in my center flared to life. I felt at once both freezing cold and flaming hot, an impossible pairing that made me feel a hostage in my own body. I should've been better prepared for what I was looking at. After all, it wasn't the first time.

In the center of the bed were two bodies. One on top of the other. Both bodies were burned to a blackened heap.

As Marcus cursed, I stepped forward, something about the position of the bodies niggling at my subconscious. I placed my hand on the top corpse. It was Caleb. "Help me pry them apart." I said.

Marcus gave me a bleak look. "We shouldn't even be touching them. In fact, we shouldn't be here at all. Kezia, we got to get outta here before someone else finds the bodies. This ... this isn't gonna end well for us."

I frowned. "What do you mean?"

Marcus stuffed his hands in his pockets. "We're the only Black faces in this whole place. Who do you think they're gonna question? No, lemme take that back. Who do you think they're gonna throw in jail first and ask questions way, way later? Assuming they don't just shoot us on sight."

I blew out a steamy sigh. My Black ass knew Marcus's paranoia was justified, but it didn't matter. In that moment, there was no rationality, no reasoning. I was moving on pure instinct and the fire that burned in my belly. I had a suspicion, and I had to confirm it. When Marcus saw that I wasn't to be dissuaded, he lent me a hand and together, we pulled the two bodies apart. Separated, it was obvious that only one body was the source of the flame.

"It was Brandy who ignited," I said softly, my eyes lingering on her corpse. "Look at her chest." As I pointed out the nature of her wounds, I wasn't sure Marcus could detect what I saw. He didn't have super senses. "It looks like an exit wound. The fire must have burst from behind her ribs. And I'm guessing Caleb threw himself on her to try to put out the flames. The fire consumed them both."

"All three of them," he corrected. "She was pregnant. God, this is awful. The man sacrificed himself. But I guess he didn't have any choice. He was compelled by biology and paternal instinct. Parents will do anything to save their child."

I didn't need to respond to that.

We sat for a while, numb and deflated, bewilderment anchoring us in place. We had been relying on Brandy and Caleb for answers. But whatever answers they had, they carried to the grave.

Suddenly, an idea struck me. I turned to face Marcus, my eyes wide. "I can still talk to them."

Marcus blinked. "Oh my God. Yes. Can you do it now? Here? And quickly?"

It wasn't ideal. As Marcus had pointed out, if anybody were to find us here, there'd be hell to pay. I couldn't imagine how we would explain this to the police, and as much as I hated to admit it, we would be the prime suspects by sheer fact of our skin. The safe thing to do was remove ourselves from the scene of the crime.

But if I wanted to find them quickly, performing the ritual here was the only way to do it.

"Let's do this now," I said, brushing past Marcus and putting some distance between myself and the two corpses. Marcus stood back, making himself melt into the shadows, giving me space to perform my work.

When I was calm and centered, I reached out with my senses towards the veil. It took only a moment to find its edge, and I was terrified that I might be attacked again. But the veil was unguarded, and I slipped through it easily.

I formed an image of Caleb in my mind. My heart called out to him. Miasma swirled as the scenery shifted, the magic seeking to bring me to Caleb.

Next, I formed an image of Brandy, who in my mind shone bright, a gleaming white ball of joy and love and goodness. I opened my heart to her and called out to the universe to reunite us in an environment of love and family. I had made that call so many times when looking for my own mother. It was almost second nature now. Brandy should have no trouble answering my summons.

Of course, that's what I thought about my mother, too.

It was only a moment before Caleb shimmered before me. We were standing in a dilapidated chapel, the air musty and dank. I heard the faint trill of children laughing outside its walls, and I realized we must be in a chapel from his youth, somewhere in Somalia. Caleb looked haggard and worn as though he had been crying for a long time. I was surprised to see him this way; the dead almost always appeared to me as their favorite versions of themselves. It was rare to come upon the dead still in mourning.

I felt a stab of guilt for interrupting his grieving. His ethereal hands shook as he reached up for his face, sinking to his knees. When his face turned up to mine, his expression was filled with anguish. "Where is she?" he asked.

I opened my mouth to explain, but there was too much and I was low on time. My explanations wouldn't do him any good now, but he almost certainly had information that would help me. "Caleb. I need you to tell me everything you can about the man you purchased this land from. His name was Hassan Torabi. Does that ring a bell?" When Caleb didn't answer, I sighed and tried again. "Caleb, this is important. We really need to find him."

"I don't know where he is," Caleb said, wiping his face with his palms. "Truly, I have no idea. I haven't seen him since I purchased this property."

I cursed, wracking my brain for another approach. He had to know *something* that would help me. "Tell me how you came to own this land," I said.

"There's not much to tell," Caleb said, his slim shoulders shrugging. He looked so sad. Broken. "The opportunity presented itself very soon after my mother died. I received a small inheritance. I was very close to my mother," he said, "though I had rejected everything she and my father believed in. I didn't believe in their God or their Bible. Those things hadn't brought me any comfort in my years growing up in Africa."

He sighed. "But when she died, I was alone. My father had passed years before, and my mother was all I had left. I remember sitting at her bedside, praying for a miracle." He laughed then, a dry, bitter sound. "Well, she prayed, anyway.

She prayed the whole time I sat with her, right until she died. Funny. I was so desperate not to be alone—not to be left on this Earth with not a soul to call my friend that instead of praying, I read that incantation of friendship again. Like I said —hoping for a miracle. I was a damn lonely fool." He hung his head, wrung his hands. "In any case, there was an earthquake that night, and my mother died shortly thereafter. A chaplain came into the room to offer me comfort; he gave me a book of poetry. I hardly looked at it, but I held onto it anyway.

"About a week later, a coworker, Eunice, reached out to me, saying she knew someone looking to sell a plot of land out in the desert. She remembered my fantasies of living off the grid. I fell in love with the place instantly. We arranged to meet with the seller, and guess who it was?" Caleb smiled at the memory. "It was the chaplain. I figured that had to be an omen, so I started reading those poems. Really reading them. Some of them ... " He dithered, rocking his head equivocally. "They were strange. Too strange for my sensibilities. But the others were life-changing. They ignited something within me that had been dormant for a long while. They were a call to action—admonishment for allowing life to happen to me. Brother Zahi's poems were all about asking for what we want—*demanding* our gifts from the universe. And that resonated with me. I'd never asked for anything, but his poetry gave me a reason to begin. And that's how the Temple was born. I reproduced his book minus the more ... *mystical* poems, and that became the basis of our faith. That's all there is to it. But I couldn't tell you where to find that chaplain."

I stroked my chin, searching for a shred of information to help in our search. I recalled Theo speculating that the land contract might've had unconventional terms. "Do you recall anything strange about the contract you signed for the land? Anything unorthodox?"

Caleb was silent a moment. "Now that you mention it, there was something. In addition to the sale price, he also requested a small percentage of the value the property would bring me. It was to be paid in perpetuity." The man sniffed. "You're probably thinking signing such a thing was ridiculous, but I was desperate. Plus, I certainly didn't see at the time how the land would bring any value. But as the retreats became more successful, I kept waiting for a request for remittance, but none ever came."

I tapped my fingers against my lips. "You never paid him any additional money?"

Caleb shook his head. "No. I never heard from him again."

"You don't still have that contract, do you? I'd like to take a look. It might have information that will help me."

Caleb leaned his head back. "I keep it in my office safe. You'll find the key beneath a loose floorboard." He paused, considering. "Since you'll find it anyway, I may as well tell you that the incantation of friendship is there, too. I hope you don't think me extremely foolish for keeping that." He shrugged with chagrin. "It doesn't work, but it's sentimental."

I nodded. "I understand. Is there anything else you can tell me?" I asked.

The man shook his head. "Nothing useful. Just reunite me with my wife," he said, his voice hoarse. "That's the only thing I ask for. I know I don't deserve her. But if you have any pity left in you, please—reunite me with my wife."

"I know where she is," I said, "and I will do everything in my power to bring her to you. I promise."

There was nothing more I could do on that side of the veil, and so I retracted my consciousness into my physical body, shaking off the last remnants of that otherworldly realm. As I blinked my eyes open, Marcus pressed a cold glass of water into my hands. I gulped it down greedily.

"You weren't gone long," Marcus said. "I'm guessing fast isn't good."

I shook my head. "Well, it wasn't exactly good, but I did get something from him." Quickly, I recounted the major points of everything I had learned. "Brandy's not with him, either," I added. "I'm pretty certain she's trapped in the temple with the others. But he did tell me where to find the contract." I sighed, shaking my head. "It's not much. But it's the only lead we have."

I rubbed my temples as a throbbing headache tried to form behind my eyes. It was late; my body wanted to sleep. But I had a feeling the night's events were not over. The fire in my own chest was burning hotter every hour, a growing reminder that we had work to do, and very little time to do it.

"We need to open Caleb's safe."

TRUE TO HIS WORD, the key to the safe was under a loose floorboard in the office beneath a potted pothos. With trembling hands, I unlocked the safe, eyes squeezed shut in anticipation.

When the door creaked open and I opened my eyes, I was surprised to see that the safe did not contain jewelry or piles of cash. In fact, the only items inside were legal documents like birth and marriage certificates, passports, social security cards, and the two articles Caleb told me about: a legal contract, and a scroll.

A *gleaming* scroll.

"My God," Marcus whispered. "Dove, please hand me that scroll."

I handed it to him. "What? What is it?"

Marcus licked his lips, his whole body shivering with excitement or fear; it was impossible to know which. "Kezia, that's no minor incantation."

I frowned. "Is there such a thing as a *major* incantation of friendship?" I said.

"Minor incantations don't glow like this," he said. "This thing practically looks ... "

He didn't need to say it. It looked like it was on fire.

Now, I, too began to shiver, and the fire in my chest flashed hotter. I peered over at the paper, but my heart sank when I saw what was written there.

"It's in Kaddare script," I groaned. "There's no telling what this is."

But Marcus again shook his head. "I know *exactly* what this is."

I balked. "What? How? What is it?"

"You see this?" He tapped the scroll's upper-right hand corner where something was scrawled in plain ink—it didn't look like Kaddare script, and it didn't glow or have any other special properties. It looked like a signature. "Back when I took Theodetta's class, we did a unit on the ethics of scroll-making. Incantations are transcribed and passed down from a magus to his student. As you know—or maybe you don't, sorry, I shouldn't presume—incantations are not written by hand. The spell creator recites the spell under the guidance of a specialized enchanter called a scribe. The scribe uses magic to etch the speaker's words onto an enchanted scroll. The more powerful the spell, the higher quality enchant is required on the scroll. This scroll," he said, indicating the brightly glowing paper in his hands, "is the highest quality I've ever seen."

I waited patiently for him to continue. I sensed the wheels of his mind whirring. "One of the ethical considerations of creating incantations is that you don't want them to fall into anyone's hands—especially major incantations such as this. Obviously, when it comes to things such as summoning demons, you don't want just anyone blundering into that." He cleared his throat and tapped the small symbol again. "Most powerful incantations are protected by codes—words transposed, meanings altered, or even encoded instructions on how the scroll should be read. One of history's most famous scribes was a man named Lysander. He invented many of the techniques used today for keeping scrolls safe. He was very religious and believed magic should only be performed in the presence of God."

I was growing impatient, and Marcus sensed my distress. "Stay with me, dove. Lysander's scrolls must be read in the presence of prayer or in a sacred place. This here is his signature. Some random who stumbled upon the scroll wouldn't know the requirement, but someone who studied the ethics of scroll-making would." He grinned at his own cleverness.

I felt like an epiphany should be dawning on me any second, but I still wasn't quite picking up what Marcus was laying down. "Okay? *Why does any of this matter?*"

"As I mentioned, this is not a minor incantation of friendship. It *is*, more to your point, a *major* incantation of friendship."

Now, I threw up my hands. "Marcus, what the hell are you talking about?"

"What do friends do, dove? What do you think of when you think of friends?"

I shook my head, frustrated. We didn't have time for riddles. "I don't know, Marcus. I don't have any friends. They're always there when you need them? Always there ... "

My eyes shot wide, and Marcus's grin grew as we completed the thought aloud together. " ... Always there when you call."

My heart turned a cartwheel in my chest. "This is a *summoning* spell," I breathed.

"Precisely that," he said with reverence. "And based on all the evidence we have, I'd bet my ass this is an incantation to summon a jinni."

"Caleb said his mother was praying when he last read the scroll," I mused. "And then the chaplain appeared and gave Caleb the book of poems." My excitement got the better of me, and I pressed my hands against my cheeks, scarcely able to believe this new development. "The chaplain land seller *was* the jinni, just like Theo said. Caleb finally summoned him by reading the scroll in the presence of prayer. So can we use this to summon Brother Zahi? To force him to appear and give us the souls back?"

"A summoning spell would force him to appear, yes, but nothing beyond that. He would not be subject to any demands from us, though of course, we could negotiate."

"That's good enough for me," I said.

"No, it's not," Marcus continued, "for several reasons."

Now, I frowned, my enthusiasm dampened. "What reasons?"

"Well, for one," he said, "the scroll is written in Kaddare script, which neither of us can read." My heart sank. I'd forgotten about that. "And for two, there's a second part. This incantation requires a reagent."

My enthusiasm turned to dread as I let my hands fall to my lap. "I'm not going to like this, am I?"

Marcus shook his head. "If a reagent is required, it will be written just before the incantation begins. Here." He tapped a symbol at the top of the paper, different from the rest. I recognized it immediately—it was the same symbol etched on the Charon's Recall Opal had given me. A triangle and a cross. "This is the reagent. And this symbol next to it?" He tapped a pair of arrows pointing in opposite directions. "This means trade. The summoner offers this reagent to the summoned."

I nodded. This all seemed like pretty standard magic to me. "Okay. What am I missing?"

Marcus took a breath. "This symbol here, this triangle and cross, is the alchemical symbol for sulfur. Again, a neophyte might assume the reagent to literally be sulfur. But it isn't." He glanced at me before looking quickly away. "Alchemically, sulfur can refer to several properties: dryness, heat, and masculinity. But in an incantation this powerful, it doesn't refer to either the chemical sulfur or any of its properties. It refers to a human soul."

"Sulfur," I whispered. "The same alchemical symbol as a human soul. That makes sense."

Marcus frowned. "What do you mean?"

"Different chemicals emit different colored light when they burn. Sodium burns yellow. Boric acid burns green. Sulfur burns bright blue. And, apparently, when lit with magical genie flames, the human soul also burns bright blue."

"The old alchemists were scientists, too," Marcus recalled.

"There's reason in their symbology. It does make a poetic kind of sense."

My mouth ran dry as I looked to Marcus. "We really need to *trade* a human soul to bring Brother Zahi here?"

Marcus nodded. "Yes. That's how the incantation works. A reagent ensures that the speaker wants what he's asking for; he's had to go through the trouble of procuring whatever the spell calls for. Iron ore, eye of newt, whatever. Reagents are supposed to be—among other things—a *safety* measure."

I frowned again as I once more fell into confusion. "But Caleb's soul isn't trapped in the temple like the others. And he didn't have the fire in his eyes. I don't think he ever made that trade."

Not like I did, I didn't add.

"No," Marcus admitted. "The summoner can't use his own soul in trade. Again, safety measure. I think Caleb got lucky—or unlucky, depending on how you look at it. Didn't you say he read the incantation at his mother's side?"

My face paled. "He offered his mother's soul to summon the jinni—and he probably didn't even know it."

"He almost certainly didn't know it," Marcus said. "Caleb really isn't a magician. If he were, he'd have known how powerful this scroll is, and he would have understood what Lysander's signature in the upper-right meant." He looked at me with sadness in his eyes. "I wanted to believe he caused all this. And maybe he did, but in ignorance. We might have to accept that he's a victim, too."

"God, that's unfair," I breathed. "What gives anyone a right to give another person's soul away? How can the universe allow such a thing?"

Marcus shrugged. "Fair has nothing to do with it. The

universe doesn't give a damn about your free will. We all must fight to make our own choices. That right isn't a given."

We sat in silence a moment, absorbing the implications of everything we'd just learned. We couldn't summon the jinni. It was impossible. That neither of us could read Kaddare script was problematic enough, but the requirement to turn a soul over to the jinni made the entire endeavor out of the question. My soul was already marked; I would never give another person's soul to the jinni. Not ever.

Not ever? I asked myself as an idea—terrible, unthinkable, brilliant—shouldered its way into my brain. *Not even the soul of someone who has already passed?*

Suddenly, with cold clarity, I understood what we needed to do.

I turned to Marcus and sucked in a breath. "How many more hours of work do you have left in you?"

Marcus shrugged. "I'm okay. Why? Do you have an idea?"

I nodded. "I have an idea. But you're not gonna like it."

CHAPTER SIXTEEN

D ESPITE THE LATE HOUR, Andromeda answered the door quickly, as though she'd been expecting us. But when she saw my expression and read my body language, her eyes hardened and her mouth settled into a grim little line. She stepped aside and beckoned us to enter.

Ben was seated on the couch. It seemed those two were inseparable. He smiled and gave a little finger wave which I returned, glad for the camaraderie, no matter how surface level. I settled down into the couch beside him. Marcus and Andromeda took seats in the chairs across from us.

"This is my ex-husband Marcus Adeyemo," I began. "Marcus, this is Andromeda Clark and Ben Matheson. I met them a few days ago."

Marcus tried to remain composed, but I knew him well enough to see that he was completely star-struck. I swallowed a chuckle; I'd have to make fun of him about his reality-TV-watching habits another time. "I'm so sorry to bother you both this late," I said. "I'm not exactly sure how to tell the story I need you to hear. And I definitely don't know how you'll react to it. But there's something going on that you need to know about. Because I really need your help."

Andromeda adjusted herself in her chair, crossing her legs. "Oh, don't worry about me. I'm something of a night owl anyway," she said. "What's going on? You look like you've seen the devil."

I exchanged a look with Ben, who jumped to his feet. "I'll make us some coffee," he said.

When Ben returned, Marcus and I took turns telling the story. It was hard to get the words out. The entire tale sounded ridiculous when spoken aloud, and I had lived it. I couldn't imagine how Andromeda and Ben who, hearing this for the first time, could process everything we were laying on them. But I was sure I couldn't execute my plan without their help.

When we finished explaining the situation, from the souls trapped in the temple to the fire jinni responsible for it, Ben retrieved the coffee from the kitchen and began passing around hot mugs. I accepted mine gratefully as I sipped on that warm brew, the caffeine reinvigorating me.

"Forgive me," Andromeda said as she folded her legs beneath her on the couch. "I'm gonna need a minute to process this. I've been an initiate of the Temple for a long while. Finding out I've been tricked by a genie ... let alone that genies are *real* ... " She let her words trail off, but I didn't need her to finish. I could only imagine the gamut of emotions she must be experiencing. "And Caleb's really dead? You're sure?" Her eyes shone with tears.

"I saw him with my own eyes," I said. "And I spoke with him. On the other side. He's in a lot of emotional pain. If we want to help him ... "

"Of course we want to help him," Ben said, glancing from

me to Andromeda and back again. "And you. I think we're just shocked." He wiped a tear from his cheek. "Caleb was special."

"I'm sorry to be the one to tell you," I said. "Believe me, none of this has been a cakewalk for us, either."

"I'm sure it hasn't," Andromeda said through her sniffles. Then, suddenly, she cleared her throat, wiped her face clean of tears. "All right. I can mourn later. So what exactly is the plan then?" Andromeda asked.

Marcus leaned forward, elbows on his knees. "I think that's what we all want to know," he said.

I took a final sip of my coffee, drawing confidence from its warmth before continuing. "We have the incantation to bring the jinni to us. But there are a few problems." I cleared my throat. "I can't read the scroll, and I only know one person who can."

I glanced over to Marcus, whose face darkened. "Caleb?"

I nodded. "Obviously, we can't take the scroll to the other side, and we can't bring Caleb back to life. But we can channel him." I turned to Andromeda. "We just need to borrow a body for him to inhabit."

Andromeda's shoulders drooped. "And you want me to do that? To host him?"

I nodded. "Yes. You're the only person who can. I need to be fully present to speak to the jinni once he arrives. But that's not the hard part." I swallowed over the lump in my throat. *Here goes nothing.* "The spell requires an offering of a human soul for the summons to work. Obviously, we're not going to sacrifice any one of us." I didn't bother to remind them that my soul had already been claimed. "But I'm betting we can use a soul that has already passed on if we call it over from the other side. Which we can do as long as we have its corpse." I paused. "I think."

I chanced a look around, but none of the faces before me bore any look of understanding. I took a deep breath. "I propose we call down the soul of Brandy and Caleb's unborn child."

At first, nothing happened. But as the true horror of what I said descended upon the group, their expressions marked a path from disgust to incredulity to anger. "Are you absolutely out of your mind?" Ben asked. "We can't sacrifice a *baby* to a *genie!*"

The fire burned hotter in my chest as adrenaline pumped through my veins. "I know that's a really ... dark request, and normally I wouldn't even entertain the idea. But hear me out." I took a breath. "The child is already gone. We can't do anything about that. We only have three corpses to work with: Brandy's, whose soul already belongs to the jinni so we can't trade it, and Caleb's, who we need to read the script and summon the jinni. You can't use your own soul as a reagent, so Caleb is out. The only corpse left is the child in Brandy's womb—who is not claimed," I added, making my voice as gentle as possible. "I know what a horrific thing I'm suggesting. But I don't see that we have any choice."

A moment of silence followed. It was Andromeda who finally asked the inevitable question. "Assuming we all agree to this," she began slowly, "I've never heard of anyone calling a soul from the other side into a corpse. Is that really something that can be done?"

I reached into a pocket and withdrew Charon's Recall. "I can use this. I think." I quickly explained how the talisman was supposed to work, that it could anchor a soul into a corpse. "The soul won't be able to animate the corpse," I said, using Opal's words. "But the body can hold the soul while we trade with the jinni."

Andromeda's expression was morose. "This sounds like torture," she said. "You're really proposing to bring the soul of an embryo back across the veil into a ruined body? It has never known this world. It's only ever known the safety of its mother's womb, and—"

"I know," I said, my voice soft. I tried to avert my eyes, but I couldn't avoid the expressions on their faces. "Believe me, I know what I'm asking. But if this all goes well, the jinni will release his claim on these souls peacefully and Caleb, Brandy, and the child will all cross over."

"And if he doesn't release his claim?" Ben asked.

I didn't blink. "Then we kill him."

Marcus grunted. "You mean we *try* to kill him," he corrected. "Killing him *would* nullify the magic. All the souls locked in this temple—and yours—would be freed."

I nodded. "That's right."

"But how do you propose we kill a *genie*?" Ben asked, incredulous.

I nodded toward Marcus. "With imps. We have a scroll."

Andromeda took in a deep, slow breath through her nostrils, eyes closed. "How many? Will imps be enough to slay a jinni?"

"I don't know," I admitted. "But none of it matters if you're not all in this with me. All of you. And hopefully it won't come to that, anyway," I said.

I didn't really believe that. But a girl could dream.

"Okay," Andromeda said finally. "I'm in." When her eyes opened again, I saw my own determination reflected back at me. "I don't like it. In fact, I *hate* it. But if that's our only plan, I'm in."

Ben nodded. "Me, too." He reached out and put his hand on Andromeda's.

I turned to Marcus, holding my breath. Marcus had always been my north star. My compass. His morals were my guiding light. And I wasn't sure this was anything he could stomach.

But even as I worried over these things, his face twisted with bewilderment. "Do you really have to ask?" he said. "I'd do anything to save you."

I stared a moment, overwhelmed. Leave it to Marcus to shred my heart into absolute pieces.

There was little to say after that. We agreed that we should perform the summons in the temple to be nearer the souls we wanted to free. But first, we needed to gather the reagent. The four of us made our way to the mansion in silence. We crept into the master bedroom and, to my enormous relief, both Andromeda and Ben handled the gruesome sight with aplomb. Ben looked a little green around the gills, but Andromeda just looked sad. We arranged the corpses side by side on the bed, covering Caleb's with a blanket. I retrieved Charon's Recall from my pocket and swallowed hard, praying silently as I none-too-gently jammed the coin into what remained of Brandy's belly.

I wasn't sure what I was supposed to do after that; I hoped the magic would guide me. I placed the flat of my palm against Brandy's ruined chest and mouthed a silent prayer as I opened myself up to the death current. I felt the change in my hands as a burning sensation that started in my palms and climbed into my fingers. At once, I sensed the cold emptiness of a charred corpse on one hand and the bright, twinkling energy of a child on the other. I reached for it, swallowing down my guilt as I stretched toward eternity, my consciousness creating a bridge from the child to its body.

The connection was swift but painful. The child's soul resisted the call, and I screamed on the astral plane, hating my part in this abomination. But I had no other options. I linked myself between the child's soul and the corpse and pulled, drawing the child's soul into it. I felt it snap into place, my hands blazing with heat as I came to, gasping, blinking back tears.

Andromeda put her hand on my shoulder and squeezed. "You did it," she said, only the barest whiff of disbelief on her words. "Can you feel it? The child's soul is inside its body."

"I feel it," I said, sick to my stomach. "She didn't want to come. She was content where she was. I *forced* her."

Andromeda's chin wobbled as it dipped to her chest, acknowledging what we'd done. "We had no choice," she whispered.

"There's always a choice," I argued.

"Always?" Andromeda shook her head. "You just said the child didn't want to come. And yet, here it is."

"Now's not the time for philosophizing," Marcus interrupted. "We have work to do. Let's get the corpse down to the temple as quickly as possible."

We fell into place wordlessly, each taking up positions to move the body. The gruesome work of loading the corpse into Marcus's car took far longer than we expected. Turns out, corpses are heavy as hell. Moving a dead body is a lot harder than it appears in movies and television. We made the short drive to the temple where we tediously maneuvered Brandy from the car. Getting her out was even more difficult than getting her in. As we struggled to get the body into the temple, my heart leaped into my chest with every sound. I kept expecting someone to find us, to ask us what in God's name we were doing. Luckily, the preserve was quiet. Dark. It seemed maybe luck was on our side.

Obviously, my definition of luck had reached a new low.

When we finally got Brandy inside, we were all bathed in sweat and cramped with exertion. Andromeda drew me to her and placed her hands on my head as she murmured an incantation. She called upon European gods that I wasn't familiar with, asking for their love, protection, and guidance. It was strange to have a White lady lay her hands on me, blessing me with the protections of her ancestors. I felt simultaneously blessed and jealous—this was the relationship with my own ancestors I so desperately wanted. As she spoke the words, the surrounding air changed. I felt a cocoon of gentle warmth, a dulcet counterpoint to the violent fire that raged inside me. I felt the protection like a welcoming bath as I slipped into it, ensconced in love and healing. I felt lighter, somehow. I could almost hear a choir of angels singing benedictions in my ears.

"You're really good at this," I whispered. "Have you considered a TV show?" She offered a light smile at the jest, wiping away a film of sweat that had formed on my brow, but didn't reply.

"Are we ready?" Marcus asked.

Andromeda slipped into place beside the ravaged corpse, laying a hand on Brandy's open chest. Then, she retreated into herself, legs crossed, eyes closed. Ben knelt before her, sweeping the hair from her face and offering loving gestures and whispers. Watching them, it became startlingly obvious that he was more than her manager—even more than a best friend. Their connection was soul deep and indelible. In that moment, I suddenly felt very alone.

She looked up at me with steely determination in her eyes. "All right then. Let's get on with this. Who goes first?"

"You do. You channel Caleb into your body, and I'll ask him to read the incantation. And then ... ?" I shrugged. "And then we'll see which way the magic crumbles." I paused. "One last thing. You probably know this, but he can only see what you see. So, please—keep your eyes off Brandy's corpse. I don't want him to see his wife like this."

We all took our places. Andromeda closed her eyes and began to chant. After a moment, the energy in the room shifted, and when Andromeda opened her eyes, the contours of her face seemed to change. Her jowls sagged; the mouth drooped. I'd never seen a medium in action before, though I'd seen Andromeda do it on television. But to see it in person was some crazy shit.

"What's happening?" came a voice from Andromeda's mouth. We all recognized it. It was Caleb's. Like I said: crazy shit.

"Caleb, there's no time to explain," I said. "I promised to bring your wife to you, but I need your help." I held out my hand and Marcus handed me the scroll, which I opened and held before Andromeda's eyes. The scroll was ablaze in the darkness. The fire in my chest surged. "I need you to read this."

Andromeda's eyes went wide. "My friendship incantation? But I told you, it doesn't work."

"Read it through, please," I said. "No questions."

I took Andromeda's hand and placed it on the corpse to indicate that the soul inside was the offering. With trembling lips, Caleb began the incantation. I held my breath, heart thundering away against my ribs. The fire in my chest grew impossibly hotter. Circles of sweat formed at my armpits, my shirt clinging to my back, slick now with perspiration.

It was only when Caleb had nearly finished the incantation that I looked at Marcus.

He was holding Andromeda's hand—the hand that I had

intentionally placed on the corpse—and pressing it against his own chest.

"Marcus," I whispered, incredulous. "What the fuck are you doing?"

His eyes were liquid, gently illuminated by the glow emanating from the scroll. "We can't sacrifice another person's soul without consent, dove. I'm sorry, but we can't." His gaze was steady in the dark; he did not blink. "But this way, no matter what happens, at least I'll be with you for eternity."

Caleb's voice halted, and I realized that the incantation was complete. I was so enraged at Marcus and scared about what he had just done and what was about to happen that I was nearly paralyzed when the walls of the temple began to shake.

The ground quaked, and I wobbled off center, my vision going blurry as the fire inside me blazed so hot and bright that I felt like a walking combustion engine. My neurons were firing on all cylinders; my amygdala went into overdrive, spilling every emotion I had ever experienced into my system. The air burned with the smell of ozone, the scent ringing in my nostrils. Then, as chemicals flooded my body and my senses became unreliable, I felt more than saw that the jinni had arrived.

On each of the eight walls surrounding us, the paintings of Brother Zahi shimmered to life. The energy in the temple shifted once again, and I sensed the familiar zing of a current being activated; the same current that had activated the day I received the flame. I didn't know what it was, but I knew now what it meant. Fear and wonder seized me as the glass ceiling above filled with white light—bright, terrible, and impossible. We cried out with pain as the light seared our retinas.

When we looked again, we were no longer alone.

Standing before us was the Resplendent Brother Zahi.

The paintings on the wall didn't even come close to doing Brother Zahi justice. He was magnificent. Black skin that shone with a blue hue, cheeks and chin all sculpted angles. A broad nose and close-cropped hair, the whites of his eyes almost iridescent against the dark skin. Full lips that pulled into a smile that was so devoid of malice that I could've melted into it. He was nothing that I expected.

He was just a man.

Or at least a man-shaped thing, and that, really, was the danger. Because in my heart, I knew I should be afraid. I knew I was outmatched. I had so little ammunition at my fingertips, so little experience under my belt. And he was so disarmingly beautiful.

The prophet smiled at me from across the room, his white teeth glinting in the dim starlight that filtered through tree branches above the temple glass. He held his hands out before him, palms up. "I've been waiting for you to come calling."

I tried to swallow around the knot in my throat, my nerves so frayed I damn near couldn't remember how to speak English. I squared my shoulders and took a deep breath as I wobbled to my feet, deciding to dispel with the niceties. But before I could speak, another voice drifted over my shoulder.

"How is this possible?" Caleb's voice said from Andromeda's body. Her eyes were trained on Brother Zahi. "You haven't aged at all. Not in all these years."

Brother Zahi's expression was soft when he said, "You served me well, old friend. And I hope I've served you, too. I'm sorry to see what's become of you."

I cleared my throat loudly, forcing the jinni to return his attention to me. We didn't have time for a sappy reunion. "You need to let the souls go," I said.

The jinni took a step towards me, and I instinctively took a step back. I felt Andromeda's protection magic squeezing closer to my skin. When he noticed my reticence, the prophet stopped moving, but his gaze never broke from mine. Beneath that stare, I felt shriveled, emaciated. Powerless.

What have I gotten myself into?

"Those souls were fairly acquired," he said. His voice was lightly accented, and though I didn't know what a Somali accent sounded like, I assumed that was what I was hearing. The vowels and the lilting cadence of his words were pleasant to my ears. I had to fight not to fall under his sway. His charisma was undeniable.

"I don't think so," I said. "I don't know what you've done or why you've done it, but no one deserves to be trapped. These souls deserve to go on to the afterlife and reunite with the friends and family waiting for them."

Brother Zahi took another step forward. "They made a bargain with me right here in this temple," he said. "They requested my divine light, and I poured it upon them. You did the same, as I recall."

"I did not," I said. "I *never* gave my soul to you."

The prophet laughed, a glittering sound that tickled the fire in my sternum. "Of course you did. Entering this temple, praying within its walls. Those who pray here, pray to me. And unlike the Creator, I answer. For a price." He shrugged lightly. "That's just the nature of my kind. Kezia, the trade is fair. How much I take all depends on you—the greater your desire and the more impossible you believe the request to be, the more of your soul you must give. Ask for something small and feasible, I take very little. Ask for something you want with *all* your soul, believing it can never be? Still I will grant it, and I will fill your whole vessel with my divine light. It's all stated in the contract inscribed right over the temple doors in my own language." He smiled as he said this, but then the smile fell away. "Don't you feel my divine light within you?"

At his words, a lick of flame flared behind my ribs. I couldn't tell if it was the jinni's power or pure anger. "*That's* what's written over the door? A contract for my *soul*? How can that be fair?"

The jinni's expression was almost mournful. "A contract is a contract. Fair has nothing to do with it. When he bought this land, Caleb agreed to give me one percent of this land's value in perpetuity. As of today, I have claimed fewer than 30 souls. And how many adherents does your religion have, Caleb?"

Behind me, Caleb answered, "At least 20,000."

"See?" Brother Zahi was smiling again. "I am entitled to one percent of this temple's yield, and yet I have claimed far less than that. According to the terms of our contract, Caleb actually owes me 200 souls. But I am nothing if not generous."

I stared in disbelief. "This is insane. But regardless of whatever deal Caleb made with you, *I* never agreed to any of this!"

"You agreed to the terms when you crossed the threshold into this temple. And I have been utterly upstanding in the fulfillment of my end of the trade. Armand Lopez wanted to destroy his political enemies, and I did that. Camilla Stevenson wanted to be beautiful—that one was easy, as she was already beautiful, she just couldn't see it. Eunice Cho wanted her name cleared of all allegations. These souls are *rightfully* mine! And isn't hastening physical death a small price to pay for everlasting harmony?"

My stomach rolled over. So that was it then. That's why Eunice had burned to death in her bed. I'd seen her in this temple, tears streaming down her face, praying for what her heart wanted most—to be cleared of all the charges against her. To have her good name restored.

He'd given her what she wanted most. But she hadn't lived to enjoy it.

It was a terrible trade.

"You're a deceitful bastard," I snarled. "You could have been honest. You could have been forthright. There are probably a million people on this planet who would *gladly* have given their souls for worldly satisfaction! You didn't have to do *this*." I clutched my own chest in despair.

"Kezia," he cooed. "I didn't want just any soul. I only wanted those I found worthy of salvation."

"Salvation?" I stared, incredulous. "How is this salvation? What do you think you'll accomplish by torturing these people for eternity?"

The jinni's eyes went wide with disbelief. "Torture? For eternity? No, you misunderstand! Oh!" He clutched at his chest, a pained look on his face. For a moment I thought he might actually cry. "When the jinn were created, we were promised a place in this beautiful, perfect universe—to sit at the feet of the Creator." Again, his face twisted, eyes growing dark with what I guessed was anguish. "But then the Creator invented angels and men which became His favorite, and the jinn were left alone, forgotten. The Creator refused to stop man from ruining everything He had created. The jinn begged to intercede, but the Creator refused. Many jinn accepted their fate, but others didn't. My ancestors were among those who refused to be content to watch the greed and lust and hate of man destroy this universe. And so my people proposed a solution. If we collected enough souls from this broken and sinful world to populate our own planets in an alternate universe separate from this one, we could be gods, too. We could seed our new worlds with the souls of the harvested, and you'd get to live *again*, but this time in peace and love in alignment with your higher purpose."

His smile was full and real, and part of me wanted to believe every word he spoke. After all, I'd felt the love and peace he spoke of right here in this very temple. He took a step nearer to me. "The jinn of my line have vowed to honor our covenants and promises to a race of men who will hold their hands to the heavens and sing *our* praises. Our universe will be what *this* one was supposed to be before the Creator let you ruin it. Who wouldn't want that? All I asked from you was a soul to take to a better place. This place, this universe that you so love, has been ruined by the greed and hate and evil of man. I want to *save* you from this."

I shook my head. "You can't save humanity from itself. Some people will always make evil choices. People can't be forced to be good. That's not who we are."

"You are not wrong," the jinni said, his head cocked to the side as he smiled. "Which is why in my universe, there will be no free will. Humanity will only be able to make choices that are graceful and loving and kind. Wouldn't you want that, Kezia? Don't you want to exist in a universe like that?"

My instinct told me to shout back that of course I didn't want to live in a universe like that, that free will with all its risks was better than the alternative, no matter how you looked at it. But before I spoke the words, I second-guessed myself. To exist in a world without sin, without evil?

But that was the fallacy. Because he was forging his world without consent—the worst kind of ethical breach. How could a world born from lies and trickery be free of sin? It was original sin all over again, just wrapped up in a different package.

"You can't force peace upon people. Taking away their free will doesn't guarantee they'll be happy—it just means they'll be unhappy on *your* terms. Why would we want to spend eternity in another universe where our families aren't?" My voice broke on the word *families*. I took a step toward Zahi. "These souls you've collected are part of *this* world. And we deserve to continue on in this world. You have no right to claim us. No more of a right than the bastards who snatched my ancestors from their homeland and enslaved them in a *better, more civilized* country." Another thought struck me. "You said your ancestors came up with this 'new universe' idea—and yet *you're still here*, on *this* plane, in *this* world. Has anyone in your line even been successful in this fantasy of yours?"

The jinni sighed, forlorn. "Not yet. But we will be."

"You will *not* be!" I cried, suddenly filled with bright rage. "I'm not going to let that happen, Zahi. If you want souls for a new world, obtain them *freely*. Let people *choose*." I looked to Marcus, my idiot ex-husband who had traded his soul for this meeting. If I failed, we would both be trapped here for centuries or longer. And then who would Lola have on the other side? I shook my head, sealing my determination. "I can't let you force anyone into an afterlife without their ancestors. I can't let you separate parents from their children. Not if it isn't their choice."

The jinni pressed his palms together at his chest in a prayerful pose. "Kezia, please. I—"

"I've been patient with you," I said. "But now I'm done negotiating. If you won't give us our sovereignty back," I growled, the fire in my chest growing white hot, "then I guess we'll just have to take it."

CHAPTER SEVENTEEN

I OPENED MYSELF to the death current, feeling it charge my core with energy. But as I extended my consciousness toward it, Brother Zahi began to transform.

The man before me went up in a pillar of flame, its heat so terrible I thought for sure we'd all combust. Then, as though Michelangelo himself took a chisel to it, the sculpted form of a man emerged from the fire. But not just any man.

A blazing, twenty-foot tall man made of prismatic, smokeless flame.

The jinni's true form was astonishing. His fire twisted and flashed, his image rippling across the flames like a reflection on water. He thrust his arm forward and scorching air rushed past me, the heat so intense it disrupted my channeling. The fire inside me rose sharply in response, reaching out toward the jinni. Feverishly, I reached for the protective magic Andromeda had cast on me. It was still there. Still strong.

And if I wanted to live to use it, I needed to move.

Suddenly, I heard something behind me like a hole being

ripped in the fabric of the universe. When I spun around, my heart leaped into my throat.

Surrounding Marcus was a small army of lesser imps.

I gulped. A small number looked to be about a dozen. The imps stood at least ten feet tall, broad shouldered and naked. They walked upright like men, with chests and arms that resembled a human on steroids, but with heads, haunches, hooves, and sometimes, tails of various semi-deformed animals. The creatures were colored in every hue, some solid, others a fabulous ombre. They bared their teeth and snarled as they readied their magic. They were terrible and awesome to look at.

If those were lesser imps, I couldn't imagine what a greater imp might look like.

I felt a jolt of heat rise as the death current quickened, its vibration growing more frenetic. I returned my focus to my part in this attack. I didn't intend to sit idly by as Marcus led the imps into battle.

I had my own plan.

I reached out, trying to connect with the current, but it was wilder than ever. It took several tries before I could lock in. But once I had it, the power flowed through me, filling me with the death smells and making my hands throb. I pushed away any self-doubt, and then I called to my patrons.

Papa Jinabbott, Mama Fat, I need you now. Guide my magic. Make me strong. Lend me your protection and strength!

I thrust out my arm, fingers extended, and imagined energy shooting from my fingers until it found the jinni, winding around him. With that image clear in my mind, I howled as I drew my fingers into my palm and yanked my arm backward. My energy connected with the jinni's, and I felt resistance, but nothing more.

The imps had begun their attack. With Marcus shouting commands, the imps had summoned enormous shields and were now creating a wall. I dropped my arm and ran behind them, thankful for the protection, which came not a moment too soon. As I dove behind the imps, the jinni began to cast.

Arrows of fire shot from the jinni's torso, raining flame down on the temple floor. We were at a disadvantage, as the jinni's height gave him the upper ground. The imps maneuvered to protect the humans as best they could, but we were still vulnerable. We needed to do more.

I gritted my teeth to try again. I stood, reaching out again toward the jinni. The monster growled as he hurled enormous balls of fire at the imps, weakening their shields. The beasts screamed as the magic hit them, their skin scorching, smelling of burning hide and fur. I choked; the stench was souring my concentration.

Hold it together, Kezia. You can do this. But my conviction wavered as the imps began to fall, crumbling away to nothing as they died.

Marcus was shouting again, and the imps went on the offensive, hurling magical projectiles at the monster. Enormous vines erupted from the ground, climbing the jinni's legs, holding him in place. The monster screamed as he ripped the vines from his body, kicking a centaur in the chest and sending it flying. The creature screamed as his man-shaped upper half burned away, leaving nothing but char. The jinni roared as he summoned a pillar of fire that filled every corner of the temple with impossible light and heat. "You cannot win this!" he shouted. "I didn't come to hurt any of you! I want to offer you salvation, Kezia! What more can I offer? What more is it you want? Your mother?" A pause. "Your daughter?"

I screamed then, raising my arms and flinging out my

hands, mentally pulling against the jinni, trying to free his life source. But I was far too weak. If I couldn't remove the life force of a plant, why did I think I could do it on a jinni? I glanced to the imps, hoping for a miracle, but though they continued to battle, they were just about used up. We were running out of time. We weren't going to win. We'd come all this way for nothing. "Just let the souls go, and take back this magic you put inside me!" I screamed.

The jinni growled, a dark, throaty sound. "You don't really want that. I can give you anything. Wish for it. Ask for it! In this temple, anything you want is yours. The only price you have to pay is your soul. And, think about it, Kezia. Isn't that a price you've already paid tenfold?"

I threw a look at Andromeda and found her countenance changed; she was once again herself. She, too, was channeling energy—but she was channeling toward me, offering me peace and protection. The peace part wasn't really working, but I felt the protection. But even as the protection grew stronger, I knew Andromeda couldn't hold out forever. Neither could Marcus or the imps. I needed to end this one way or another.

"This is the last time I'll ask," I said through a clenched jaw. "Release the souls and you can go. I have no beef with you. Just leave these people alone!"

This time, the jinni ignored me completely. The imp army was nearly destroyed. With the imps wiped out, the certainty of our loss hit me like a wave, and I had to catch myself from giving in to the crushing enormity of it. I couldn't let the jinni have the souls he trapped—or the soul my ex-husband had traded away.

But what more could I do? I didn't have any more magic at my disposal. I had used everything I had.

"No, you ain't," came a voice in my head. Papa Jinabbott

smirked in my mind's eye, arms folded across his chest. *"You got a chest full of genie magic you ain't even* touched."

The last of the imps screamed as a pillar of fire exploded around it, scorching the creature into dust. Panic rose in my throat. *"What am I supposed to do?"* I thought at him frantically. *"I don't know how to access it! I don't know how to use it!"*

Papa Jinabbott grinned. *"Guess you best wish for it."*

"Wish for it," I whispered, understanding. *Make the choice. No matter how much it hurts.*

I closed my eyes, and instead of swallowing down the jinni's dark wildfire that tried to consume me, I surrendered to it. I let it into my heart and soul. I let its energy permeate my whole being, infusing me with a power normally far beyond my grasp. And as I accepted it, breathing it into my scalp, my fingertips, the furthest corners of my body, I threw impossible wishes to the universe.

I prayed in the temple.

I prayed for the most outrageous things I could think of. Riches. Fame. Love. I asked for it all. And I wanted it *now*.

But nothing happened.

In a fury, I turned to the jinni, tears and sweat streaming down my face. "Grant my wishes!" I screamed, my body shaking with the fight-or-flight chemicals that flooded my bloodstream. "It was so easy with Eunice and Camilla. I asked you for one thing before, but you didn't grant it. Why didn't you grant my wish?"

Dimly, I was aware of Marcus shouting in the background. "Kezia! What are you doing? Now's not the time, dove! Stand down! Don't incite him further!"

But I ignored these pleas. "Tell me why," I said, curling my hands into fists. "Tell me why you couldn't grant my wish, you bastard."

The jinni threw his head back, laughing. "Idiot child!" he puffed. "You wished to find your family. Your wish was the easiest of all. Remove the mote from your eyes, Kezia; you have to want to see that everything you asked for has been with you from the beginning!"

His words made no sense. I had been trying to find my mother and ancestors on the other side since I was a teenager, and nothing had worked. With me from the beginning, my ass. That they weren't with me was the crux of every problem: my absent friendships, my failed marriage, my lost child ...

A blinding idea struck me, and I spun around, seeking Marcus. And when my eyes landed on him, I heard Mrs. Harrison's voice one more time, rasping softly in my ears.

Family's what stick around to clean up your mess after everybody else done hitched up they skirts and gone on.

Another wave of endorphins flooded my bloodstream as my last conscious thought unfolded in my mind: *Marcus is your family. Big Ginny is your family. Papa Jinabbott and Mama Fat are your family. And they have been with you from the beginning.*

With that final thought, I burst into flame.

The death current that I had been channeling blazed a hot, brilliant blue, visible to my naked eye in a rare moment of clarity. The jinni's fire exploded painfully from my chest, igniting the death current like a match dropped onto a stream of gasoline. The two became one, the death current no longer merely a force of decay and deceleration but now also chaos and heat and rampant destruction.

It felt like pure power. I'd never experienced anything like it.

As I ignited, the screaming began—Marcus, Ben, Andromeda. But they seemed distant, underwater. The pain in my chest was nearly unbearable, but I had to fight through if I wanted us all to survive. I pushed all thoughts and external stimuli from my mind and concentrated on channeling the fire-infused death current. If I wasn't careful, I would burn down the whole temple and everyone in it. Thank God for Andromeda's protection, otherwise channeling the super current might have destroyed me. Even so, her magic was almost depleted.

Here we go, I thought. *I can do this. Papa Jinabbott, Mama Fat, guide and protect me now.*

I turned my attention to the jinni. My ears were filled with his triumphant howls and the mingled screams of my companions as they watched what they must have thought was my body burning. They didn't know that I was in control, that I was using the flames to my advantage, my body protected by Andromeda's magic.

This has to work, I thought in my fevered frenzy. *Please, God, let this work.*

I threw out my arms, activating every muscle in my body until I was as tense as a coiled spring. I imagined my power as a grappling hook as I thrust it into the monster's soul. I thought of every person who'd had their choices ripped from them. I thought of the people the jinni had tricked and the souls he'd stolen, and I let that anger fuel me as I thrust out my arms.

"*Fuck you!*" I screamed.

Then everything happened at once.

Marcus found his footing and was barreling toward me, screaming something about putting out my fire. He careened past the jinni, eyes wild as he ran for me. I screamed, curling my fingers into my palms and jerking my arms back just as Marcus shot between me and the monster.

An explosion of light and sound filled the temple, momentarily blinding me as a crack like thunder boomed against my eardrums. The explosion sent Marcus flying. He hit the floor with a yowl, clutching his chest. His skin pulsed with a kaleidoscopic aura, intense and painful to look at. And just as quickly as it appeared, the light vanished.

I tore my eyes away from Marcus to find the jinni still standing, but his face had gone slack, his jaw hanging limply open as the color faded from his fire. His knees buckled as he gasped one last, choking breath before crashing to the floor. When his body hit, the ground shook and a wave of heat rushed from the spot where he lay lifeless.

The jinni's fire went out, his body fading to a dull, inorganic gray. Its surface cracked and plumes of black smoke rose from the ragged fissures before evaporating into nothing.

I stared, panting as the energy I had been channeling fizzled before draining away altogether. I was suddenly cold, and I shivered.

But I wasn't cold, exactly. I just wasn't hot anymore. The fire in my chest was gone.

Tentatively, I moved toward the jinni's corpse, fearful now of some trick, that the monster would roar to life the minute I was close. But as I neared his head, I saw that his face was crumbling to ash. The decay moved into his cheeks, traveling to his scalp, his neck, his shoulders, each piece flaking into slag and soot until the beast was nothing more than a pile of ash.

Convinced now that the jinni was dead, I hurried over to Brandy's corpse as Ben ran to Andromeda. Carefully, I removed Charon's Recall from Brandy's belly. As it came free, I felt a shock of calm as the child's soul lifted from its prison, returning to the other side. I stuffed the cursed object into a pocket. I really needed to get rid of it. Opal was right; no one should own an object like that.

Marcus came up to me then, eyes wild with confusion. "What happened?" he demanded, holding out his hands. "What just happened?"

I lifted my arm, displaying the bracelet. "One of Opal's spells," I said. "Telekinesis. I snatched the vital spark out of him."

"Telekinesis?" he repeated. "How? Telekinesis doesn't—"

I tried to smile, but I was so tired. "I'll explain later," I said. "You'll like Opal's theory. It's right up your alley."

For a moment, Marcus only stared. Then, he pulled me into an embrace, crushing me with his strength and shaking with sobs. "I can't believe it," he whimpered, fingers sinking in my hair, holding me close. "You did it. You saved us all. You did it."

I entertained his emotions as long as I could before pulling away, grimacing in pain. He stepped back, eyes traveling over my body. "What is it? What's wrong?"

But I didn't need to answer. His eyes found the wound at my chest where the jinni's fire magic had burst free. It was about the size of my fist, and it didn't bleed. Its edges were blackened. Burned.

"Kezia," he rasped. "Are you all right? Does it hurt?"

"Yes," I admitted. "A lot, actually."

"We need to get you to a doctor," he said. "Burns are serious. You need—"

"Not yet," I said. "When we're done here, you'll take me to see Opal. She can heal this; I know she can. But first, we have work to do."

With my last reserves of energy, I reached out to the veil. I was so tired. My connection was not as strong as I wanted it to be. The call wasn't as magnetic.

Yet, as I slipped my energy into the veil, parting the inky

membrane, no fire magic slapped me back. I met no resistance. Pure relief flooded through me as the souls, one by one, realized that the veil was penetrable, and they could cross over.

Their joy was palpable. They shouted, cried. Someone was laughing. I crossed over first, guiding them through the veil. As they appeared on the other side, I finally saw their faces. It felt good to look upon the people I had freed. It felt like justice.

They finally achieved what death was always supposed to bring them: peace.

As soon as they appeared in their afterlife, the souls hurried on, vanishing from my view. Only one soul lingered, turning to face me with a smile. "I always knew you could do it," Brandy said, her hands folded neatly before her. She looked beautiful—whole and complete, as perfect in death as she had been in life. "I wish I could've been with you. I wish it hadn't ended like this."

I readied my mouth to ask what wish the jinni had granted her; what had been so important that she opened herself to the fire within even though she knew what the price would be. But I couldn't ask. It wasn't my business. Tears formed in my eyes, and I blinked them back, wiping them away with the heel of my hand. "You'll like it on the other side," I promised. "You and Caleb will be happy together."

She hesitated only a moment, her fingers fluttering toward her belly. "And the baby?"

My smile widened. "She's here too. I'm sure you'll see her—however she chooses to appear to you—when I leave you. Go ahead now. Your purpose here has been served. Rest in peace, Brandy."

She hesitated only a moment longer before pressing her

fingers to her lips in a farewell kiss and disappearing into her afterlife where I would likely never see her again.

I took a moment to collect myself before making my way over to Marcus, who was sitting with his head in his hands as Andromeda caressed his back and whispered calming words to him. I sat down next to him, placed my hand on his knee. "Marcus? Are you okay?"

My ex-husband looked up at me, his eyes shining with tears. "I thought we were all going to die," he said, his voice trembling with emotion.

"I thought so, too," I admitted, wiping away my own tears and biting back laughter. "You were great with those imps. They really saved the day."

Andromeda turned her attention to me then, her eyes bright with admiration. "You did it, Kezia. The light in your eyes is gone. You're free." She touched me, fresh tears stinging her eyes. "You removed the vital spark with magic." She sounded so awe-struck I couldn't help but grin. "They're going to write papers about this, you know. You'll be famous." She grinned and gestured at Marcus, eyes still wide. "And have you ever seen anything like that? I'd never ... I couldn't imagine ... Marcus, you're an incredible mage!"

He chuckled good-naturedly, shaking his head but offering no reply. What could he say? He'd promised Theo that he wouldn't reveal where he'd gotten the scroll. I smiled at Andromeda and offered a slight shrug. "Every man has his secrets, I suppose," I said.

Now, Marcus reached out to me, clasped my hand in his own. "Did the souls all make it safely across?"

I nodded. "Everybody made it. It's over," I said.

It was only at that moment that I let myself succumb to exhaustion and pain. I swayed, and instinctively, Marcus reached out to catch me. I leaned against him, breathing in his smell, the warmth and comfort of him, and never before had I been so grateful to have him as my chosen family.

Andromeda and Ben were sitting with their legs crossed, holding hands, facing each other. They were humming together, a chilling and strangely beautiful discordant duet. I wasn't sure if it was supposed to sound that way or if one of them was just tone deaf, but in either case, I could almost see the glow around both of them. I had to say one thing about Andromeda: she was an excellent magic worker in her own right. If I had ever doubted her as just a TV psychic, those doubts had been blown away.

Andromeda drew to her feet and brushed away invisible wrinkles from her dress. "Well, I don't know about the rest of you, but I'm feeling like we should probably get out of this goddamn temple. Any takers?"

It was very late by the time Marcus and I returned to our bungalows, and neither one of us wanted to be alone. And so, despite our better judgment, we slipped into bed together, wrapped in each other's arms, and thankfully, fell asleep long before lust could rear its head, fucking everything up.

I didn't mean that as a pun.

It wasn't until I awoke from a nightmare in the middle of the night that I realized the nacreous light that knocked Marcus to the ground hadn't so much vanished as been absorbed.

CHAPTER EIGHTEEN

I AWOKE EARLY, sneaking out of bed to bury Charon's Recall in a remote part of the desert. I buried it deep, leaving no marker, hoping it would lie in the ground forever, never finding its way to another necromancer's hands.

We left the compound at daybreak, and even as I crested the mountains making my way back toward Los Angeles, I saw the news vans and police cars passing me from the other direction, making a beeline for the preserve. I watched the flashing lights and chaos in the rearview mirror, thankful to be leaving all of that behind.

Days passed; I slept through most of them. Opal came to check on me and tend to my wounds, but otherwise, I was alone. When I finally felt rested enough to think about going back to my regular life, my phone rang.

"Marcus," I said. "It's good to hear from you."

"I wasn't sure I should call," he admitted.

I chuckled under my breath. "After everything we've been through?"

He was silent on the other end. Then, "Is Big Ginny still in the hospital or is she back home with you?"

I deflated a little, disappointed at the direction of this conversation. I think I half wanted him to use my words as an invitation. "Oh, she's out. Yeah, she's okay, Lamont says she's good. She's still with him because I'm not a hundred percent, yet. I've been damn near in a coma since I got home."

"Yeah, me, too. Mum's been watching Lola." He paused. "I just wanted to hear that you were okay."

I nodded. "Do you want to go get Big Ginny with me?"

He hesitated a moment too long; I thought he would demur. But then, "Do you want me to?"

I squeezed my eyes shut. "Yes," I breathed.

"Okay. Just let me know when to come by." He disconnected.

I dialed my brother, who picked up on the first ring. "Was wondering if you was ever gonna call," he chastised. "Big Ginny's been asking for you."

"I bet she has," I joked. "Let me guess: she needs some supplies from Opal's and your wife won't get them for her, right?"

Lamont grunted on the other end before giving in to chuckles. "Sis, you know Nadine think magic come from the devil. Y'all lucky she let this ole Conjure woman in the house at all."

"Luck ain't got shit to do with it," I said. "Nadine scared of me. Like she should be."

"Yeah, yeah, well, if you don't want her to divorce me, you best come get your grandmama."

I laughed. "She only *my* grandmama when she out here causing problems. Anyway. How she doing?"

"She's been good ever since they released her. She was

ornery at the hospital; you know how she get. Doctor told me to keep an eye on her, and if anything strange surfaces or she has another episode to let the hospital know. So far, so good, though. She in the kitchen right now cooking up a grip of okra. I hate that shit; just because she was sick a couple days ago don't mean I'mma eat that."

I chuckled. "Just stick it in the freezer. She'll probably eat most of it, anyway. Is it okay if I swing by your place and pick her up? I'm sure she wants to get home."

Lamont pretended to think on the other line so as not to appear too eager to be rid of her. "Yeah, that should be okay. I'm heading out in a couple hours for the bar. You comin' in to work tonight?"

I rolled my eyes, a slight smile spreading over my lips. "Can I have one more day? I promise to come in tomorrow."

Lamont grunted on the other end. "Don't be late," was all he said before hanging up.

I called the hospice next and asked when I could return to work. My supervisor sounded happy to hear from me, and once again I was reminded how nice it was to have people around who were understanding of my circumstances and only asked from me as much as I could give. She said I was welcome to return to work whenever I was ready, and I accepted a midweek shift gratefully. Lord knew I was gonna need groceries sooner or later.

Cuz I sure enough wasn't finna eat okra, either.

HOURS LATER, after Marcus and I picked up Big Ginny and got her settled in, the three of us stood around the kitchen, Big Ginny making coffee, and Marcus joking and jostling her like we were back in the good old days before Lola got sick. I was thankful for the familiar rhythm, and even more grateful for the delightful aroma of coffee that wafted throughout the house. Being home felt good. Safe.

We piled up plates with sandwiches, pickles, and chips and carted them into the living room. I poured coffee for all of us and placed the carafe on the table between us. Big Ginny brought her mug to her face, closing her eyes as she inhaled the aroma deeply. "This here some witch's brew," she crooned. "Nobody makes coffee like Kezia." She shifted her eyes to me. "You must've gotten that from your mama."

My heart skipped and I raised my eyes to meet Big Ginny's. It was rare that my grandmother spoke of my mom, but whenever she doled out samples like this, more was sure to follow. "Mom was a barista, wasn't she?"

"She had all kinds of jobs," Big Ginny said. "Nobody worked harder than that woman. Had to, I guess. Wasn't like she was getting much help from her husband." She frowned, and I knew it pained her that my father, her stepson, had been such a miserable excuse for a human. "But that's not why your mama had a gift for coffee. It's because she woke up a memory of her Ethiopian heritage."

I balked, hardly daring to breathe. "She did what?"

Big Ginny nodded. "She went up to North Hollywood one day to get her hair done, and while she was up there, she stopped in to see a new necromancer—someone she ain't never visited before. When he laid his hands on her, it woke up a memory of how to perform *bun*. That's a traditional Ethiopian coffee ceremony." She chuckled at the memory. "Girl you shoulda *seen* her! She had to send away for raw Ethiopian beans, and they was hard to come by. But when she finally got them, you couldn't stop her. She roasted beans like it was going out of style. Then she'd grind 'em up and put them in a clay pitcher with boiling water and she'd put the whole thing on the stove. She didn't have no fancy coffee pitcher like she was supposed to have, and boy did that piss her off. But it ain't stop her none. That child used whatever she could get her hands on. Resourceful. Woulda made a good Conjure woman if she'd had the heart for it, but she didn't."

Big Ginny took a sip of her coffee. "She would serve us coffee with a little brown sugar and butter. Nothing in the world tastes as good as your mama's coffee. After she passed away, I couldn't get nothing like it, of course. I had to make do with this here business," she said, holding up her mug. "And you do make a fine brew. It just ain't like nothing your mama ever made."

I stared at her in disbelief. "How have you never told me this before?"

My grandmother shrugged. "You always seemed so bent outta shape about all the magic you don't have. It ain't seem fitting to tell you your mama woke up a genetic memory."

"Big Ginny, that memory means my mother was of Ethiopian heritage. Which means *I* have Ethiopian heritage! You really thought after all these years that that's something I wouldn't want to know?"

Marcus placed a hand on my arm, a gentle admonition to calm down. I sighed. "*Anything* you can tell me about my mother could help me find her," I said. "Please don't keep things from me. This is important. You know that."

My grandmother said nothing, and I let the subject drop. I knew enough about old people to know they had their reasons for keeping secrets. I couldn't count the number of times a son or daughter cried in my arms after learning of a secret at their parent's death bed. The secrets were often innocuous, too: a woman who was a few years older than everyone thought, a man whose twin brother died in the war. And yet discovering that their parents were not who they thought left some people bitter. Angry.

The irony, of course, was that the secrecy was the problem, not the secret. No one cared that Willem O'Malley had been married when he met his children's mother, or that Rose Jasperson's life-long roommate was actually her lover, or that Mike Harrow was born Micah Horowitz and shed his Jewishness before entering college. The families only cared that they didn't know their loved ones as well as they believed.

Understanding that, I chose not to be angry at Big Ginny. Maybe she had a reason for keeping my mother's genetic memory a secret, maybe she didn't. But carrying anger for what little family I had left seemed a poor choice.

And God knows I wanted to start making better choices.

The important thing was that I knew something more about my mother. *Ethiopian!* That was surprising; I had always figured that like most American Blacks, I was primarily descended from West Africans captured and enslaved. And that was still likely. But knowing that my mother awoke a genetic memory of Ethiopian heritage meant somewhere in my blood and DNA, an ancestor drank in Ethiopian sun. Bathed in Ethiopian waters.

That knowledge warmed my heart. Not only did it give me a sense of connection to a past that had always been a black hole, it also meant I had a new clue I could use to locate my mother and finally receive my Godsend.

And maybe then I could finally cure my affliction and get my daughter back.

Big Ginny finished her coffee and pushed away from the table. "Well, I'll let y'all get to it. Thanks for comin' to get me.

I'm 'bout to go have me a little catnap. Don't make too much noise. If I wake up to the sound of the bed squeaking ... "

My face turned bright red, but Marcus pretended like Big Ginny had made a hilarious joke, slapping his knee and laughing. They kissed and hugged as Big Ginny shuffled off to her bedroom, the door clicking softly shut behind her. When I was sure Big Ginny wasn't standing at her door listening, I turned to Marcus. "Why don't you come take a walk with me?"

Outside, the neighborhood was quiet, the sky above a deep, rich blue. But even though the day itself was delightful, I felt uneasy, butterflies creating a windstorm in my stomach. Even Marcus looked concerned. "Everything okay? You're not still worried about Big Ginny, are you? Or are you thinking of your mother?"

I waved this concern away, shaking my head. "No, nothing like that. This is actually about you." I paused. "How are you feeling?"

"Good. Really good, actually." He stretched then as if to prove his point. "Must be the adrenaline of our adventure or something. I feel like I slept for twenty years."

I tried not to sigh; under any other circumstances, that would have been good news. But it just confirmed my deepest fear. "Marcus, remember when, right as I was killing the jinni, you flew forward? Like you got hit from behind?"

Marcus frowned. "Yeah?"

God, I didn't even know where or how to begin. My palms were sweating; I swallowed around a lump in my throat. "How long do jinn normally live?" I asked.

Marcus's pace slowed as he dug his hands into his pockets and cocked his head to the side, glancing at me out of the corner of his eye. "I don't know. Estimates range anywhere from five hundred or so to a thousand years. Why do you ask?"

I swooned at the number. I knew he was going to say some ridiculous time span, but I hoped 150-200 years would be the upper end. But I guess it was a stupid hope. I swallowed hard and cleared my throat. "Marcus, there's something I need to tell you."

Marcus stopped then, the light in his eyes clouding over. "What is it?"

I drew in a deep breath to calm my nerves. "As I already told you, I killed the jinni by yanking his vital spark out of him. Outside of the body, the vital spark is volatile; it wouldn't have lasted more than a few moments on its own. It seemed rational at the time, though I guess it wasn't like being rational was my priority."

I was rambling. I blew out my anxiety in a hot, noisy breath. "The force with which it exploded from him ... the momentum that knocked you down ... " I closed my eyes and leaned my head back. "You were standing between us, remember? When I pulled, his vital spark collided with your body. Your vital spark ... "

I shrugged, let my hands fall lamely at my side. "It's like in a displacement reaction," I said. "One element replaces another in a compound. For example, if you have a metal in an aqueous solution—"

"Kezia. I need you to get to the point."

I dropped my eyes to the ground. "When I yanked out the jinni's vital spark, it collided with you, knocking your vital spark loose. *His* vital spark held onto your body." I sighed. "I displaced your vital spark with the jinni's. Your own was used up in the reaction."

It was a long moment before Marcus spoke. When he did, his expression was ominous. "Are you telling me that my life energy has been replaced by the jinni's?"

I nodded. "Yes, but of course, it's *just* your life energy. Not your soul. You're still you. A human man. You're not a jinni. But you are different now. I've changed you. And it might not be permanent," I plundered on, desperate to save what I could of the situation. "I don't know how to fix this right now, but with time and study—"

"Kezia." Marcus took a step toward me and though I cowered, I didn't step away. "How much life energy do I have?"

I looked up tentatively. "I don't know. All I could tell was that he had a lot of life left in him. He wasn't close to natural death. So, if jinn can live, say, 500 years? I'd say I extended your life by at least half that."

The color drained from Marcus's face as he leaned his head backward, his eyes closed. I recognized the way his muscles tensed, the way his body became otherwise so still. He was reeling. Of course he was. I could practically sense the cells in his being slow down as he said, "You've extended my life by more than two centuries?"

"I'll find a way to fix it," I whispered. "I know something can be done. I'm certain that there somewhere, someone has the research or the knowledge to fix this. I'm sorry. I know this is a lot to take in. I didn't mean for this to happen."

When Marcus met my gaze again, all the earlier warmth was gone. The distance between us had grown vast. Even his voice sounded different, all traces of affection gone. That alone made me want to die. "I admit that I'm grateful as hell not to have died in that temple," he began, "and this isn't your fault. It was an accident. But this is unnatural, Kezia. I don't even know if my body can stay healthy that long, or if ... "

He didn't finish the thought, but he didn't need to. Just because I had given him the ability to live another several centuries didn't mean those would be healthy years. Perhaps I had only cursed him to two centuries of decay.

"I know. I understand the gravity of what I've done. But just because I've extended your life doesn't mean you have to accept that fate. You still have a choice. If you get tired of living, you could always ... "

My unfinished sentence hung heavy in the air between us, and the look Marcus gave me was neither angry nor incredulous. It was full of grief. "After all this time," he whispered, "it's like you don't know me at all." He paused before adding, "Maybe I've been wrong. Maybe you are not my *ayanmo* after all."

Now that was a slap in the face. "Marcus—"

My phone buzzed in my pocket, but I ignored it. I stepped toward my ex-husband, who backed away. I stopped, dispirited. "Marcus, please. Can we talk about this? You know so much more about this kind of thing than I do. Please, can we—"

He didn't let me finish. Saying nothing, he turned away from me and headed back toward the house. I followed far enough behind to give him a bit of space, but to my heartbreak, he didn't go back inside. He got into his car and drove away.

I watched Marcus's car, every ounce of me hoping he would turn around long after he disappeared around the corner. My heart thumped in my chest as a dull pain crept up from the soles of my feet to the crown of my head. Human emotions are so strange. When I first saw Marcus standing there after my arrival at the preserve, I had experienced a range of emotions: pain, surprise, anger, longing. But now that he was driving away from me, all I wanted was for him to come back. I was like everybody else in that regard. Always wanting what I couldn't have.

When I was sure that Marcus wasn't coming back, I pulled out my phone to see who had called.

But it wasn't a phone call that had interrupted me. I'd received an email. The sender was Evangeline Morris.

My heart stopped. With shaking hands, I navigated to my email program where I opened Evangeline's message. It looked like Andromeda was right: my escapades at the temple had reached the right ears. Maybe after all these years, Evangeline Morris was giving me the time of day.

I opened the short message. It read:

Hello, Kezia,

Congratulations on your recent accomplishment. I'd like to talk to you about it more in person. Perhaps we can share information beneficial to us both. Please accept this invitation to come stay at my home in Atlanta. The timing is up to you, but the sooner the better.

Walk with God,
Evangeline

An invitation to meet with Evangeline in person? I almost couldn't believe it. How long had I searched for a mentor? How many failed attempts to find my mother had I suffered? And now, after all this time, I had a standing invitation to convene with the one person who stood the greatest chance of helping me.

If I hadn't been so upset about the confrontation with Marcus, I might have cried with joy.

Instead, I headed back into the house. To my surprise, Big Ginny was sitting on the couch, flipping through television channels, the remote control poised on her lap. She scarcely glanced up at me as I came into the house and settled down beside her. "You didn't tell me Marcus was leaving," she said. It was almost a question, almost an accusation.

"I didn't know myself," I said. "We should have, though. I cut him loose years ago. I don't know why I keep expecting he'll always be mine."

Big Ginny sucked her teeth. "The hell you don't know. You keep expecting it because you ain't never let him go. Not really."

I frowned. "What do you mean? Divorce seems like the ultimate letting go."

"You a lie," Big Ginny said, shaking her head. "Divorce was for the government. It ain't got a damn thing to do with your heart. You and Marcus is destiny, baby girl, and I know you know it. He needs you like the desert needs rain, and you need him twice as much. So he might be gone now, but he'll be back."

I looked down into my lap. "I might have really pushed him away this time. What happened at the temple ... "

I couldn't bring myself to explain it to her, but she didn't really want to know, anyway. She waved a hand in front of her face. "My name's Paul and that's between y'all. All I'm saying is you can't choose your fate. God chooses for you."

I closed my eyes, pressed my fingertips into the hollows beneath my brows. Did I believe that we couldn't choose our own fate? Of course I didn't. I'd just killed a jinni to prove the point. And yet, no matter the choices I made to stay away from Marcus, the universe brought him right back to me.

If that wasn't fate despite my choosing, then what was it?

I leaned over and gave Big Ginny a kiss on her soft cheek before standing up. "You need anything?"

Big Ginny shook her head. "Naw. I really am about to go

take that nap. I was just waiting to see if you and Marcus was gonna come back home together or not."

I saw the question and the sparkle in her eyes, and I didn't have the heart to tell her that Marcus might not be coming back for a long time, if ever. Instead, I just gave her a smile before disappearing into my bedroom.

I sat down on the bed, mulling over Big Ginny's words. Did God choose our fate for us?

Maybe on some level. But I also knew that the Lord helped those that helped themselves. We had free will for a reason, and it was never too late to do the right thing.

I wasn't sure what I was doing, but I knew it was the right thing. I dug my laptop out of the corner of my bedroom and set it up to record. I ran my fingers through my curls and shook my hair out, but it didn't really matter how I looked. This wasn't about looks. This was about making up for lost time.

I wasn't ready to see my daughter. I wasn't ready to ache for her little arms, to yearn for her smiles, to feel my heart break into a million pieces every time I had to say goodbye. But just because I wasn't ready to see her didn't mean she wasn't ready to see me.

I hit the record button and let my eyes flutter to the camera. I offered the most genuine smile I could, trying hard to mask my grief as I said, "Hi, Lola baby. It's me. I'm your mom."

ABOUT THE AUTHOR

Amber Fisher is the author of urban and contemporary fantasy books ranging from sweet and delightful to dark and morbid. She lives in Austin, Texas, in a near-empty house now that her two kids have flown the coop. She would enjoy the silence except her husband is noisy as hell.

Connect with me at: amberfishermedia.com

Facebook at: facebook.com/amberfisherauthor

Twitter: @amberla

Sign up for the newsletter: bit.ly/332eurl

Made in United States
North Haven, CT
18 October 2021

10398643R00162